RHODES TO LOVE

DARING WITH THE SINGLE DAD

DANIKA BLOOM

FIRE LILY PRESS

Published by Fire Lily Press

Library and Archives Canada Cataloguing in Publication

Bloom, Danika, 1966- , author
Rhodes To Love / Danika Bloom

ISBN 978-1-7774865-3-2 (ebook)
ISBN 978-1-7780384-7-1 (paperback)

1. Title

This is a work of fiction. Names, characters, businesses, and events are from the author's imagination. Any resemblance to actual people, living or dead, is coincidental. Funny … but coincidental.

Copy Editor: Jennifer Sommersby, SGA Books

Proofreaders: Viper Spaulding & Kate Amberg

Cover design: L.J. Anderson, Mayhem Cover Creations (ebook); 100Covers.com (paperback)

To my readers. Thank you for loving the Rhodes brothers and for giving me the encouragement to keep guiding star-crossed lovers to their happily ever afters.

ABOUT RHODES TO LOVE: DARING WITH THE SINGLE DAD

I needed a job and he needed a fake wife for three months. How hard could it be? Turns out, deliciously, devilishly, dizzyingly hard ... so hard ...

"The story will tug at your heartstrings – there is passion, romance, friendship, facing your fears, communication, ups and downs, twists and turns, and family. Wonderful story with great characters!" ★★★★★

Lizzy

My mother taught me from an early age that kids will derail a woman's plans. Before I even consider settling down, I'm determined to see my number one dream accomplished: to travel through Europe—on my own. A trip that expensive requires a chunk of money I haven't been able to save.

So when an opportunity falls into my lap to earn it in one summer, I jump. The hitch ... well, I have to get hitched. Thankfully, it's a marriage in name only. Paris, here I come!

Adam

I used to live my life chasing danger and the hard hit of adrenaline. But all of that changed two years ago. Now I live my life for a flame-haired five-year-old named Olivia. Being a single dad to my best friends' daughter was not my plan, but I'll be damned if I let anyone swoop in and take this fire cracker from my big extended family, now that she's part of it.

Best way to combat the threat is to show the courts I'm

not the free-loving, risk-taker I used to be. I need a wife. And avalanche fast! Lizzy is the perfect choice because, like me, she doesn't want to be married. It's just the reminder I need to keep things light. Except nothing about the way my feelings develop for Lizzy feel temporary.

~~~

Rhodes to Love is the fourth stand-alone book in the new adult, contemporary romance series, the Mixed Six-Pack. If you like generous heroes, goal-oriented heroines, and cute-as-kitten kids you'll adore Danika Bloom's steamy friends-to-lovers romance.

~

"The splendid romance is always front and center, but the background is a cornucopia of family togetherness through thick and thin. There are many truly laugh-out-loud moments … The author exquisitely built up their growing feelings for each other little by little, one mini-crisis after another, until it's clear to everyone involved that theirs is a love story for the ages." ~Viper Spaulding, Goodreads

"Another heart-filling HEA from Danika Bloom! The road to love for these two is a bit rocky, but well worth the trip. It felt 100% real and my heart was invested in their story right away. It helped I already feel part of the Rhodes family from reading the previous books in the series. (Side note: This book will stand alone, so don't feel like you can't pick it up if you haven't read the others!)" ~Cecilia Dawn, Goodreads
~~~

1

____

LIZZY

The new dress code could kiss my ass—because that's about all it was covering.

More men had hit on me in the last two hours than in the entire five years I'd worn my old hostess uniform. Not that I used to dress like a nun, but the bare-skin-to-covered ratio of my restaurant-appointed skirt and blouse would make a stripper proud.

The new owner made it clear that I could leave if I didn't like it. The servers—all women, a legacy of the previous owner—had muttered complaints at first, but their tips had doubled in the last few weeks, since Burgersio had finished its face-lift. That quieted them down.

It had never been a restaurant that catered to families, but now, if I had a child, I'd walk out before even being seated. From the deep bass of the music to the new, hundred-inch TV screens, to the change in the menu from more substantial offerings to what's not much more than bar food, the fact that I'd only led small groups of men to tables tonight didn't surprise me. It pissed me off, but I wasn't surprised.

So when a young couple with what looked like a four- or

five-year-old girl walked in, smiling, I couldn't stop myself from making a face that screamed, "Get back in your car! Don't follow the serial killer into the woods."

With my body positioned directly behind the podium to hide the overabundance of bare skin that my clothes didn't, I dropped my eyebrows and unscrunched my nose.

"Hello! Welcome to Burgersio. Table for three?"

We swapped expressions—while I held a smile, the mom and dad looked from me to the other waitstaff, their eyes wide and mouths agape.

The man spoke first. "I'm sorry. I think we're in the wrong restaurant. We're looking for …" He paused, and the woman finished, "Burgersio. Hon, this is the place."

"Well, that makes no sense at all," he said. "Mom would never come here."

I leaned toward them. "Sorry to eavesdrop. Your mom probably came here at least a month ago. New owner," I said, trying not to scowl.

"Daddy, I'm starving," the little girl whined, pulling on the man's shirt.

"Hang tight a minute, sweetheart." He looked to me. "We have a hundred-dollar gift certificate. Any chance we can get a refund?"

I nodded. "I'm sure Joe will do that for you. This is … yeah, not a family restaurant. He's right over there." Stepping out from behind my podium, I wanted to ask them to turn away so they wouldn't see how long my legs were and how little of their shape was left to the imagination.

I explained the situation to Joe. He showed no sympathy, told me to seat them in the rear corner with their daughter facing the wall, if they didn't like what they saw.

"I am not telling them that. You tell them yourself." I knew I was pushing my luck, that he could replace me with any one of the other servers in a short-skirt second. I returned to the podium, expecting Joe to follow. He did not.

"I am so sorry. The owner's not willing to refund your gift card," I said to the couple and the hungry little girl. "He'd like me to seat you in the corner." I pointed. "We can set the table so you're not watching the meat market."

"That's bullshit," the man said.

"Bruce!"

The couple shared a look—reading each other's minds? I sighed, wondering if I'd ever have that kind of relationship.

"I have an idea," I offered, knowing if I got caught I'd probably be fired. "If you're willing to have your meal here, I'll arrange to comp it for you and"—I looked across the room at Joe who was watching over his kingdom like a sick pervert—"if you give me your gift card, I'll use it to pay another customer's tab. That way I can cash it out to you."

"I don't understand," said the woman. "You're offering to give us a free meal *and* the value of the gift card?"

I nodded. "One favor, though. Please don't punish your waitress. If the service is good, please leave her a twenty percent tip. I'd appreciate it."

"Twenty bucks for a free hundred-dollar meal? Take us to our table," the man said.

"Don't mention anything to your server. I don't want her to get in trouble. I've got authority to comp a meal once a month. I'd like it to be yours." *Since my boss is such a dick.* I pointed at the little girl. "Do you like chicken nuggets?"

"They're my favorite," she said, nodding and bouncing on her toes.

"We've got the best nuggets in town. Let's get you to a table and order those up for you." I nodded at the parents, hoping that was okay. The mom smiled.

While I changed the place settings, Bruce moved the chairs from facing out into the restaurant to the two sides of the table facing the wall.

"I am so sorry about this. Can I start you off with drinks?"

I put their orders into the system and returned to my podium, half hoping, half terrified Joe would be pissed. My best friend's voice sang in my head, "What's it going to take for you to quit that job and do what you studied? How much did your master's cost you? Time to use it, girlfriend."

Kama was right. I'd busted my butt putting myself through university to earn a degree so I'd have a marketable skill that didn't require having to stand in a drafty doorway for eight hours a night. But now that I was free from studies and before I got settled into my career, I wanted to travel, to do the gap-year thing I hadn't had the courage to do after high school—and couldn't afford between my bachelor and master's degrees.

I was twenty-five and had never been east of the Rocky Mountains. I'd made it as far south as Seattle once for a conference, but I'd never had a holiday. Never had my passport stamped. Never gone to a place where I'd have to pantomime to be understood. I wanted to do all those things before I committed myself to my career.

I had enough money saved for a flight to London and a couple of months staying in youth hostels. As soon as I had another thousand dollars in the bank, I'd be handing in my notice.

The door to the restaurant opened, and a group of four men sauntered in.

"Told ya," the first man in said.

I watched as they looked around. I wanted to suggest they work together and decide on one body spray because their mix of Axe scents made my eyes burn.

"Dude! Serious spank-bank material." They high-fived each other and turned to me.

"Lizzy," Mr. Spank Bank said, staring at my name tag, pinned in the only spot it could be—right on my breast.

I smiled big and died a little inside. "Table for four ...

gentlemen?" I said, knowing my sarcasm would be lost on them.

"Lead the way, Lizzy," guy number one said.

"Nice legs," I heard from behind, as if having random guys check me out was a compliment.

Still smiling, I placed menus on the table and said through clenched teeth, "Your server will be right with you. Do you know what you'd like to drink? I can get that started for you."

"Some of what *you've* got on tap would be fine with me, Lizzy," Spanky said with a wink.

I bit the inside of my lower lip and maintained my poker face, inhaling calm before answering. "We've got over twenty beers on tap, sir. Have a look at the menu, and your server will be with you in a couple minutes."

"I didn't mean beer, sugar," Mr. Obvious said.

"We have cider on tap too." I gave them my sweetest smile and turned to walk away, knowing they were watching me. I wanted to shrink into the floor and flip them the finger at the same time.

Nobody was waiting at the podium to be seated, so I checked in on my family guests. "Find anything on the menu for yourselves?" I asked the mom.

"Since this is a little like winning a small lottery, we're indulging in the surf 'n' turf with a twice-baked potato." She smiled like this was the best meal imaginable.

"Just want to be one hundred percent clear so we're not surprised," the man said. "When you said you'd comp our meal, did you mean up to the hundred dollars or …" He let me fill in the end of the sentence.

"Go crazy." I smiled. "We make a mean Manhattan. The beer on tap is local, microbrew. And be sure to save room for dessert."

The woman beamed. "We haven't been out for dinner in

a restaurant that serves alcohol in … how long, babe? Three years?"

"Not since your thirtieth birthday," he said.

"Sorry as I am about the"—I waved my arm toward the room—"the *not* kid-friendly environment, I hope we can make your first date in three years a memorable one, in a good way. Order anything you like. On the house. And I've got a table that's about to settle up, so I can get you your refund in a few minutes."

The dad understood my request without me asking and pulled the gift card from his wallet.

From my spot at the front-of-house, I kept my eye on the table where Sandy had placed the check, quite certain at least a couple of the five men would be paying cash. As soon as I saw them pull out their wallets and fill the billfold, I made my way over.

"Anyone need change?" I asked.

The guys who used cash said they were good. Once all the card payments had been processed I said, "Thanks so much for coming to Burgersio. Hope to see you real soon," drawing out the word *real* as part of the new required send-off.

I took the billfold and cash to the register and made sure nobody was looking, then worked my sleight of hand, counting the bills and putting the amount for food, drinks, and tax in the till—less a hundred, which I replaced with the gift card. I dropped a loonie and knelt behind the counter to pick it up, stuffing five twenties into my bra while I was hidden. Standing, I put the tip amount into the tip drawer and smiled at Joe, who was now giving me the hairy eyeball.

When the restaurant was packed and my family were about ready to leave, having indulged in desserts, I headed over. "I had a look at your bill. It comes to one hundred sixty-four dollars."

The woman whistled, then giggled. She was three tequila sunrises to the wind.

"Was the service okay?" I asked, looking from the woman to the man.

"Exceptional," he answered.

"Worth a twenty percent tip?" I pulled the bills from my blouse as discreetly as possible. "Sorry. No pockets."

The woman giggled again. The man nodded.

He took the money and placed two twenties on the table.

"Would you like any change?"

"No. I hope it's shared with you," he said. "And that we haven't gotten you in trouble. What you did … well, thank you. The food was fantastic, and we had a wonderful evening, though I don't think we'll be back."

"Aww, Daddy, why not? They were the best chicken nuggets I ever had in my entire life," the little girl said with award-worthy drama.

I leaned over to her, making sure my arms were covering my cleavage. "I'll tell you a secret. They're just normal chicken nuggets. Want to know how we make them so tasty?"

She nodded with so much enthusiasm, I laughed. "The cook fries them in a bit of bacon fat after they've been heated." I looked from the dad to the mom.

"Copy that. Fried in bacon fat."

On my way to the register, I pulled Brandy, one of the new servers, to the side. "Your family of three in the corner has settled. Left you a forty-dollar tip. Well done!"

She beamed. "Man, I love this job!"

I printed the receipt, wrote 'Comped by Lizzy' across it, and put it in the register. It would be a couple of days before the bookkeeper would give Joe the news. In other words, a couple of days for me to worry—or maybe hope, I wasn't sure—that I'd be applying for a new job by this time next week.

2

———

ADAM

Olivia's absentee aunt could kiss my ass—thinking she could waltz in and assume full custody of her niece after three years of once-a-month video chats. She was delusional. As far as I was concerned and Olivia remembered, I was her dad now.

I'd been hiding my stress and anger for two weeks, since Brigitte announced she was coming back to Vancouver—and that I'd better find a lawyer.

I slid open the van door to let Olivia out. She was dressed for her first kindergarten class performance in front of the whole school. To add to her nerves, she'd be meeting Auntie Brigitte in real life for the first time tonight.

"Do you think she'll recognize me, Dadam? Oh no!" She hit her head against her car seat with Disney-caliber princess drama. "What if *I* don't recognize *her*? Will she be mad?"

I undid her seat belt and stood back. "Chill, pumpkin. I am one hundred percent sure you'll recognize her. And there is no way she won't be able to tell you apart from every kid in the school."

"Because I'm the only one with hair on fire." She pouted and slid from her seat to the ground.

"No." I rubbed the top of her bright red curls. "Because you're the one who lights up the room when you smile. Stop stressing. You'll recognize her, and she'll love you. I promise."

As I said those last words, I regretted it. I had no doubt Brigitte would be able to pick Olivia out from the two hundred students. She was the spitting image of her mom, Brigitte's older sister. I also had no doubt Brigitte would love her. And that's what scared me.

Scared the crap out of me. She'd been clear—she was in town from London to assume a more active role in Olivia's life. A life, in my opinion, she gave up the right to have more than a passing interest in when she chose to let me assume full guardianship responsibilities after her sister, Maggie, died.

"Let's get inside. I want a seat in the front row so I can embarrass you when I stand up and sing along."

Olivia rolled her eyes, knowing I was being a goof. But then she held her hands across her stomach and stared up at me with pleading eyes.

"Five, four, three, two, one?" I asked.

She nodded. "You first."

"Okay, me first." I scanned the parking lot and side yard of the school. "I see a garbage can, a soccer net, a crow"—I touched Olivia's nose—"a talented five-year-old, and ..." I spun in a circle and came right back to Olivia. "Another talented five-year-old. How many talented five-year-olds are there here?"

She giggled and shook her head then pointed to different kids getting out of cars and walking toward the school. "I see Tyler and Maddy and Sarah and Sarah's little brother and Sarah's mom."

The therapist Olivia saw twice a month had taught us this grounding exercise. At first, I was skeptical, but truthfully, it worked as well for me as it did for Olivia.

She'd developed intense separation anxiety when school first started. I couldn't blame her, given her parents never came home after she'd been dropped off at daycare when she was two and a half.

Not the time to think about that. Not now.

"My turn?" I cupped a hand around one ear. "I *hear* … kids laughing and a piano from inside the school and that crow and a motorcycle." I looked up to see another dad pull up to the curb and a girl several grades ahead of Olivia hop off the Harley. "What do you hear?"

"Um, I hear a motorcycle and—"

"Cheater."

"Am not! And kids yelling and other kids singing and …"

I burped for fun, and to speed up the game a little, since I wanted to be in a chair before Brigitte arrived. I didn't want to have to make small talk, or worse, sit beside her. I'd be seeing her in court on Monday, and that was already more time breathing her air than I wanted.

"Gross, Dadam! And I hear a disgusting burp."

"Only human." I scrunched my nose to mimic her expression. "I *feel*," I said, emphasizing the word, "these silly shoes pinching my toes, and the cut where I nicked myself when I was shaving, and giant pride in my heart to see my favorite girl on stage tonight."

"Of course, I'm your favorite because I'm your *only* girl." She frowned.

"Fine, fine, what do you feel?"

"I feel fuzzy stuff in my pocket—"

"Hey! That's my fuzzy stuff. I thought I'd lost it!"

"Dadam, be serious. And I feel my hair is pulling because you put the scrunchy too tight and can you fix it?"

"One more," I said, loosening the elastic keeping her hair out of her face.

"And I feel … like …"

Please don't say throwing up or going home.

"… singing so loud, Uncle Dylan and Auntie Kama can hear me even though they're not here."

As if on cue, my brother and his wife popped out from beside the van. He winked, and Kama nodded hello.

"My turn?" Dylan asked.

Olivia jumped into his arms. "Uncle Dylan! What do you smell?" she asked.

He sniffed her and said, "Chocolate chip cookies and stinky armpits."

"Uncle Dylan, be serious."

Kama held out a paper bag. "Chocolate chip cookies for after the show. And the stinky armpits are Uncle Dylan's. I told him to shower, but he said we'd be late if he did."

Dylan put Olivia on her feet. She took Kama by the hand and walked her toward the school.

"Hey, there's one more. I taste toothpaste," I called after her.

Olivia looked up at Kama, then at the bag. Kama held it open, and a small hand shot in and back out, clutching a cookie. Before I could argue, she'd taken a bite. "I taste chocolate chip cookies!"

Mission accomplished. Olivia waved a happy goodbye to us and skipped away to a group of her classmates.

"Didn't think you could make it," I said to my brother.

"I booked a fake meeting so I could leave work early."

"Nice."

"Have you seen—"

"No, and don't risk conjuring her by saying her name. I told Olivia I'd sit in the front row. You with me, or are you bugging out after her class performs?"

"Have you got beer?"

"Not on me."

"No, dumbass. At home. If you have beer, we'll stay and come over after."

We made our way to the small school's multipurpose room—which was also my classroom, the gymnasium. Not a job I ever expected to find myself in during the years I was being paid millions by sponsors as a stunt snowboarder.

I'd set up the five hundred folding chairs after my last class this afternoon. The students in my first class in the morning would have the displeasure of putting them all away.

The only seats we could find together were close to the gym's side entrance at the end of the row. Unfortunately, Brigitte would be sure to see us when she arrived. Fortunately, there wasn't an empty fourth seat available.

The lights flashed. Kids screamed and then laughed.

The principal stepped onto the stage. "We'll get underway in five minutes. Children, please find your homeroom teachers now. Parents, family, and friends, find your seats."

I scoped the room for Brigitte, glad not to see her. It wasn't very considerate of me, but then, it wasn't very considerate of her to come crashing back into my life. Into Olivia's 'in real life' life.

As far as I was concerned, her niece was my daughter now. And as far as Olivia remembered, I was her dad, my parents were her grandparents, my brothers, her uncles, their wives, her aunts, and Nana? She was, without a doubt, the best thing that ever could have happened to that little girl.

Olivia's kindergarten class was up first. They sang and did an interesting dance number to a song called "Stomp and Clap." Each kid had a one-line solo that the rest of the class repeated. Olivia nailed her line and she knew it. Dylan and I stood and cheered when it was over.

Grades one through six had two performances each, wrapping with the grand finale, a painful rendition of the perennial school concert classic, "Eye of the Tiger," played on recorders.

The door to the gym opened, and on instinct I looked over. Ugh. Brigitte. She caught my eye and silently asked if I'd saved her a seat. I shrugged. She scowled.

What the heck? The concert would be over in another three minutes.

Brigitte, looking quite relaxed, stood with the heel of her stiletto against the wall. The song ended. Everyone cheered —if they were like Dylan, Kama, and me, the celebration was that the tiger had been put back in his cage. It was brutal. Then we were surrounded by the chaos of close to two hundred kids trying to find their parents.

Brigitte approached. She nodded at Dylan, whom she'd known almost as long as she'd known me, then extended her hand to Kama.

"Hello. I'm Brigitte. Olivia's aunt." She said *aunt* with a pronounced British accent even though she'd only been living there for three years.

"Kama. I'm also Olivia's auntie."

"Sure, sure. But I'm her *real* aunt. Not by marriage, by birth."

"I am aware." Kama smiled politely, then turned her shoulder toward Brigitte, presumably to speak to Dylan, but her lips turned down so quickly I was pretty sure Brigitte saw the real meaning in her change of posture.

Olivia ran up, full of energy. "You're here!" She tried to jump into Brigitte's arms, but was blocked by a quick elbow in a designer jacket.

Before Olivia could register the rebuff, I scooped her into my arms and gave her a hug. "Congratulations! You nailed your part!"

Olivia beamed and turned her head to Brigitte. "Did you see me?"

"I wouldn't have missed it for the world," Brigitte lied.

"Goody. I didn't see you. Where were you sitting?"

Brigitte waved to the far end of the room. "Over there. Well done, Olivia. Your mum and dad would be proud."

My muscles contracted at the passive-aggressive comment. *I'm her dad, and you cannot take her away now.* It was a good thing Olivia had started to wiggle free, because at that moment, my instinct was to take her and run.

"Can I go play with my friends?"

"Don't leave the gym."

"I won't." Olivia skipped a few feet away, then turned and waved. "Bye, Uncle Dylan and Auntie Kama. And Auntie Brigitte."

"I noticed a bake table on my way in. Dylan, will you buy me a cupcake?" Kama took my brother's hand and the two left me alone with my very own Ghost of Christmas Past.

I grabbed at my jaw and massaged the joints, concentrating on finding my inner diplomat. "Brigitte, I saw you come in five minutes ago. *Wouldn't have missed it for the world?* So what *did* you miss Olivia's first performance for?"

"Not that it's any of your business, but I had a mani-pedi appointment and—"

"You've got to be kidding." I flashed on a vivid memory of waiting at a hockey game for her years earlier and her showing up at halftime with a new cut and color, entirely unapologetic.

"What? It usually takes months to get an appointment with this woman. I was on her wait-list if there was a cancellation, and ..." She waved long, bright, multicolored nails in my face. They looked like they could draw blood.

I took a step away. "Why bother showing up if you're not even here to see Olivia sing?"

"How was I supposed to know her class would be first?"

I hadn't realized the depth of the anger I was harboring against Brigitte until that moment. The tension in my gut, like a tight, heavy metal spring, uncoiled too fast. My arms rose quickly, then opened wide. "Whatever."

She smirked, and I knew she'd made a mental note of my impatience, something to use against me. "Relax, she'll have other little concerts. I'll be on time for the next one. And she thinks I was here. That's all that matters, right? That her Auntie Brigitte loves her so much, she came all the way from London to see her sing her little song. What was it, by the way, in case she asks?"

I shook my head and left my ex-wife standing on her own, an electric eel in a toddler pool.

3

ADAM

I didn't hear from Brigitte over the weekend, which worked for me. Not that she wasn't on my mind every waking minute.

On Monday afternoon we met again, this time with lawyers in tow, to appeal to the family court judge for primary guardianship of Olivia. It did not go well. My lawyer—my brother Dylan—invited me to his place to process and talk about next steps.

Dylan pushed open the door to his condo and held it for me.

I stopped. Dead in my tracks.

Before I even saw her, I knew Lizzy was here. Her signature scent greeted me. It was a perfume I never remembered the name of but wished every woman would wear.

Dylan hadn't given me a heads-up, which I would have appreciated. In fact, if I'd known she was going to be here, I'd have passed on his offer of beer and bro time. I gave him a look, a silent, "What the heck? Why didn't you tell me?" He returned an expression that told me he had no idea she'd be here.

It had been six months since we'd seen each other, and our last goodbye had been as uncomfortable as a snowball to the face. I inhaled long and slow to ground myself for her reaction. Colossal mistake on the deep breath since the Lizzy-infused jacket was hanging on a hook right beside my face. The name of her perfume came to me, sort of, in the shape of a semi-chub and the not-quite-right name—Fuck Me Green Tea.

Stepping around the corner, I expected she'd be sitting on the couch several yards away, but she caught me off guard and was right there. Her smile and open expression suggested she was happy to see me.

Okay, good start.

I relaxed a little. Well, part of me did. My right hand dropped to block any possible chance of her registering what her presence was doing to me. Mistake since her eyes followed my hand.

Ahem. I cleared my throat to bring her gaze back to my face.

Lizzy tilted her head and leaned forward with open arms.

Okay. So we're hugging. Not what I expected, but not unwelcome.

She wrapped her arms around my chest and mine fell over her shoulders with my hands landing lightly on her middle back. Her short, chestnut hair was loose and tickled my chin.

I sighed.

She looked up at me.

I extended my sigh, as though I was trying to remember something.

"That perfume. What's it called again?"

"That's like the tenth time you've asked. Fuji Green Tea. Why do you have such a hard time with it?" She rolled her eyes and laughed.

If you don't move right now, you're going to find out exactly how hard a time it gives me.

I released her and pressed myself against the wall, away from her, to put some distance between Mr. Jumpy and the object of his desire. "It's … been awhile," I stated the obvious like an idiot.

"Sorry for the sneak attack. I got fired today. Kama insisted I come over and chill. She didn't tell me you'd be here until Dylan was opening the door."

I laughed. Classic Kama.

"I hope it's okay. I can leave if you want." She pointed toward her jacket as if I'd grab it from the hook and hand it to her.

"No. Of course not. I'm happy to see you."

She nodded and whispered, *Me too.* "Kama mentioned you were in court about Olivia. Did our favorite lawyer make the bad lady go away?"

I shook my head.

"I'm so sorry." She squeezed my bare forearm, which was pressed against my stomach. The touch sent a shiver into my gut and then down. This woman. She had an unwelcome effect on me.

"It is what it is. Hey, I'm sorry about your job. That sucks. You've been there forever."

"It's a bit of pickle. But I'll find another job. Preferably one that lets me wear clothes."

Dylan didn't give me a chance to ask for an explanation. He called from his wet bar in the living room. "Whisky all around?"

"Yes!" we said in unison.

Once we were settled with drinks in the living room, Dylan and Kama on the couch, Lizzy and I in armchairs with a side table between us. Everyone focused on me and what happened in court.

"So," Kama prompted, "was my husband brilliant?"

I turned to Dylan, wanting him to field the question since I was still too shocked to believe that I didn't get the court's immediate blessing to maintain legal guardianship of Olivia until she turned nineteen.

"Not so much," Dylan said. "Brigitte's not going to go away easily. On the upside, the judge does not want to see us in her chambers again. But, on the flip, if we can't figure out a shared custody arrangement on our own, I'm worried she'll award guardianship to Brigitte."

"Why? The judge knows Adam's been her father for over three years and is doing an amazing job. Why would she take that away?"

"Because," I growled, "I drew the short straw with that particular judge. She, too, was orphaned when she was about Olivia's age."

"Isn't that a positive thing? Something in your favor?"

"No, she told this touching story about her parents dying in a car crash when she was seven and how she was raised by her mom's sister and her uncle. In her memory, it was the best childhood she could have hoped for. So even if she doesn't acknowledge it consciously, she'll be biased toward Brigitte," Dylan said.

"That sounds kind of judgy, not very judge-like. Can't you ask for someone else?" Lizzy scowled.

Dylan shook his head. "Despite their power, judges are only human. And they all have biases."

"And one of hers," I added, not helping change Lizzy's expression, "is that she also said something about blood being thicker than water and that family ties should be respected." I swallowed the rest of my scotch and stood to pour myself some more.

"That's bullshit!" Lizzy said. "Has she ever met your family?"

"I think that's one reason she's looking as kindly on Adam as she is," Dylan said. "She's sat as the judge for a half dozen cases I've argued. We've gone for drinks. She likes me. She's heard enough stories about our mixed-up family that I think that's why she decided to send us away to figure this out ourselves. That, and the fact that no judge wants to make this decision when neither applicant appears to be a sociopath and could presumably be a reasonable parent."

Kama spoke up, "How can she say Brigitte would be the better parent? She doesn't even know Olivia. And did you mention the recital?"

"It wasn't the time."

The truth was that even though Brigitte, Maggie's sister, never made it to Vancouver to visit Olivia, they did have a relationship via FaceTime. Brigitte called about once a month and would spend as long as Olivia had patience to sit still, telling her stories, making faces and goofing around. They had as close a relationship as a relative who lives on the other side of the world could have.

The thing that pissed me off was we had an understanding: since this was working, she wouldn't challenge my role as Olivia's primary caregiver. When Brigitte's sister, Maggie, and her husband Dalton, my best friend, found out they were pregnant, they named Brigitte and me as joint legal guardians. It made sense at the time since we never considered we'd actually have to take it seriously.

But when Maggie and Dalton died three years ago, Brigitte was in grad school in London, so caring for a two-year-old would have been impossible without disrupting her studies.

Me?

I was twenty-nine, single (since Brigitte had buggered off and left me a few months before Olivia was born), and on the road for weeks at a time, extreme snowboarding for extreme pay checks all over the world.

That said, after the deaths of my stunt buddies and best

friends, I was in no shape to get on a board. With Nana willing to help me through those first few months, nothing was keeping me from figuring out the dad thing. After half a year with Olivia, I loved that little girl like she was my own. So did everyone else in my family.

"This is such bullshit!" Lizzy banged her fist on the arm of her chair. "What can I do to help? You want me to arrange to have her poisoned? Nothing to kill her, just some bad seafood to make her realize that taking care of a child is a full-time gig, even when you're ejecting fluid from both ends of your body?"

That got a laugh.

"You can help by being my friend. Keep being Olivia's favorite auntie," I said, giving her a wink and realizing what an absolute ass I'd been for the last six months.

"You really are, Lizzy," Dylan said. "She asks about you every time we have a family event."

"But apparently," Kama glared at me, "some people have more sway than others about who's invited to Rhodes' family gatherings."

"*Anyway,*" Dylan said, kissing Kama's cheek. He turned his attention to Lizzy, "Olivia really does love you and channels Kama's disappointment that you haven't been included in all the festivities lately, in her own five-year-old way."

I was standing now, holding a fresh tumbler of scotch. Lizzy reached her hand up, holding her own empty glass. I handed her mine and took hers to refill.

"Well," she said, "my twenty-five-year-old way of expressing my rage that you and Olivia are being put through this, Adam, has me wanting to do things best kept secret from your lawyer. Tell me if there's anything, anything at all, that I can do to help you keep her."

I believed her. I had no doubt she loved Olivia. I felt bad that I'd been keeping them apart. It was selfish, but it was for the best since I'd started to feel things for Lizzy that were not aligned with my life goals. Or with hers.

I dropped into my chair with a three-finger pour. Lizzy held up the glass I'd handed her to swap back. I shook my head. "This one has more. I'm keeping it." We clinked glasses, and I took a long sip. "That's enough about my day. I want to hear about yours. Why'd you get fired? Poisoning patrons who pissed you off?"

"Wish I could poison the new owner. He seems to think that waitresses should make our male customers think of foreplay. We have a new dress code. Doesn't leave much to the imagination."

"You should take Olivia there for dinner," Kama said. "And then complain that you thought the place was family friendly, but that you can tell it's clearly a front for a brothel."

"As if anyone would believe that you and your window-shopping-for-women ways would be upset by a waitress showing too much skin," Dylan scoffed.

"Hey! I resemble that remark," I joked.

Lizzy nodded, almost imperceptibly, then examined her hands in her lap.

By the way she was shaking her head, I knew we were having the same memory—the last conversation we had at Josh and Paige's wedding. She'd helped Olivia catch the bridal bouquet, and I put my foot in it. Not the bouquet. That would have been much less destructive.

I wish I could claim I was drunk when I said what I did. Sadly, I was expressing exactly what I was thinking, how I was feeling.

～

Lizzy put Olivia on her feet and she ran over to show Nana the flowers. "So, looks like you're next in line to tie the noose."

Lizzy shook her head. "Not until I'm at least thirty. I've got too much living to do before I let some guy and a family tie me down."

That was a surprise. I'd taken her as a clinger.

"Good news for you, then, because I've been looking forward to you being all wedding drunk, the way women get, so I could seduce you. But I was worried you might take it the wrong way."

"Sorry? Wedding drunk? The way women get?" Lizzy's forehead crinkled and her eyebrows pressed closer together.

"Yeah, you know, easy to seduce, all googly-eyed thinking about love and stuff."

She tried to push by me, but I caught her arm. "Yeah, no. You're the one who's wedding drunk"—she made air quotes—"or just drunk *drunk."*

"I'm not too drunk to show you what I think about, every time I see you."

She crossed her arms and scowled. "Oh yeah, and what's that?"

"You really want to know?"

"Tell me," she said without any hint of flirtation; it was pure pissed off, which had the strange effect of really turning me on. So I told her exactly what I thought of when I saw her at our family events.

"You want me to tell you how I want to lick every last damn inch of your body, to figure out why you always smell so damn edible? You want me to tell you that my dick is like the needle on a compass and you're true north? You want—"

"Wait. Your dick is like a needle?" She threw her head back and laughed.

I considered biting her neck.

"Not the point," I growled.

"You're saying your needle dick does not have a point? I'm so turned on right now."

"You want to see how turned on you make me?"

"Dream on, Romeo. Never going to happen."

"Because you're afraid you can't handle me. You're worried—and rightfully so—that you'd fall in love with me."

And I'm worried I'd fall way too hard for you.

"You're delusional." She gave me a somewhat gentle shove.

I grabbed her wrists and pressed her palms against my chest. When I released them, she bunched my shirt in closed fists.

"You want me. Admit it," I whispered in her ear.

I want you.

"No, Adam. I have zero interest in my vagina being one of the hundreds you've tested. I like being your friend, having auntie time with Olivia, but sex with you?" Her fists pulled back, then landed hard against my ribs. "Thanks, but no thanks. That free-love schtick isn't sexy for a guy who's over thirty. No wonder you're the last single brother."

And then she did the evilest thing possible. She pressed her hand to my cheek, turned my head so my ear was touching her lips, and whispered, "One night with me would break you. I would ride you so hard you'd need to see a chiropractor to realign your spine. You, drunk man, can't handle me."

That's when I pulled her close and pressed my hard-on into her abdomen. "One night with this giant Space Needle, and I promise, you'll have memories to live on for years."

Lizzy pulled away, still smiling, but shook her head. "I'm happy to come over any Friday night and babysit Olivia while you space needle your way into some other lucky woman's orbit."

And then she walked away.

Lizzy pushed a coaster off the side table and into my lap.

"Hey. You're looking kind of … spaced out." A smile played on her face, from her mouth to her forehead.

"Just remembering the bad old days."

"The days when a dick made an ass of himself?" Lizzy laughed.

Dylan and Kama exchanged glances.

"Fine. I was an ass that night." I glared at my brother, then turned to Lizzy. "Can I make it up to you? Why don't you come over Sunday morning and have brunch with us? Olivia would be thrilled to see you, and I'd be thrilled to have a woman do the cooking—ouch!" Kama kicked me. "While I do manly stuff, like wash and fold three weeks of laundry and put away toys."

Lizzy laughed again.

I kicked myself for having assumed she'd be pissed off and for having actively avoided her these last six months.

"You know what? I've changed my mind," I said.

Her smiled dropped, and she appeared to be truly disappointed.

"I don't want you to cook. I'm still not convinced this whole poison thing won't be turned on me since you have a legit reason to want me to suffer for a day—"

"Or three."

She held my gaze, her sparkling blue eyes playful.

"I'd like to take you out to Olivia's favorite restaurant. We can pick you up, if you're not too cool to be seen in the Dad Mobile."

She brightened. "Lucky for you, Olivia's cuteness outshines the butt-boring ugliness of that minivan."

"Butt? Boring? Ugly? Rude. You have no taste. And, you've never experienced the luxury of the ride. All the bells and whistles available for a safety first, family van."

"Have you ever thought of painting a bell or whistle on it, to give it some style?"

As soon as Lizzy said that, I had an epiphany. "It was you!"

"What?" Lizzy sucked in her top and bottom lips. It was quite a face, but it didn't hide the smile she was fighting.

I pointed an accusatory finger at her. "You're the one who

planted the idea in Olivia's head that I should paint the van princess pink."

"I would never!" Lizzy looked at Kama, who was wide-eyed, laughing. "I suggested *bubblegum* pink, but Olivia didn't know what color that was. She's the one who came up with princess pink."

I sat back and the tension of the afternoon melted. Lizzy did that. She made things feel easy, possible. But she was so far off-limits, no matter what reasons my little head argued to make me change my big head's mind.

She was my sister-in-law's best friend. If I crossed a line with her and things went south—in the aftermath of things going south—I'd still have surprise encounters like this dropping in to see my brother. But she and Olivia had hit it off, and I enjoyed hanging out with her. I'd simply have to ignore the carnal desires that came along with seeing her. I could do that. I was thirty-two years old. I could control my dick.

"Do you have plans after Sunday brunch?" I asked her.

She shook her head.

"I have an idea that will let you and Olivia express your inner artists. You game to do something messy and fun?"

4

LIZZY

In the five days between unexpectedly seeing Adam and our brunch date, I thought far too much about how my senses came alive when my body was pressed against his. I realized that in all the months I'd been hanging out with the Rhodes, Adam and I had never hugged. It was strange since I'd hugged Olivia hundreds of times. But if Adam had ever wrapped his arms around me before, I'd have remembered. The way the electricity sparked and clashed between us was something a woman does not forget.

Of the four brothers I'd met, Adam was by far the most handsome—the only one who showed up at events with messy hair and probably only shaved once a week. He was also the most aloof and hardest to get to know. Were it not for Olivia, who was always with him, I probably never would have said more than hello to him.

I knew Dylan the best, since he'd basically stolen my best friend from me when they started dating. And then Josh, Adam's half brother and the youngest of the guys, who had been dealing with losing his favorite brother to my best friend. Josh and I did a lot of double *not*-dating with Dylan and Kama until his girlfriend, Paige came home from being away.

I knew Nick, their firefighter brother who lived about an hour from Vancouver in Lily Valley, the least well. He was married to Sophie who was two years younger than me—married at twenty-three—which blew my mind since she seemed really happy. Happy to be married at twenty-three? She was out to lunch and one tomato shy of a BLT, in my opinion. I could not understand wanting to settle down that young.

And I didn't need to. What I had to wrap my head around was the fact that Adam "International Superstar Snowboarder (Retired)" Rhodes was taking me out for brunch with his daughter. *For* his daughter. *Because of* his daughter.

This was not a date; it was an apology for acting like a tool. That's all. And that was perfect, no matter what traitorous ideas my lady bits whispered.

He and Olivia picked me up at my place, as planned, at 10:30 a.m. sharp. Adam hadn't told me what fun we'd be getting up to, only that I should dress to make a mess—but also be clean enough that we'd be allowed into Olivia's favorite brunch restaurant: Bacon Brothers Diner.

The closest spot we could find to park was several blocks away, down a steep hill. I tried to be less of a whiner than the five-year-old, but my feet were killing me, having walked a thousand miles in the last four days, going from restaurant to restaurant trying to find a new job. And I was overtired since I'd hardly slept, wondering if Adam would hug me again, if he'd been zapped the way I had. And then worrying about it, since the very last thing in the world I wanted was any kind of magical connection to anyone or anything other than my travel savings account.

But in this moment, the only thing I wanted was to melt into the café's old, padded bench seats.

Olivia, on the other hand, was full of beans. We were halfway there when she stopped and threw her arms in the air with dramatic flair.

"Dadam, stop! We have to go back to the van. I forgot my backpack." She hung her head and shook it.

"Don't worry. They have paper and crayons."

She put her hands on her tiny hips and huffed, "I know that. But that's not what I need in my bag." Olivia grabbed Adam's hand and started to drag him down the hill. I wanted to cry.

"They have toys to play with, Olivia."

"You're not listening! I need what's in my backpack." She pointed in the direction of the van and emphasized with a roll of her eyes, "It's your Father's Day present."

I laughed. "You guys go and get the bag. I'll keep dragging my butt up this hill and stand in line for a table."

Adam frowned. "They won't let you in the line until your full party has arrived."

"Oh, for fuck-accia bread," I said, catching myself, I hoped in time.

"They don't have focaccia bread, Auntie Lizzy," Olivia said. "They have really yummy pancakes, though! Come on, let's go!"

I looked down the hill to the van, then at the strip of grass between the sidewalk and the road. "I'll be right here," I said, dropping to the ground and closing my eyes.

By the time the fearless hikers returned, I was almost dozing.

"You think we should wake her up?" Adam whispered.

"Mmm, I don't know. Maybe you should carry her to the restaurant so she can keep sleeping until we eat," Olivia suggested.

"But if my arms are full, who will hold your hand?" Adam asked.

"I'm five. I don't need anyone to hold my hand."

Five going on fifteen, I thought.

Adam raised his eyebrows and nodded. "Okay, then. I think carrying Auntie Lizzy is a stellar idea."

My heart did a backflip …

I opened my eyes to find Adam kneeling in front of me. He winked and whispered, "You want to play along?"

… and then it fainted.

Did I? Yeah, I did. I nodded and closed my eyes again. Adam scooped me into his arms and held me like I'd seen him carry Olivia, with my chest pressed to his and my legs hanging around his hips, his arm making a seat under my bum.

I rested my head on his shoulder and breathed in the scent of his soap. My lady bits woke up, and without thinking, I clenched to tell them to settle down. Of course, my butt muscles contracted too. Against Adam's forearm. He chuckled.

"You smell nice," I whispered, hoping to distract him from what my nether region was communicating to his arm. His arm!

"You're supposed to be asleep."

Little Miss Bat Hearing piped up. "Yeah, if you start talking, Dadam will put you down and make you walk. So even if you wake up again, pretend you're asleep. That's what I do."

I made a snoring noise.

"She's asleep again, Dadam. You have to keep carrying her."

How he managed to carry me up that hill and halfway down the block to the restaurant without any sign of exerting himself was beyond me. I'm not an Amazon, but at five foot seven, I'm not a waif, either. As he came to a stop, I opened my eyes and saw the window of the restaurant beside us. I was disappointed that we'd arrived; it felt way too nice to be held like this.

"Auntie Lizzy, wake up," Olivia said in a singsong voice as she tugged the leg of my jeans. "We're here. You have to stand up now."

"I don't mind carrying you until we're ready to go in. We'll be in this line for at least thirty minutes." Adam bumped me up a little higher in his arms, so my head was level height with his.

Every cell in my body screamed, urging me to kiss him. His mouth was so close it was out of focus. I pressed my nose to his neck to keep myself from acting, but that was a mistake since he smelled so delicious, all I could imagine was licking him.

Adam relaxed his hold and my body leaned away a few inches. "You okay? Your heart is pounding like you've run a half-marathon."

"Just … need coffee." *And to feel my lips against your skin.*

"Well, we can go somewhere else. Someplace without a lineup."

Or back to your place. Your place would be good.

A plaintive little moan murmured in my throat.

"Lizzy, are you okay?" He rubbed his hand between my shoulder blades.

"Can you put me down? I need to …" I couldn't catch my breath. "Down."

Adam pulled one arm from under my butt. My legs fell free. But he was still holding me up with an arm across my back. I twisted and landed on my feet. I bent forward and rested my forearms on my thighs, focused on breathing.

This man was like a dangerous drug. One hug. How much trouble can you get into with a hug? Yeah, right. One hug, a gateway drug to needing a kiss, and then an intimate touch, and then … nope. That line of thought was not settling my rattled nerves at all.

"That is one heck of a caffeine withdrawal." Adam laughed and touched my shoulder. I flinched. "Whoa! Okay.

Olivia, I think Auntie Lizzy is really desperate for a coffee. You two stay here while I wrangle something up."

"People are staring at you, Auntie Lizzie."

"Well, I guess they've never met a true coffee addict before."

"I'm never drinking coffee," Olivia said in earnest.

Once he was out of my force field, I recovered quickly. Adam was gone several minutes before he came back down the line of people, all patiently waiting for their hit of Bacon Brother's brunch. He was carrying a coffee carafe in one hand and a tray with paper cups, creamers, and sugar in the other. He was as relaxed as an experienced server.

"Madame, some coffee to keep you from passing out again?"

"Oh my god, I love you!" I slapped my hand against my mouth as soon as the words in my head betrayed me. "I mean, coffee. I love coffee. And I thank you for getting me some. Thank you. That's what I meant to say." *Shut up, shut up, shut up.*

Adam did an exceptional job of keeping the tray balanced while he laughed.

I took a cup from the stack and held it out so he could fill it. I grabbed two creamers, a pack of sugar, and a stir stick.

He winked and nodded down the street, away from the entrance to the restaurant and the people in line behind us. "Anyone else need some liquid love?"

Several people called, "Over here," and "Me, please."

I watched as he interacted with a half dozen people, smiling, laughing, sharing his joyful energy. That's just who he is. He's a friendly, touchy-feely kind of man. *Get a grip, Elizabeth. Control your hormones.*

He was back in line with us, tray emptied, in under five minutes.

"How did you swing that?" I nodded to the empty carafe.

"I said I had a coffee-deprived woman in line with me who was ready to pass out. When they offered me a cup, I thought it would be fun to play server for a minute. You know, see how it feels to walk a block in your shoes."

I couldn't tell if he was making fun of me. I kind of hoped he was, since if he was trying to empathize with how hard my old job could be … that would make him even more irresistible. And dangerous.

"And? How does it feel?"

"I'm exhausted!" He pressed his hand against his forehead.

"You're an ass-sociate server now." I looked at Olivia, wide-eyed, then turned to face Adam. "How do you manage not to swear when little ears are present?"

"It took awhile, but I trained myself to use alternative words. The thing is, now that's all I use. You've never noticed the guys razz me for saying, 'Ah, shhh-atner' or 'dadgum it'?"

"Don't forget 'son of a biscuit,'" Olivia chimed in. "He's so weird. As if biscuits have babies!"

With coffee in my veins and maintaining at least twelve inches of space between Adam and me, time passed quickly before we were seated in a booth in the crowded little café. As soon as our bums hit the benches—Olivia and I on one side, Adam across from Olivia so I wouldn't have to spend my whole meal trying not to bump knees with him—she pulled a small, wrapped package from her backpack and placed it on the table.

"Don't open it yet," she warned. She pulled a homemade card from the bag and put it on top of the present. "Nana helped me spell for the card and choose a present. But I wrapped it and did the printing and the drawing all by myself. Happy Father's Day, Dadam."

"That is a beautiful card," I said.

"I know," she said in the way only a child can without sounding obnoxious.

As Adam appreciated the card Olivia had made, a pang of grief and anger overcame me that someone—a relative stranger in both senses of the phrase—was trying to break this dynamic duo apart.

Adam unwrapped his gift—a Bart Simpson mini-figure— and laughed so loud, he drowned out all the background chatter.

Olivia glowed.

Adam beamed.

I melted.

I was moved by the sweetness of their relationship and the thought that Olivia might lose her second dad, her entire second family, before her sixth birthday. It was too much.

Adam gave me the "Are you okay? What's wrong?" look.

I grabbed a napkin and pretended I had something in my eye.

"Auntie Lizzy, it's okay. I'll make you a card too. You don't have to cry."

"Thank you, sweetie. I would love you to make me a card." I gave her arm a rub and tried to distract us all from my wet eyes by asking why the present made them laugh so hard.

"I've been coming here since I was younger than Olivia."

"And not as well-behaved," she interrupted.

Adam laughed. "Yes, and not nearly as well-behaved." He pointed to the shelf on the wall behind the diner counter. It was covered with hundreds of small, colorful toys from Slinkys to Rubik's Cubes to Teenage Mutant Ninja Turtles. Every generation's best sellers were on display. "According to family history, when I was five, I *really* wanted to play with the Bart Simpson figure that was up on that shelf and was so … how shall I put it … vocal about it, we were asked to leave."

"And Nana said that one day, Dadam would understand when he had kids who embarrassed him. Right, Dadam?"

"Yup. But joke's on Nana because you've never embarrassed me."

"Nana said this would be the perfect day to test my lungs."

I almost spat out my coffee. Olivia was too much. You'd never guess she'd suffered the amount of trauma she had. It was a testament to how adored she was by the Rhodes family.

Adam made his Bart Simpson toy talk to Olivia's pink, purple, and blue glittering monkey finger puppets. Another wave of emotion hit me, but different from the feeling a few minutes earlier. It wasn't based in anger or sadness about the upheaval Olivia could soon be facing again; it felt more like a longing or regret. Here was a man and a little girl I could so easily imagine myself loving as my own family. If only I'd met them five years from now.

5

ADAM

"Okay, little miss," I said, faking a giant yawn as we pulled into the driveway after the best Father's Day brunch ever, "that was fun, and now I think it's time for you to have a nap."

"What?" Olivia was indignant. "What do you think I am? A baby? Dadam, if you're so tired, *you* can have a nap," she whined. "I want Auntie Lizzy to play with me. Please, Auntie Lizzy, will you stay and play?"

"If you're not going to nap," I said with my best dad authority voice, "I'm going to put you to work."

"No-o. I don't want to work. I'm *only* five."

Lizzy sucked in her bottom lip, trying not to laugh. I hadn't told either of them what I had in store. Weeks earlier, Olivia had mentioned how much she wished trees weren't all boring brown.

"I wish the tree in our yard was a rainbow tree. Then I'd be happy every single time I went outside," she'd said one afternoon while I was trying to convince her that riding her bike would be more fun than watching *Brave* for the hundredth time.

It was Kama's brilliant idea to grant Olivia's wish. While

we were out having brunch, she snuck over to the house and wrapped the trunk of the maple tree in my front yard in a bright yellow sheet. I had no idea how she was going to do it, so it was a surprise for me too.

"Well, Lizzy is going to be working with me."

"What, pray tell, am I going to be working on? Will we be … washing this ugly van?"

"Stop calling Betsy ugly. She's beautiful, isn't she, Olivia?"

"Well …," Olivia started.

"Women! How do you not appreciate the beauty in gun-metal gray? But no, we're not washing the van. Everyone out and gather at the tree."

Lizzy and Olivia walked hand in hand to the tree by the living room window and said almost simultaneously, "What in the world?"

It was my turn to laugh.

Kama had left bottles of a dozen colors of tempera paint at the foot of the tree and a sign that said, "Paint me!"

After an hour, not only was the tree "so, so beautiful," according to Olivia, our jeans, T-shirts, hands, and faces were too.

"Shower or bath, Miss Messy?" I asked.

Lizzy answered, "Shower." A very cute blush told me she realized I was talking to Olivia, who jumped on the mistake.

"Yay! Auntie Lizzy and I can have a shower together. Dadam never lets me have a shower with him, and when he washes my hair in the bath, he *always* gets soap in my eyes," she accused.

There was no point arguing. I faked exasperation and turned to Lizzy. "If you're not comfortable showering with her, I totally understand."

Lizzy made a face and Olivia's shoulders slumped forward. "Please?"

"How about we pretend we're at the community pool?

You can wear your bathing suit and I'll … make do with what I have on." Lizzy gave me a questioning look. "Can I toss my *bikini* in the dryer after?"

"Of course. All right, find me in the laundry room matching socks and ironing dresses to meet this princess's exacting standards." I was only half kidding.

While Olivia was singing in the shower, the doorbell rang. I expected it to be Dylan and Kama over to admire the results of our artistic afternoon. I couldn't have been more off.

"Brigitte." Her name tasted like poison on my tongue. "Why are you here?"

"I didn't realize I had to make an appointment to spend time with my niece," she said, hand on her hip.

"A call would have been nice. You know, to make sure we were home."

"You are home, so what's the difference? Where is she?" Brigitte took a step toward me so we were almost touching and leaned around my side. She smelled nice, and I swore at myself for noticing. "Olli! Your favorite aunt is here to visit." She stood straight again. "Aren't you going to invite me in?"

I stepped to the side and waved my arm. A silent invitation to the bloodsucking vampire.

"Where is she?" Brigitte asked.

"She's taking a shower."

"Oh. I didn't realize five-year-olds could shower on their own. I guess I have to brush up on the age milestones."

"What? No. She's way too young to be left on her own in the shower or bath for more than a minute or two."

"Then what the hell are you doing down here?"

Before I could answer, she'd turned and moved toward the stairs.

"Wait. Where are you going? Come back," I called after her.

Brigitte didn't answer. She took the steps two at a time.

"Brigitte! Don't go in—"

"What the hell?" she screamed.

"—the bathroom."

"Hi, Auntie Brigitte!" Olivia's joyful voice carried down the stairs. "Auntie Lizzy and me are taking a shower."

And then, without a pause, Lizzy's voice, firm and confident, "Excuse me. Do you mind? Close the door." There was ice in her tone.

"Yeah, you're letting all the steam out, right, Auntie Lizzy?"

This was going to be a three-beer afternoon. I pulled one from the fridge, cracked it open, took a swig, then realized how a judge would react to Brigitte telling the court I was a day drinker. I put the open bottle in the fridge and grabbed a soda water.

Brigitte stormed into the kitchen, doing a fantastic impression of Mother Gothel, the old crone in *Tangled* who locked Rapunzel away in a tower.

"What the hell, Adam? Letting Olivia see your flings half-naked? And you think you're the better parent," she scoffed. "If you don't agree to let me have full guardianship starting immediately, we *will* go to court over this." She pointed to the stairs. "That is disgusting, and it's child abuse."

I breathed in through my nose to control my anger and heart rate. Expelled hard out of my mouth, concentrating on not allowing words to accompany the breath. I sat and listened as she told me how incompetent and irresponsible I was. How she should never have left Olivia with me. How Olivia would have been better off in boarding school until Brigitte finished her PhD. I took a long pull of my soda, wishing it was stronger.

"You're not even going to argue because you know I'm right," she said.

"No, I'm not going to argue because I'm not going to

argue. I can tell you where you've made bad assumptions, but not now, and not here."

"Because you need time to come up with arguments," she huffed.

"No, because Olivia will be down any second and I don't want her to see my anger toward her loving aunt," I said through gritted teeth.

Right on cue, Olivia bounced into the room in fresh pajamas. "Auntie Lizzy said I should put on my pajamas since I'm not going out again. It doesn't mean I'm going to bed, though." She leveled her most threatening stare at me.

"Not till seven," I said.

"What time is it now?"

"It's only four. And the chef needs to make dinner, so why don't you take Auntie Brigitte out and show her the rainbow tree." I gave myself serious points for how well I hid my feelings.

Brigitte glared at me, then plastered on a giant smile and took Olivia's hand. "I would love to see your rainbow tree."

I grabbed the open beer and a fresh one from the fridge and carried them upstairs.

"Knock, knock," I said, slowly pushing open Olivia's bedroom door. "You okay in here?"

"That was … uncomfortable. I wasn't sure I should come down. I didn't want to make things worse."

"Don't think you can. She's decided what the reality is and …" I put the beer on Olivia's nightstand, sat on the bed, and put my arm around Lizzy's shoulders. She stiffened for a second, then relaxed against me. As if in sync, most of my body relaxed too. All but one rogue appendage that had ideas of its own.

"And what?" She nudged my shoulder.

"And now you're, um, some nameless hookup." I let her go and crossed my arms so my hands landed on my lap. Seriously, was I sixteen?

"Gosh, sorry. I must have slept through it. What was *your* name again?"

She amazed me at how easygoing she was about things that would upset most people.

"Hey." She bumped her head against my arm. "I'm sorry. Do you want me to talk to Brigitte? Do you think she'd listen to me?"

I shrugged.

"Well," she said, mimicking Olivia's negotiation voice perfectly, "if you hand me that beer, I'll talk to her. You know, auntie to auntie."

"Yeah. I guess … What could possibly go wrong?"

6

LIZZY

A untie to auntie. What was I thinking? The conversation with Brigitte was more like predator to prey or intellectual powerhouse to village idiot. Me being the preyed-upon village idiot, of course.

In the end, I don't think I hurt Adam's chance of maintaining guardianship of Olivia, but I wasn't looking forward to telling him the little white lie that came out of nowhere when Brigitte cornered me.

She and I met for coffee on Monday morning. I figured it would be best to not let her assumptions grow in the absence of facts. She got right to the point. I didn't even have time for a sip of my latte before her interrogation started.

"So. Olivia tells me you've been hanging around for some time."

I nodded, opened my mouth to speak, but Brigitte raised one finger and an eyebrow. I shut my mouth.

"She tells me you spent Christmas with the family. And that she made you a special card."

I smiled. "It was really sweet—"

"I'm not done," Brigitte interrupted. "She also tells me her wish came true at her uncle Josh's wedding."

I waited.

"Well?" Brigitte asked.

"Um, I, uh, okay? I wasn't aware of that."

Her eyes bored into me. Anxiety swirled in my chest. My mind raced, as I searched for an answer to a test I hadn't studied for.

"Is it true?" She pushed.

I panicked; I should know what Olivia's wish was to prove that I wasn't some random stranger taking showers with her niece. "Olivia makes a lot of wishes. Which one came true at Josh and Paige's wedding?"

I put my cup to my lips and inhaled the rich aroma before taking my first sip.

"She said she caught the bouquet. And that you were holding her."

I nodded as I swallowed. "That's true. And her reward was to spend every Friday night for the next six months with Josh and Paige, so that Adam would be free to—" I stopped myself from saying "do his horndog thing."

"So he'd be free to what?" Brigitte asked, cocking one eyebrow again. Maybe she's half Vulcan. I wished her long hair wasn't covering the tops of her ears.

"Um, free to take me out without, um, having to hire a babysitter." Dammit, I shouldn't have said that. "Which I've never known him to do. If family aren't available to look after Olivia, he doesn't go out."

I picked up my coffee again to keep myself from saying anything more.

She nodded, as if that sounded like what she already knew. Thank god. But then she added a ringer to my understanding, of her understanding, of my relationship with Adam.

"And Olivia told me that her wish, the one that's finally come true, is that you and Adam are getting married and that you're going to be her new mom."

It was a miracle I didn't spit my coffee at Brigitte with that nugget. Nope. I inhaled it. Right into my lungs. And once I'd recovered my ability to breathe, I was so shocked it was all I could do to stay sitting upright and try to listen to what Brigitte was saying. But my brain spun with how much shit I'd dropped Adam into, trying to figure out if I should correct her misassumption or leave it for the lawyers to sort out.

By the time I'd decided to come clean, to tell her Olivia's wish had not actually fallen on any fairy godmother's ears, Brigitte stood.

"Thank you for initiating this meeting, Lizzy. It's been helpful."

She gave me a hug before we parted ways. And all I could think was, "Her hair smells so nice. This must be the scent of true power."

I called Adam as soon as Brigitte was out of sight. I was frantic.

"Where are you? We need to talk, like, ten minutes ago."

"At school." He sounded as if everything was peachy in the world. What was wrong with him?

"When do you have a break? What school are you at? Where's your office? I'll be there as fast as I can."

"Whoa, Nelly! Can't this wait until I get home?"

"No! And whatever you do, if Brigitte calls, do *not* answer it."

"Lizzy … what have you done?" Thank the goddess, he finally understood the gravity of the situation.

"Which school? I'm coming right over. And don't talk to Brigitte. I'm serious, Adam."

He gave me the address and I waved down a cab, even though the fare was going to cost me a full week of groceries.

~

It had only been eight years since I'd graduated from high school. A lot more since I'd been inside an elementary school. The strange but familiar scent of crayons and bleach transported me right back to wearing ugly, corrective shoes to fix my pigeon-toed gait. Even though I wasn't super tall, everything felt miniature—the lockers that went up to my chin and the one chair outside each classroom that would have been a tight squeeze, even for my butt.

Adam told me to go to the main office and have him paged, since he said he'd be teaching a class and didn't take his cell phone into the gym with him.

"Hello," I said to the focused woman sitting behind a low counter, working on her computer.

Her concentration face changed to a smile as she raised her head to greet me but was replaced by a look of caution when our eyes met. "How can I help you?"

"I'm here to see Adam Rhodes." I hoped I sounded more confident than I felt.

"I believe he's in class."

"He said he would be. If you point me in the right direction, I can find him myself."

"Are you a parent?" she asked.

"Um, no."

"I didn't think so," she muttered. "I'm sorry, but you can't go wandering the school if you're not a parent." She flipped through some papers. "Mr. Rhodes will be done in thirty-five minutes. You can have a seat in the hall and wait for him."

I looked at my phone. I didn't want to wait.

"I sort of have a child who goes here. I'm Olivia's aunt. She's in kindergarten. Does that qualify me for a hall pass?"

That piqued her interest. "So, which one of the Rhodes brothers are you married to?"

"Oh no, it's not like that. I'm not married to any of them." And then, because apparently I had me some hardcore village-idiot disease, I muttered, "Yet," under my breath.

Her eyes widened. "Just a minute, please." She picked up her phone and dialed, then swiveled her chair away from me and spoke so I couldn't hear. When she turned to face me, there was a sparkle in her eye. "Someone will be here to escort you to Mr. Rhodes in a few minutes. Please have a seat while you wait."

A minute later, Olivia came skipping down the hall.

"Auntie Lizzy," she called. "What in the world are you doing here?"

My heart sank. I stood, smiled, and waved as she continued toward me. When Olivia was still a good twenty feet away, the woman from the office moved to the doorway. "Ms. Blain. Walking, please."

"Oops. Forgot," Olivia said, stopping dead in her tracks.

I turned to the lady and whispered, "I need to speak to Adam alone, without Olivia."

She tilted her ear toward her shoulder, as if she didn't understand.

Olivia had started a deliberate walk toward us and jumped into my arms when she was within touching distance. "Are you picking me up today? Did Dadam have to leave? Where's Nana?"

I gave the lady at the desk a desperate look, then answered Olivia. "No, sweetie, I'm just here because I need to talk to Dadam. I'm pretty sure he's still going to be taking you home after school."

"Are you coming with us?"

"Not sure. Maybe."

"Goody!"

The desk lady handed Olivia a folded piece of paper. "Please take this to your teacher. Thank you very much for doing such a good job. But please walk on your way back to your classroom."

"Okay. Bye, Auntie Lizzy. See you later, alligator."

"In a while, with my toothy smile!" I gave her a goofy grin.

She waved before she turned the corner. Office Lady was already behind her desk.

"Looks like you check out. Congratulations. I have to say, it's a bit of a surprise. I had no idea Adam was … well, congratulations."

Congratulations? Married to the most unapologetic player I've ever met? At twenty-five? More like condolences.

"To get to the gym," she continued, "you go to the end of the hall and turn right. Down a flight of stairs. You won't miss it."

"Thank you." As I walked, I debated whether to let Adam know that his colleagues had heard the news of our new relationship status before he had.

The gym was indeed easy to find. The sound of twenty ten-year-olds yelling "Over here!" and "Knock it to me!" was the tip-off.

Adam waved for me to join him on the sideline at the volleyball net.

"Can we talk in your office?"

"Kids, when I'm finished with my meeting, I want to know that every single one of you has touched the ball at least twice. No hogging. Team game means everyone plays. Got it?"

"Yes, Mr. Rhodes," a chorus of voices called.

He jogged and I walked behind him to his office.

"What couldn't wait one hour to tell me?"

"Check your phone. Has Brigitte called?"

Adam pulled his phone from his desk drawer and his eyebrows shot up. "Three missed calls. And"—he wiped his finger across his screen—"seven text messages. Lizzy, what the heck did you say to her?"

7

———

ADAM

Lizzy waited in my office while I finished teaching my class, which looked less like teaching and more like clutching the volleyball net to keep from punching a wall. She came home with me and Olivia since we had a lot to talk about. I was in no mood to make dinner, so I ordered pizza. And after we ate, I plunked Olivia in front of the TV, then hit play on the DVD compilation of sing-along animations.

I directed Lizzy upstairs so we could talk without being overheard. She'd dropped a nuclear bomb on me in a place and at a time when I couldn't even respond. I'd spent the last two hours clenching my teeth so hard, my jaw ached.

On one hand, she'd made the mess, so she should darn well clean it up. But it was obvious I couldn't trust her to do it on her own. I was in this, like it or not, for better or worse … and right now, it felt like a whole lot of worse.

"Sit," I ordered after I closed my bedroom door.

She glanced from me to the bed with fear in her eyes.

"I'd rather stand."

"Sit."

She sat with her butt barely touching the mattress and kept her feet firmly planted on the floor. I sighed and walked toward her. She stiffened. I easily lifted her and gently tossed her into the middle of the bed.

"I'd like to be facing you while you tell me the whole story." I sat against the headboard with my legs outstretched. She settled herself to my side with her knees pulled to her chest, hugged by her arms. If I weren't so upset, having Lizzy on my bed would have had me wishing Olivia was at Nana's for the night. I blinked away that thought. "Talk." Apparently, I'd become a single-syllable caveman.

"I'm so sorry. I didn't mean for … I don't know how I … bloody hell, I screwed up." She looked so worried that I wanted to hold her and tell her it was fine, that there was nothing to worry about. Except I also wanted to throttle her.

"We can fix this, though. Right?" She continued. "We can tell Brigitte she misunderstood. I never lied. Well, not a big lie, at least. I might have said we've been spending Friday nights together, but that was so she didn't find out that you …" She stopped midsentence and grimaced. Then she perked up again. "I never agreed with what she was saying. I just didn't correct her when she made assumptions."

"Lizzy, slow down." I tapped her thigh with my foot. "You still haven't told me what Brigitte said. How on earth did she leave that coffee meeting thinking we were engaged?" I would have been laughing if the repercussion wasn't that I could lose Olivia.

Lizzy grimaced. "Not engaged. Getting married."

"That is the implied next step—"

"Adam, you're not hearing me. She believes we're getting married on Canada Day."

I squeezed my eyes shut and saw a white out as my nervous system kicked into full-on fight, flight, or freeze mode. Not helpful. Making eye contact with Lizzy, I exhaled slowly and tried to keep my voice level. "Canada Day as in ten days from now? Or as in some random July first in the future?"

She hung her head. Shook it.

"Fuuughh." My chest constricted. Blood pounded in my temples. "How?" Caveman Adam had resumed in control.

"I don't know. She's like some kind of witch with language manipulation powers. She was saying things that were true, and I just sat there. She didn't give me space to clarify. All I keep thinking was, she seems happy about this. And that's good—if she thinks Olivia is in a healthy, happy, safe place with Adam, she'll go back to London and let you keep doing what you're doing."

"Lizzy. What did she say?"

"I don't remember her exact words, but basically, Olivia told her that some wish she'd made when she and I caught Paige's bouquet at the wedding was coming true."

"Nana did not help with that. Nana told her it meant you'd be the next person to get married. And since you were holding her, Olivia decided it meant she'd be getting married, too ... but Nana said more likely she'd be a flower girl at my wedding ... and in her five-year-old logic, that meant you and I would be tying the knot next."

"Oh, dear," Lizzy sighed.

"Yeah, oh, dear. She must have said something to Brigitte on one of their calls. And then what?"

"Brigitte acted like I was playing coy, and I felt like an idiot, as if I should know what Olivia's wish was since I was the one holding her and was claiming to be so close to her."

Lizzy relaxed her arms and let her legs drop open, then she fell backward on the bed with her knees still in the air. She moaned. I know it was a moan of distress, but my dick didn't have the same emotional intelligence and it jumped to life. I pulled a pillow onto my lap.

"And?" I prompted.

"And I don't know." Lizzy rolled onto her side and faced

me. "She said it's obvious Olivia loves me. That she never expected you'd end up with someone like me. What does that even mean?"

I growled a non-answer. "What else?"

"Something about a big party on July 1 the whole family will be at and that Olivia is really excited about."

"Canada Day. Nick and Sophie's," I muttered. "And?"

"And …she wished me good luck. And I know I should have corrected her, but Adam, she didn't stop talking, and it sounded like she wasn't going to push for guardianship and I …" Lizzy grabbed the pillow from my lap and used it to cover her head.

"Hey." I grabbed to get it away, but she held it tight. "You need to breathe. And give that back." I tugged at the edge of the pillowcase, but she rolled away, keeping the cushion against her face. "Elizabeth …" I was about to use her full name, to assert my dad authority, but I realized too late that I didn't know it. "Lizzy, what's your full name?" I poked her in the side.

"Don't," she mumbled through the pillow.

Each time I tried to touch or comfort her, she jerked away. I tried to picture her sitting across from Brigitte, wanting to do the best for me and Olivia and getting sucked into a story that sounded plausible—to a five-year-old. And a vindictive thirty-year-old.

It was hard to be mad when she was trying to do the right thing and was so torn up about the lie she'd reinforced by not correcting it. After several minutes, she sat up.

"Mona Elizabeth Sheila Hillhouse," she said.

"Pardon?"

"If you want to use my full name to yell at me, it's Mona Elizabeth Sheila Hillhouse," she repeated without humor.

"Mona Elizabeth … heck, by the time I'd get through your whole name, I wouldn't remember why I was mad."

That got a small smile.

"All my mom had to say was 'Elizabeth' in her special, serious way for me to know I was in trouble."

"Like this? *Elizabeth*!"

"No, you need to get louder with each syllable and end with lots of emphasis on the 'beth' part." Her lips tilted up at the corners but her eyes looked down.

"E-liz-a-BETH!" I barked, then used my normal voice. "Did I nail it?"

She chuckled. "Close enough." And then she looked away. "I'm so, so sorry."

"Hey." I sat beside her and wrapped my arm around her shoulders. "It's not an ideal situation, but none of this is. Brigitte was going to find something to use against me. That was clear from the day she decided she was ready to be a mommy and that it was her turn to play. She has no idea what it takes to be a full-time parent."

"So why now?" Lizzy leaned into me. Fuji Green Tea filled my lungs. I turned away from her and inhaled normal-smelling air before Mr. Jumpy came to life again.

"No idea. Something's changed in her personal life, I assume. Maybe she found out she can't have kids. I haven't asked. I don't want to know."

"You and she have history." Lizzy said it as a statement.

"Mmm." I nodded but felt no desire to elaborate. "Okay." I sighed. "We need to get out of this. I suppose the smartest move would be to ask for advice from my lawyer."

Lizzy groaned. "He'll never let me live this down."

"You and me both. I can already picture how the family saga will be spun and shared with the generations to come, how Adam Rhodes, perennial player and single dad, tossed away the perfect woman to mother his child and that's why he ended up as the angry old uncle all the kids are afraid to visit."

"You think I'd be a good mother?"

"What? No. I mean," I muttered and stumbled with my

words. "I mean … that wasn't supposed to be the takeaway of my imaginary future. It was supposed to be a funny … never mind. I'd better call Dylan."

Lizzy wiggled her shoulder and pulled out from under my arm. She got up and walked to the door, looking deflated. "Speaking of bad parents, we should really check on Olivia, don't you think?"

She left ahead of me and was already sitting on the couch by the time I got to the squeaky step on the stairs. I paused to listen.

"What were you and Dadam doing up there?" Olivia asked.

"Just talking. We didn't want to interrupt your movie," Lizzy said, leaning her chin on top of Olivia's curls.

"Why was he mad at you?"

"He wasn't. Why'd you think he was mad?"

"'Cause he yelled 'Elizabeth' two times in his frustrated voice."

"We were goofing around, sweetie. He's not mad at me. I don't think. Your dad is very patient. You're an incredibly lucky little girl."

"I know. Oh, you have to be quiet. This is my favorite song in the whole movie. Want to sing it with me?"

"I don't think I know it. I've never seen this one."

"Dadam always sings it with me." Olivia lowered her voice. "He's not a very good singer. But you can't tell him or it would hurt his feelings."

I stepped forward, triggered the squeaky stair, and said, "Oh, good! I'm here just in time to sing my favorite song." I dropped onto the couch.

Olivia squirmed away from Lizzy and into my lap. She pressed her finger to her mouth and said to Lizzy, "Shh."

A guitar strummed and was joined by a keyboard. Olivia swayed to the beat as we watched a little girl make a snowman, and then the snowman came to life when she put a hat on him. She gazed up into my eyes as she sang the first line of the song, "Stay with me."

Normally, I'd join in, but for some darn reason, I couldn't find my voice.

"Auntie Lizzy sing too. Read the words. See, they're at the bottom of the movie." Olivia rejoined the song. "… If ever I need you."

Lizzy was silent, her lashes working overtime, but a tear managed to escape. Not helpful. I looked back to the TV to see the snowman making shadow movies on the fence for the little girl. I'd watched *Lily and the Snowman* a hundred times, heard the Vapor cover of the old Genesis song "Follow You, Follow Me" as many. And maybe I wasn't the best singer, but I never missed singing backup with my little girl.

I wasn't embarrassed to sing in front of Lizzy but I couldn't seem to push a sound out past the mogul in my throat. The combination of the lyrics, the image of the little girl growing up and forgetting about her snowman, and Lizzy sniffling beside me was too much.

I lifted Olivia and placed her on Lizzy's lap. She snuggled in easily as Lizzy wrapped her arms around her.

"Where are you going, Dadam?"

"Bathroom." I went upstairs, locked myself in, and called my lawyer brother.

"Dylan, we have a new snafu with the guardianship situation."

8

LIZZY

Adam didn't come downstairs until Olivia was asleep. He'd been gone almost an hour, but I didn't want to disturb him since he looked pretty shell-shocked when he joined us to watch Olivia's movie. I couldn't blame him.

Here was a guy who could control a slab of wood and fiberglass hurtling over cliffs, out of helicopters, riding triggered avalanches down a mountain. He could control a class full of preteen girls. I don't imagine there was anything he wasn't able to control. Until Brigitte showed up. And I let her over-egg the pudding without correcting her.

I was shocked at how calm he'd stayed as I told him the story of how we had become engaged—and the date of our shotgun wedding.

We didn't speak as he gathered Olivia into his arms and carried her up to her room. My Converse were already tied by the time he came back down.

"You're leaving?"

"I didn't expect to stay this long."

"Stay. Have a beer with me. God knows I need one." He ran his fingers through his messy hair and made it even sexier. Messier. He made it messier.

I laughed, hoping to distract him from what I'm sure was a blooming blush.

"What?"

Without permission from my brain, my legs carried me to him and my hand rose to smooth out the sticking-up bits. His hair was ridiculously soft and my mouth went ridiculously dry. "You sure you want to offer me a beer? The last time we had an idea after one beer, look how that ended." I made a face, hoping it wasn't too soon to joke about the pickle I'd put him in.

My heart beat double-time and I'm certain my blush intensified as I drew a mental image of his pickle. And what I'd like to put it in.

"Maybe," he said with a said smile, "the takeaway is to have two beers before making new plans. Or three." Adam moved toward the kitchen and left me with my idiotic, insensitive thoughts.

I pulled off my shoes, sat on the overstuffed leather couch, and reminded myself how it felt to be objectified. *Adam is more than eye candy and I am not a female frat boy. I am a respectful woman.* It was easy to repeat the mantras when he was out of sight, but as soon he sauntered back to the living room, all broad chest, toned arms, muscular thighs and full lips? *Mm, mm, finger lickin good.*

Adam was carrying four bottles of Granville Island lager. He handed me one, placed another on each end table, and kept one for himself. They were all open.

"You weren't joking."

"No. I talked to Dylan. He told me not to accept any calls or reply to any texts from Brigitte so this doesn't snowball into something even worse. He wanted to think about options, best- and worst-case scenarios."

His tone was flat. I wondered if this was like the calm before the storm. It freaked me out.

"Why aren't you furious with me? Hell, I think I'm

madder at myself than you are." My stomach was in knots, but I couldn't name the feeling—there were too many of them tangled up like headphone wires at the bottom of a purse. I placed the beer on the side table without drinking.

"What's done is done. And you didn't do anything on purpose. I know your heart was in the right place; I can't be angry at you for that. What's one more thing to deal with in an already sucky situation, right?" He took a long pull of his beer and then fell against the couch looking exhausted.

"I'm really to blame, anyway. I let myself believe she wouldn't ever come for Olivia, even though she told me she would, once she was ready for the responsibility. I guess I thought or hoped, really, that day would never come. And I also convinced myself a judge would never take Olivia from this family after she'd bonded with us all. If I'm mad at anyone, it's with myself."

"Is shared guardianship on the table, like joint custody after divorce?" I asked.

"Maybe? Honestly, she's kept the cards close to her chest. My big concern is how cagey she is about where she's planning to live."

"What do you mean?"

"As I understand, she's in a short-term rental. And when she mentioned her fiancé in court, it seemed like he was planning to stay in London, so … I don't know."

"You can't be serious. She wouldn't be allowed to take Olivia away, would she? This is her home. What about her friends? What about her aunts and uncles? What about Nana? It'll be like having her parents die all over again." I snapped my mouth shut and regretted those last words before I'd even finished the sentence.

Adam studied the ceiling. "Yup. And if we don't settle this ourselves, there's no doubt that will come up in court. The fact I was with them doesn't help my case as the more responsible parent. Part of me thinks I should give her what she wants to avoid the aggro a court situation will create."

"No, you can't give up." I tapped his arm with a fist. "I shouldn't have mentioned … ugh. I'm sorry. You can cut out my tongue. Save us both from me. Talking when I should shut up and keeping quiet when I should speak up."

As Olivia's so-called "favorite auntie," I'd failed her dramatically. Maybe that's why I felt so invested. This positive little human had bonded with me over the year that I was Josh's platonic plus-one. But when invitations to family events dried up, I didn't make any effort to maintain my relationship with Olivia, because I wasn't sure I had a place at the table anymore once Paige came back. And then there was the whole weirdness with Adam.

"I suck," I said. "Olivia would have been better off if I'd stayed away. If she'd never met me."

Adam lifted his bottle, clinked it against mine. "I'm feeling the same way."

"That is so untrue, and you know it." I didn't hide the frustration in my voice. "I've never met a man who's as good a dad as you are."

Adam grunted. "And this is in a survey of how many dads? Two? Three?"

"Um, hundreds."

Adam's eyes opened wide for a second. Then he scowled and squeezed them shut. "Sorry. That was a judgmental reaction. Who am I to judge how many guys you've dated?"

"Dated?" I laughed out loud and smacked his leg. "No, dummy, for my master's thesis."

"You have a master's degree? In what?"

"Psychology, with a focus on family dynamics in divorced families. Funny, eh?"

Adam looked like this was the craziest thing he'd ever heard. "How the heck did I not know that? And why in the world were you working as a hostess in a restaurant?"

"You sound like my mom," I muttered. "You didn't know about my degree?"

"No. But I guess it makes sense, you being Kama's best friend and all. You met in school?"

"First year undergrad. Been best friends since."

"Wow, for my fiancée, you've got a few things you need to fill me in on, Mona Elizabeth … uh …"

"Sheila."

"Right. Mona Elizabeth Sheila Hillhouse. What kind of family name is Hillhouse? It sounds very hoity-toity. Not the kind of family who would let their daughter date, let alone marry, a professional snowboarder. Your mother must be beside herself."

"Ha. Mommie Dearest doesn't believe in marriage. Or kids for that matter." I reached for my beer. "Which is exactly why I'd date and marry a bad boy like you."

Adam was half finished his second beer, leaned over and whispered close to my ear, "I've always had a thing for rebels."

My stomach lurched. Was he flirting with me? I could not see this ending well. I leaned away, but he caught my neck and gently pulled my head toward him.

"And your hair smells really nice," he said.

"Thank you." I dipped my chin, escaping his grasp. "I think I should go. You're getting drunk and the last thing we need is … yeah. Never mind."

I tried to stand, but he pulled me down. My left butt cheek landed on his right leg and I squirmed away.

Adam stared at the television, which was muted but playing a kids' movie. "Takes a lot more than two beers to get me drunk. Look, it's not even eight. If you leave now I'll drive myself crazy thinking about what Brigitte is going to do once she finds out the truth. You can stay and distract me for an hour, can't you? By then, if I focus really hard, I can have a nice buzz to help me sleep."

I relaxed into the cushions and watched him finish his second beer. When I passed him the second bottle he'd opened for me, he caught my hand under his and wouldn't let go. Adam took a long swig. I had to lean forward for my arm to reach far enough, my free hand pressed on his chest to avoid collapsing into his lap.

This was not going to end well.

"Can I …," I tilted my chin toward the table with my own beer and he released me. "You and Dylan were talking for a long time. What else did he say?"

"You want the tweet or the full story? Actually, I don't feel like watching that movie again. Basically, I'm screwed."

Afraid to utter the question on my mind, I let silence sit between us for a minute before the need to know took over. "Because of me?"

He inhaled long and exhaled hard. "Because if I don't marry you, that will give Brigitte the impression that I was lying to cover up what she actually believes about me, and which is the truth—that, for the past few years, I have been bringing a different woman home virtually every weekend. What court in their right mind would let me raise a daughter knowing that?"

"But Olivia isn't here when you … do that."

"Of course not. But Dylan says the judge we drew is conservative and won't think much of my moral compass, which doesn't bode well for earning her trust as the better guardian."

"But you *are* the better guardian!" I argued.

"It's too bad you're not a judge."

"Didn't Dylan have *any* helpful advice?"

The look in Adam's eyes made me simultaneously want to hug him and run away. Fast. It was a combination of regret and remorse, grief and guilt. It was a look I'd seen in the eyes of a handful of parents in my thesis research. A look that said, "If only I could turn back time, I'd make different decisions. Better decisions."

And then his face changed. He plastered on a big, fake smile that wouldn't fool anyone and said, "Dylan suggested I send out wedding invitations."

I guess my eyes communicated what I was too stunned to say out loud.

He chuckled, "So, you like the idea as much as I do, eh?"

"Adam, we can't get married. I don't even know your middle name or … I'm … it would be …"

A hundred excuses ran through my brain. Before I could mutter out one complete sentence, the doorbell rang, and the door opened before Adam had time to get up off the couch.

9

______

ADAM

"**W**here's my little girl?" a singsong voice called. Brigitte.

She rounded the corner as I stood.

"What the heck, Brigitte? You can't barge into my house like this."

"Yes, well, you can't ghost me. Did you lose your phone? I've left you at least five messages and texts," she hissed. Then she spun toward the foot of the stairs and said again in her sweet voice, "Olivia, your favorite aunt is here. And she has a present for you."

"Brigitte, she's asleep."

"But it's only eight o'clock. Is she grounded?"

I eyed her, not sure if she was serious. "She's five. You don't ground a five-year-old. She needs twelve hours of sleep. Her bedtime is seven. Every night."

"That's inconvenient. I'll just look in on her. Leave the present at the foot of her bed." Brigitte turned toward the stairs.

"Brigitte!"

She stopped and looked over her shoulder at me.

"Stop. She's a light sleeper. You'll wake her. Come and

see her tomorrow. You can pick her up from school if you want. Take her to Brownies. I'm sure she'd love to have you be her show-and-tell."

Lizzy stood. "I think I should go. Leave you to talk."

Before she could walk away, I put my arm around her shoulders. "No, stay. We're not done yet, and Brigitte is leaving," I said in as balanced a tone as I could muster, given how angry I was.

"Actually," Brigitte said, kicking off her sandals, "you and I have something we need to talk about. Since you're not returning my calls, and I'm here, I vote we talk now." She dropped into a recliner and triggered the footrest, making herself right at home. Lizzy and I stood facing her.

"I really think I should go," Lizzy said again.

"As you're so deeply entrenched in my niece's life, you should stay, too, since this involves you," Brigitte said, pointing at the couch.

"Yeah, about that—" Lizzy started.

"Funny enough, we were talking about the wedding when you barged in," I interrupted. Lizzy's eyes widened as I spun her so we were face-to-face. I whispered but expected Brigitte could hear, so I chose my words carefully. "I know you're getting anxious about all the plans we still have to make, and all the packing you have to do. But we'll get it done. We'll get up early tomorrow and have Olivia help."

Lizzy sat and pressed herself against the arm of the couch. Sitting cross-legged with two cushions in her lap. She looked nervous. I hoped that meant she'd sit quietly and agree with everything I said. The last thing I needed was for her to challenge me in front of Brigitte.

Dylan had painted a grim picture of my odds if this went to court. He said the best thing I could do was figure something out with Brigitte that worked. It wouldn't be perfect, since perfect would be if Brigitte went back to London and remained happy with video chats once a month.

But I knew better than anyone—you can't always get what you want. And worse? What I want isn't always the best thing for other people involved. The very fact this conversation was even taking place was proof. And if Brigitte ever found out *that* truth … I clapped my hands to break the negative thought spiral.

Play nice. Give her what she wants.

"Can I get you something to drink?" I pasted on a smile and nodded to Brigitte.

"Do you have a sparkling blush?"

"Sorry."

"A sparkling white?"

I sighed, picked up my beer, and raised my eyebrows.

"Any wine at all?"

"If I put a few drops of cranberry juice in some carbonated water and give it to you in a wine glass, will that do?"

"Fine, I'll have a beer." She looked at the bottles Lizzy and I were drinking from and pointed a bright red and gold nail at me. "In a glass."

I grabbed a bottle from the fridge. As I poured the lager into a wine glass—because she was pissing me off—I replayed my conversation with Dylan, trying to remember the most important points, aside from basically giving Brigitte anything she wanted in exchange for keeping co-guardianship rights. The best-case scenario, the one I could live with, was Olivia living half-time with me and half-time with Brigitte. But I wanted full weeks. None of that "I'll take Friday to Monday and you can have the middle of the week" BS.

Brigitte accepted the glass with a scowl. "So," she said, leaning her chin on her hand, directing her poisonous gaze at Lizzy, "how are you feeling about the big day?"

Lizzy seemed quite invested in examining the fabric of

the pillow in her lap. "Good," she answered without looking away from the cushion.

"Nervous?"

"A little."

I dropped down beside Lizzy, coaxed one of her feet onto my lap, and rubbed her calf. "Not much to be nervous about. It's just a small party. Family only. Nothing we haven't done a hundred times. Right, Sheila?" I added in a decent Australian accent.

That got a small laugh from Lizzy, and she relaxed.

"But it *is* different. You don't plan to get married *a hundred times*. At least, I hope you don't. Divorce can be ... messy. You know?" Brigitte asked.

If looks could kill, Brigitte would have been a pile of ash. She and I had a deal that we would never talk about our short-lived foray into matrimonial misery. My family didn't know and didn't need to know about that lapse in my judgement. "Then it's a good thing divorce isn't part of our wedding plan."

"Is it true you haven't done a stunt since ..." Brigitte's spiky energy softened a little.

I nodded.

Lizzy's calf muscle tightened, and I turned to her. She raised her eyebrows, asking for permission to speak? I nodded.

"Since he became a full-time dad? Adam gave up the thing he loved most in the world to be here for Olivia."

I could hear the subtext in Lizzy's tone: *Something you weren't willing to do.*

Clearly Brigitte heard it too. Her eyes flashed. "You think I didn't give up anything? Maybe I didn't quit university to rush home and be an unemployed single mother with half a doctorate, but I gave up opportunities, too, knowing I'd come for Olivia once I was able to provide a good life for her."

"Sure," Lizzy said with a shrug.

"Don't presume you know me." Brigitte scowled.

Lizzy took a breath and opened her mouth. I squeezed her leg hard enough that she gasped, which had the desired effect. She didn't say whatever she was about to.

Brigitte's reasons were bullshit and we both knew it. Dalton and Maggie left a trust for Olivia worth millions. They had more money than I did and her guardian would be given a monthly living allowance—if they were inclined to use it. I was not. I wanted Olivia to have everything her mom and dad had earned, to use as she saw fit when she turned twenty-one.

"You dropped over with a present?" I asked, pointing to the oversized handbag that Brigitte had placed on the floor by her chair.

"It's a puzzle. She told me she loved them, so I found one I thought we could do together, just her and me. Special Auntie Brigitte time." She sounded genuinely interested.

"That's a …. that's a great idea. She'll love it." I was surprised, and my mood shifted. "Hopefully, she doesn't already have it. She and Nana have puzzle time every Sunday afternoon. She's done every pet puzzle that Toys 'R' Us sells."

"Guaranteed she hasn't done this one." Brigitte sipped her beer and made a face.

"So … is there anything else? You don't have to force yourself to finish that." I pointed to the glass she'd put on the side table. I felt the smallest bit bad that I hadn't opened a bottle of wine for her.

"There is," she said. "We need to talk about how we're going to resolve the guardianship question."

"I was talking to Dylan—"

"Must be nice to get free legal counsel," Brigitte said, crossing her arms over her chest. Then she pointed with one hand. "Adam, I have no desire to drag this into court and waste thousands on a lawyer. I'm confident we can agree to an arrangement that works for everyone."

I relaxed even more upon hearing those words. I'd misjudged her intentions. Or maybe the judge's words had made an impact on her. Either way, I felt the tension in my chest release. "You cannot know how happy that makes me. Thank you, Brigitte. I'm sorry I've been—"

Brigitte waved her hand and interrupted. "Good. Now, I have to admit that learning you're getting married, and that Olivia has what I assume, at least hope, is a positive female role model in her life, caught me by surprise."

You and me both.

"About that—"

"But after careful reflection," Brigitte straightened and tilted her chin as she spoke, "I don't think that should change my original plan."

Something in her tone triggered me. My jaw tightened. That was the old Brigitte I knew and loved. Then hated. She had a plan, which meant she wasn't here to discuss or negotiate, she was here to dictate. There are old exes and there are bold exes, and the old, bold exes are the ones who will kill you.

"What is your plan, Brigitte? Let's see how it meshes with mine."

"Since Olivia will be finished with school for the summer at the end of the week, I'll let her keep the schedule she's used to."

How generous of you.

"I had hoped to take her for a girl getaway over the Canada Day long weekend, but it doesn't seem fair to make her miss your wedding, so I've booked a suite for the following weekend, Friday to Monday."

"Sorry, you're planning to take her where?"

"Not far. Just up to Whistler. Nowhere you probably haven't taken her yourself."

I lifted Lizzy's foot from my lap and stood, not sure where I was planning to walk, only knowing I had to circulate the hit of adrenaline her tone had triggered. I took a deep breath to calm myself. "For your infor—"

"Excuse me. Please stop interrupting. That will give us a chance to spend quality time together without having to worry about bedtimes and such."

"Brigitte—"

"Adam, let me finish. I've found a tolerable short-term rental downtown. Do you know how hard it was to find a nice place that allowed children? I had no idea how many buildings are adult only. Anyway, I've got it for the rest of July and August so Olivia can spend part of her time with me"—she nodded toward Lizzy—"and be part time with you and your new wife."

Brigitte picked up her glass and tipped it to her mouth, made another face and put it down without drinking. I was happy I'd not given her wine.

"Can I share my thoughts on this idea now?" I snarled through clenched teeth.

"I'm not done. I'd originally planned this to roll out over the eight weeks of summer, but in accommodating your news, I have compressed it to seven."

"Compressed *what* to seven?" I said, losing patience.

"I'd forgotten how you always interrupted me. It's very annoying, you know. I hope Olivia hasn't picked up the habit."

I bit my tongue. *I'd forgotten how you always manipulated me.*

Brigitte continued. "I thought it would be unfair to both you and Olivia to make this transition too quickly, so I've come up with the following schedule."

She reached into her purse and pulled out a folded paper, flattened it, and then smiled at it, as if it were a report a teacher had lovingly stuck a gold star on. She held it out but not far enough for either Lizzy or me to reach.

"I'm not going to fold it into an airplane and send it to you special delivery," she said, dropping her arm.

I crossed the room and took the paper. Lizzy reached out and motioned for me to sit again. I did, then squeezed Lizzy's leg as hard as I was clenching my jaw. She squeaked. I mouthed, "Sorry."

Lizzy leaned against me and we looked at the sheet together.

"I don't understand. It's a blank calendar," I said.

Brigitte didn't offer any explanation.

Lizzy pointed to the fine print at the bottom, then up to Brigitte. "This," she said, matter-of-factly, "is not happening."

"I'm afraid this isn't a democracy where each person gets an equal vote and your vote is the tie breaker," Brigitte replied.

"What am I missing?" I leaned against Lizzy and whispered.

"Dates with a red dot are the days Olivia is with Brigitte. Days with a blue—"

I grabbed the calendar from Lizzy's hand. "No fucking way. This"—I tore the calendar in half—"is not happening."

Brigitte smirked.

Six years ago that look would have made me lose my shit. I closed my eyes and inhaled for a count of five.

"Not happening," I repeated.

"Don't get your knickers in a twist, Rhodes. You know me, I'm accommodating. I've changed it once to allow for the whole wedding surprise."

"And what do you think gives you the right to walk into Olivia's life after over three years and disrupt everything she knows—"

"And loves," Lizzy added.

"She has a whole extended family. The time with me is also time with them. If you limit me to one day a week, she won't have time with Nana or Dylan or Nick or Josh."

"And your new wife, of course."

"Brigitte …" I warned.

She looked and sounded entirely blasé about this conversation. Emotionless. She was in the power position and knew it. Brigitte smiled and tapped her chin. "I assume Olivia has a passport. If she doesn't, we'll have to get her one."

"Brigitte—"

"What? I have her enrolled in a elite school in London starting in—"

"Are you out of your fucking mind?" I spoke way too loudly and reflexively looked toward the stairs.

Brigitte sighed. "You didn't think I was planning to raise her in backwater Vancouver, did you? Don't be ridiculous. My home is London. Olivia will have the best of everything with me. What are you giving her? Subpar education, mediocre culture, limited opportunities—"

"She's five years old." Lizzy was on her feet now. "She needs love from a family she knows and trusts, not trips to the ballet with a stranger."

"I'm sorry, Elizabeth, your opinion isn't needed. Or quite frankly, wanted." Brigitte dismissed Lizzy, then addressed me. "Adam, once you get over the shock of not being in control, I'm confident you'll see this is for the best. I seem to recall years ago you saying you never wanted kids. Think of it as me doing you a favor. And anyway, I'm sure it's what my sister would have wanted for her."

I clenched my teeth so hard my jaw throbbed. Only my lips moved when I replied, "What would you know about what Maggie and Dalton wanted for Olivia? I seem to recall you buggering off to London when your sister was six months pregnant," I spit, literally. Brigitte wiped her chin with her finger.

"Of course, I remember, Adam. I wasn't the one living the life of a rock star."

"The rock star life didn't seem to bother you when you were tagging along with us."

"Is that what I was doing? Tagging along? Lizzy, do you have any idea who you're marrying?"

I'd had enough. I stood and walked to the front entry, grabbed Brigitte's sandals, and tossed them in front of her.

"You don't get to bulldoze into my life after six years and play like I'm the bad guy. I need you to leave. You're good at that, at leaving, when you don't get what you want."

Brigitte smiled, unmoved. "Not until I see my niece."

"Brigitte, get the hell out of my house."

"Dadam, why are you yelling?" Olivia padded down the stairs, rubbing her eyes. "Hi, Auntie Lizzy. Hi, Auntie Brigitte." She gave a tired wave.

10

LIZZY

Olivia said she'd heard Adam yell, "Are you out of your fucking mind?" so she came down.

"I'm sorry I woke you, sweetheart," Adam said, scooping her into his arms and against his chest, the same way he'd carried me two days earlier. It seemed like a lifetime ago.

"Who were you yelling at?" she asked.

"At myself."

"That's strange."

"Well, I'm strange, so that shouldn't surprise you, should it?" He tickled her lightly, and she snuggled closer against him.

"Why is Auntie Brigitte here?"

"I brought you a present," Brigitte said, reaching her arms out, clearly an encouragement for Olivia to go to her, but she didn't move from Adam. Good girl. "Would you like to see it?"

"Okay." Olivia yawned and Adam adjusted her. She leaned her head on his shoulder and closed her eyes.

Brigitte walked over and shook the puzzle box by Olivia's ear to get her attention. "It's a puzzle of London landmarks. Do you know what landmarks are?"

"No."

"They're fun and interesting places to visit. Places I'm going to take you."

"Okay." She yawned. "Can I go back to bed now?"

Once Adam and Olivia disappeared into her bedroom, I glared at Brigitte without apology. "That's an adult puzzle. A five-year-old can do a fifty-piece, maybe a hundred-piece puzzle with help. That has a thousand pieces? She won't enjoy it. It's going to frustrate her."

"Oh, as if you know everything there is to know about five-year-olds. Did you learn that bit of trivia at the restaurant where you waitress?" She put on a fake voice of concern. "Oh no, don't give *that* doodle sheet to the little boy. It's for ten-year-olds—he's not ready for it yet."

"MSc in child psychology, actually." Not that I was trying to impress her.

Brigitte brushed away my statement with a swish of her hand. "Whatever. You think that's going to make *you* a better mother than *me*? I saw your disapproval with my plan for Olivia."

"Why? Why take her away from her family only to shove her into a boarding school?"

"Number one, she's not with her family. I'm her family. And number two, by making me her legal guardian, Maggie trusted me to act in Olivia's best interest. And I don't have to explain that to you or anyone."

"Yeah, well, she also trusted Adam, didn't she?"

"Maybe she didn't know him as well as she should have."

"What is that supposed—"

"You're still here?" Adam interrupted me but spoke quietly. "You've given Olivia her gift, given me your plan. There can't be anything else, so, thanks for coming, Brigitte. Next time you want to see Olivia, text me with the request.

And next time you have something to tell *me*, have your lawyer tell my lawyer. I'm done talking to you."

"Adam, don't be like that, after all we've shared." Brigitte made a pouty face, then reached her clawed fingers out to stroke his arm. He grabbed her hand before she made contact and pushed it forcefully away. "Ouch. So rough. Not very patient." She rubbed her fingers as if he'd hurt her. "Judges don't like rough, impatient fathers. I think you should consider my offer because if you insist on taking this to court and I win, I'll fight for no contact with you."

Brigitte smiled as if she'd presented us with a homemade cherry pie to welcome us into her world. Then she opened the door and gave a wave as she crossed the threshold to her alternate reality.

Adam locked the door.

Rage roiled in my chest. Unkind names filled my head. I wanted to punch her. I'd seen her type before—and the emotional damage those women did to the fathers and children they separated. There was no way I could sit by and let her win.

"Anything you need, Adam, anything at all, you've got it." I dropped onto the couch and squeezed a cushion, hoping it would absorb the angry energy that was making my muscles vibrate.

"Thanks, but … I haven't got a clue what to do. Dylan didn't consider that she might be planning to leave the country with Olivia. Fine lawyer I've got myself, eh?" He looked miserable. His slight, asymmetric smile was shadowed by the sadness pasted over top of it. All I could see in it was defeat.

"Call him. Tell him what happened. See what he says." I patted the spot beside me, and he sat.

"What's the point? She knows me—at least, she used to. And really, my behavior as a role model for a young girl in the last three years? Shit, on paper I wouldn't want me fathering a child."

"Are you kidding me? I didn't know you before, but I know you've not let your ..." How could I say this without sounding judgmental? Adam gave me a look that told me he knew what I was thinking. "Your active social life intersect with Olivia. Adam, I was around for a year and never once saw you with another woman. And from what Kama has told me, neither has she."

"It's true. Olivia's never met one of my hookups. But that doesn't matter. Dylan isn't very confident I'll win if this is left to the judge we drew. That's why he's encouraging me to work with Brigitte."

"But you said he thought you being married would help your case. So, why don't we get married?"

He sighed. "Lizzy, you're the kid psychologist. You know why not. How fair would it be bringing you into our lives like a mom figure and then, once the guardianship is decided—assuming that even works and I do win—have Olivia lose yet another parent? No. I won't do that to her."

"So you'd rather have her lose you and everyone else in your family? Kids are resilient. Hell, look at me."

"What about you?"

Damn, I hadn't meant to mention my whole screwed-up childhood. "Never mind. As long as kids know they're unconditionally loved and safe, they can weather all kinds of change without turning into serial killers. If Dylan truly thinks that you being married could sway the judge, get married. Marry me. I'll do it to make sure that witch does not steal Olivia from us."

"Uh-huh. Make the offer again tomorrow when you're stone-cold sober and you've had time to think about what this means for you. It's not as simple as signing some document we ignore, you know. You'll have to move in with us. It's kind of a must, to convince a court that I didn't just marry you for … well, for the only reason I'd ever marry you."

I winced. *The only reason I'd ever marry you.* What was I doing? Was this the worst idea ever? To put myself through another round of being included as a member of this family, only to be left out as soon as I wasn't needed anymore? Adam was right. This was a terrible idea. It might work, and he might get primary guardianship of Olivia. But at what cost to me?

As we sat in silence, I convinced myself this wasn't my battle to fight, even though I might have been part of the reason it was started.

"What are you thinking?" Adam asked, tapping my leg.

"You're right. Marrying me would be a terrible idea."

"Oh, that's too bad because I was thinking of all the reasons marrying you might be a good idea."

"Like what?" I expected him to say something like "I'll have a live-in babysitter for my Friday nights out," but he surprised me.

"You don't have a boyfriend, right?" He raised his brows in question and while I was focused on the fine wrinkles in his forehead, his fingertips landed on my leg again, this time higher up my thigh. He stroked upward, toward that place only boyfriends get to visit.

As much as my hips longed to thrust toward the warmth of his touch, my brain stayed miraculously in control. I looked down at his long, strong fingers and placed my hand over his, then lifted them together, placing his hand on his leg.

"No." Dammit, I could hear the breathiness of my voice. I sounded more needy than resolute, so I added, "Because I don't want a boyfriend."

I realized I was still staring at his fingers, willing them to slide a few inches to the left, toward me, and stroke a few inches higher than they had been ten seconds earlier. When I looked up at him, his gaze was boring a hole right above the spot he'd been touching. Was he a mind reader? Oh please, let him be a mind reader.

"I feel the same way."

I gasped as his fingertip made contact with the spot I'd just willed him to connect with.

"But I assume," he continued, "like me, you enjoy company in your bed from time to time." He inched a little higher.

"From … time to time." Apparently the oxygen in the air had been replaced by helium.

He licked his lips. "That's one upside of being married—I won't have to wait until Friday night when Olivia is away to, you know …"

My heart and mind raced, and the way my girl gear contracted expressed that it liked the idea a great deal.

I realized I was gawking, my mouth half-open as I tried to figure out if he was serious.

"What?" He took my hand and placed it on the same spot on his leg, on bare skin, under the fabric of his shorts.

Oh, sweet Jesus, I was a soufflé rising far too fast. The parts of me that hadn't been intimate with a man in over a year cheered. But the smart organ in my body waved a red flag in the form of a quick memory—the last guy I'd ghosted because we'd started to enjoy time together a little too much for someone who wasn't going to settle down until she was thirty.

"You see our fake marriage as a real, on-demand, booty-call service?"

"I suppose you could call it that." His fingertip made contact with what I had no doubt was a moist spot on my panties.

I jumped. Literally, leapt off the couch and threw myself into the chair where Brigitte had been sitting. I could barely breathe let alone think. Without shame, I finished the lager in the wine glass. "You said," I virtually panted, "sex was one upside. What are some others?"

He adjusted himself. And by that, I mean he did not hide the fact that he had a boner that needed attention and room to breathe.

"Adult conversation at meals …"

Not sure how 'adult' my conversation will be since all I can think is how sorry I am to have assumed you had a pickle, because that is … phew. I fanned myself.

"… someone to have a beer and watch movies with after Olivia's in bed …"

Thank the goddess for seven o'clock bedtime.

"… someone to go with me on bike rides and hikes, who will take the 'desperate single dad' neon sign off my back."

"Ha! You? Desperate?"

"I'm feeling pretty darned desperate right now." There was hunger in his eyes. And in the way his tongue continued to run over his lip.

I had to look away. We sat in a comfortable silence for long enough that my twitterpated nerves stopped tingling and my brain cells were no longer blood-starved.

"But what about downsides? What if Brigitte argues this marriage is fake and uses it against you."

"Dylan said the marriage can't be fake. It has to be legal. So I suppose that could be a downside for you since once this is over, you'd be a divorcée with all that baggage."

I scoffed. "As if that matters anymore."

"I don't want to assume it won't matter to you. Some people care. Are you willing to risk being side-eyed by eligible suitors in the future?"

"What, are you from the 1950s?"

"Nana might have influenced me a little." He winked.

I tried to think of all the ways marrying Adam would change my life in the short term.

"One upside for me is that I'd be able to sublet my

apartment for a few months and save some money. And you're in a more convenient location for most of the restaurants that would pay better tips. I've never looked for work on this side of town since I don't have a car, and transit is always shut down by the time I get off."

"Wait. You've been walking home from work at what, two, three in the morning? That's ridiculous."

"Says a guy who can afford a car."

"But why can't you afford a car? Get something used."

"Maybe I could if it mattered enough. But saving money to travel to Europe has been my priority since I graduated. I've got $6000 saved. I promised myself that as soon as I had ten, I'd finally do my gap-year trip. I'm just gapping a few years late."

"You've never been to Europe?"

"I've never been east of the Rockies."

Adam stared at the ceiling and seemed engaged in an inner dialogue if the faces he was making were an indication of his thought process. He tilted his head left and scowled. Then he tilted it toward his right shoulder and nodded. He looked at his hand and mouthed without making a sound as he pointed those lovely long fingers one by one, as if counting.

After a minute, I tossed a cushion at him. "Hey, what's going on over there?"

He knit his eyebrows together. "I have an idea. Something that would make me feel a lot better about even asking you to *consider* helping me with this whole fake-marriage thing."

"Okay ..."

"What if I paid you $25,000 once this is over? That'll get you to Europe a lot sooner—"

I laughed.

"What's so funny?" he asked.

"You said $25,000. You mean twenty-five *hundred*."

"No, I mean twenty-five *thousand*."

"Adam, that's ridiculous. That's like a whole year's take-home pay. You can't give me that much for, what? A couple months of … free rent."

"Lizzy, I made $10 million on the last stunt I did. My net worth is … significant. Twenty-five thousand is not going to make any difference in my quality of life. I won't even notice it's gone."

He looked serious.

I was confused. "Something doesn't make sense. If you have enough money to"—I waved my arms as if swatting mosquitoes from face—"toss away a normal person's annual wages willy-nilly, why are you working as a gym teacher?"

"Lots of reasons. I can't—actually, I *won't* do stunt work anymore, since I have a daughter who needs me in one piece." Adam closed his eyes and took a deep breath. "When Olivia started kindergarten, I got bored. The days were suddenly very, very long. So, I volunteered to coach the ski club at her school. That was only a few hours a week, so I made it more, to keep busy. The guy who'd been teaching gym retired at Christmas, and I grabbed his position as a volunteer until they could hire someone with a proper degree … apparently, they've either stopped looking or nobody is qualified."

"You're a full-time *volunteer*?"

"In effect."

I sat with this information. Adam had enough money banked that he didn't need to work, and he was willing to pay me a stupid amount to be his fake wife. On the upside, if I accepted the money, I'd finally be able to do my gap-year travels and maybe even stay in Airbnbs instead of hostels. Take trains instead of buses. Look at the sights from the inside, not only from the streets.

And on the downside, I could end up annihilating my one unbreakable rule: don't develop feelings for anyone.

Parts of my body had already decided they wanted to get to know Adam more intimately. And if I gave them the keys, they'd have me driving off into the sunset in an ugly gray minivan. I could not let that happen.

"Sex," I said.

Adam's eyes went wide. "Non sequitur, but yes." He stood and reached for my hands.

I pulled them tight against my chest. "No. That's not what I mean. If I agree to be your fake wife, sex has to be off the table. Sleeping in the same bed, kissing, some light cuddling, all good. But I draw the line at anything that would light my panties on fire."

I gazed into his deep brown eyes for an eternity. He finally spoke.

"So, *bad* sex only. That's what I hear you saying."

I tried to look serious but couldn't help laughing.

He frowned. "That might be a deal breaker because I don't know how *not* to leave a woman begging for more."

"That, Mr. Rhodes, is exactly what I figured. And it is why your penis and my vagina can never, *ever* get to know each other on a first-name basis."

11

———

ADAM

I assumed she was joking. The wildness in her eyes and the quickness of her breath clearly communicated she wanted to know my dick's first name.

"Belvedere," I said.

"Belvedere?"

I pointed at my zipper.

"Oh my god! Are you serious? Why the—"

"Oh, don't act so shocked. What do you call her?" I pointed at the pillow in Lizzy's lap.

"Nothing! My vagina. That's the only name … I mean, when I said 'first-name basis,' it was a figure of speech. Not literal."

She covered her flushed cheeks with her hands and peeked at me through her fingers. She was too damn cute when flustered, and I couldn't help but push her.

"I don't believe you."

She shot me a withering stare; huffed a few times.

"Belvedere says he's sad your lady parts don't have a name. What's that, Belvedere? You think we should give Lizzy's most special place a most special name? What a good idea."

Lizzy squirmed and shook her head but refused to say anything.

"Okay," I said. "Gretchen."

She wrinkled her nose. "Ew. No. I'd never ..."

"Tell me what you call her, or I will make up a name for her myself. How about Harriet? Edna?"

"Stop. Those are all so ..."

"What? They're better than Vagina. What kind of name is that?"

"Fine. Fine." She inhaled a long breath and closed her eyes. "I call it"—she exhaled and spoke really fast—"Gigi. Short for Girl Gear."

"Girl gear? Gigi? That's a great name. Don't you agree, Belvedere?" I tipped my hips up and back a few times, as if my dick were nodding.

"Stop. Stop, stop, stop," Lizzy pleaded, blocking the movement from her sight with a pillow. There was no hint of humor or desire in her eyes. She looked almost scared as she sunk her teeth into her lower lip. "This is embarrassing to admit, but I cannot fake marry you because I'd almost certainly fall in some kind of fake-wife love with you. And that would mess everything up."

She was right. The last thing I needed was another angry, vengeful ex-wife.

"I like you," she continued. "A lot. And I'd like to be friends with you. To help you. But I can't cross that line. I know myself, and if we have sex, odds are way too high that I'll turn your affection into something I shouldn't. It would ruin everything. Does that make sense?"

"Perfect sense. I don't want that either." We held eye contact for several long minutes. Thoughts tumbled through my mind. Short- and long-term wants, needs, and desires made their arguments. The consensus seems to be that Lizzy was nothing like Brigitte so I had no reason to fear vindictive post-marriage actions from her. And, of all the women I knew, she was the only one who could pull off being my wife for a few months. I needed to convince her she had nothing to worry about.

"Adam, I ghosted the last guy I sort of dated, even though we were both clear we didn't want anything more than a good time while it lasted. But when I started to think it might be nice if it lasted longer ..." She shrugged. "I can't let anything get in the way of my travel plans."

I respected how self-aware she was. And her determination to achieve her goals before having to negotiate life with a partner. We were on the same page in that respect.

"The way I see it, a short-term gig as Mrs. Adam Rhodes is the perfect solution then. It will get you to the other side of the world faster than you would if you had to earn the money in tips."

"No argument. But you missed the point."

"You're worried about getting attached."

She nodded.

"So, what if we have sex, but I give you daily reminders that this is a short-term thing?" I suggested.

She scowled. "Oh yeah, that'll be great for my self-esteem." She deepened her voice, I assume to sound like me. "Good morning, Lizzy. Don't forget that I don't actually *want* you here. You're a means to an end."

I felt like an ass. "Sorry. I didn't mean ... I have no interest in anything long term either. Did that once. It didn't end well."

"You know why I kept working as a hostess, even though I could get a job as a counselor now?"

"The money is better?" I guessed.

"No, it's because once I get a job working with emotionally vulnerable kids, building those relationships, I won't have the freedom to do all the things on my bucket list. I need to experience life before I settle into something more permanent. Work, relationships, everything."

"It's like meeting a female version of myself." I laughed. "I get it. We both have plans that don't include a spouse. It's perfect. Except for not having sex. I still don't understand that part," I admitted.

"Sex is crossing the line from a friend helping out, to a friend who might become more. So, no sex. No intercourse. No oral. No orgasms. If we can keep that in check, this fake marriage thing could work." She held her hands up in prayer position. "Please promise me you won't cross that line," she said.

I'd pretty well convinced myself that the risks of marrying Lizzy for a few months would be worth the payoff. But I assumed since we'd be living together, sleeping in the same bed, I'd be having *more* regular sex, not no sex at all. I'd put that in the pros column. But having her in my bed every night and inaccessible? That was a definite con.

I rubbed my face, suddenly exhausted and emotionally beat. When I looked back at Lizzy, she was staring at me with her big blue eyes. The problem was, I found her dangerously attractive. Always had. The night of Josh and Paige's wedding, I would have taken her home without a second thought if anyone had offered to have Olivia sleep at their place. That, and if I hadn't totally humiliated myself.

"I don't know," I admitted. "The truth is, I don't think I can make that promise. I don't *want* to make that promise. I want to have sex with you, and I'm not sure I could resist you. That's me being honest."

Lizzy rocked side to side, never taking her eyes off me. "I'm so conflicted. I want to help you keep custody of Olivia. Really, I do. And the idea of being able to travel in two or three months with more money than I could ever save in two years? That's obviously really appealing too. Part of me is screaming to give this a try. The problem is, I'm not sure I'd be able to resist you either. And that's what scares me. One of us has to put up an impenetrable wall for this to work."

"We're both assuming worst-case scenario here, that neither of us has willpower. It's kind of a pleasant worst case, but you know what I mean."

She nodded. "Yeah."

"So, instead of assuming we're both too weak to be responsible adults, what if we try tonight? See if we can share a bed without crossing the line?"

"And if we fail?" Lizzy asked.

"If we fail, we tell Brigitte the whole wedding thing was a big, unfortunate misunderstanding," I answered.

"We agree to be just friends. And I still get to visit Olivia now and then."

"Friends. No benefits—other than puzzle time with my kid."

I stood and walked to Lizzy with my arm out. She put her hand in my mine and let me pull her up so our bodies were almost touching. My cock did a little jump, and I prayed Lizzy had solid wall-building skills.

"Kissing. Caressing your nonsexy parts. Rubbing your back. All those things are within limits?" I asked.

"Cuddling. Touching me anywhere except Gigi."

"Is oral defined as touching?" I asked.

She moaned and looked like she was in pain. "Definitely no going down on me. But *maybe* a blowjob would be okay. We'll have to see," she said.

Of course, now my cock had to voice its opinion. I used my free hand to cover myself.

"One night. See if we can do this," I said.

"Push it to the limit and make sure we can stop," she said, brushing her mouth lightly on my ear, then turning her neck so the spot where she dabbed perfume was right under my nose.

"And if we can't—" I groaned.

"We call off the fake wedding."

"Deal."

Lizzy looked from my outstretched hand to my zipper, to my eyes, and down to my zipper again.

"So, if two to three months of being your fake wife is worth $25,000, what do you figure one night is worth? You know, in case this doesn't work out?" By her tone and her smirk, I could tell she was trying to lighten the mood.

"You fancy yourself a negotiator? Okay, that's a fair question. Hmm … well, if we can't control ourselves and things go too far tonight, I think *you're* going to have to pay *me* for what I give you."

That got the smile I wanted. I took her hand and led her upstairs to my room, gently clicking the door closed, to not wake Olivia.

Lizzy walked to the window. "It feels weird, going to bed while it's still light out."

No, it feels weird going to bed with a woman I want to ride like a black diamond slope, knowing we can't move past the bunny hill.

"Keep underwear on," she said, as if whispering to the neighbors through the window.

My body and brain battled with competing desires. G-rated, my brain warned. Hey, just because we can't have sex doesn't mean we can't make this experiment sexy, my cock replied, leading the way to her. I placed a hand on the small of her back, and she turned to me.

"Is this a bad idea?"

"Terrible." I leaned down and kissed her. I couldn't help it.

She returned the kiss. A slow, exploratory meeting. Lips pressed to mine, she opened her mouth. Mine followed her lead. She inhaled and drew air from me. I pressed my mouth harder against hers as she exhaled. I breathed her in. Our tongues touched but lay still for three more shared breaths. It was dizzying. And so freaking hot.

If we kept this up, there was no way I'd make it ten minutes without needing release. "Slow down." I pulled away and cupped my cock, straining against my zipper.

"Yeah." Lizzy exhaled the word. She was flushed and wide-eyed. "No kissing. Too intimate."

"No argument."

She looked from my face to my hand, still pressed over my zipper, then up to my chest. "I want to see you. But also I don't." She ran her tongue over her bottom lip, and I lost control. My jeans were on the floor before she could look away. Boxers still on, but barely. My T-shirt landed beside my pants. Lizzy took a step away, but never took her eyes off me.

I felt like a god. And an asshole. She wanted me, but I couldn't let her have me.

"I should go," she whispered.

"You should."

"It's going to end badly."

"It will."

"But I don't want to leave."

"Then stay."

As she studied my near-naked body, I undressed her in my mind. What I imagined kept me hard.

"One hour," she said.

"Set a timer."

"Turn around."

I did and heard fabric moving. Her dress coming off, I assumed.

"Can you get in bed and roll so your back is to me? My sundress has a built-in bra, so I don't have—"

"Yup," I cut her off, not wanting to hear anything about naked breasts.

12

LIZZY

I stood at the side of the bed, debating how to handle this. I could keep six inches between us and spend the next hour talking to him. That would be good. Set the right tone for a fake marriage.

Or I could crawl in and press my belly against his ridiculously broad back. That would be safe. Not sexy at all. He'd only pulled the duvet over his legs and bum. I watched his shoulders move as he breathed.

Keep a safe distance.

And what will that prove?

That you can resist him.

For one hour.

One hour at a time. One day at a time.

"You okay? You sound like you need a paper bag to breathe into," Adam said but didn't turn to face me.

My heart raced. I had that feeling you get the second you finally have the courage to jump into a cold lake. It'll be okay. You've done this before. Short-term pain for long-term gain. I grabbed the corner of the blanket and dove under. Perhaps with a bit too much enthusiasm.

My plan to keep space between us evaporated as my

breasts brushed against Adam's spine. More accurately, as my rock-hard nipple reached out and tried to become one with his vertebrae.

"Jesus," he moaned as he reached his arm behind him and pulled my body tight against his.

I adjusted my bottom arm under the pillow and placed my other hand on his thigh as we moved into a comfortable, spooning position. My mouth was an inch from his shoulder. I had an uncontrollable urge to kiss, to bite, to lick him.

Adam's scent, his taste, and his heat enveloped me. Fueled me. I reached over his hip and cupped my hand around his hard-on.

"Lizzy," he warned.

"Do you have lube? I know it's a double standard but as long as that thing is all… I just want to feel you. Is that okay?"

He answered by leaning away, moving out of my grasp. Then he opened a drawer on his bedside table, rolled onto his back, and handed me a small bottle of liquid lube. I put some in my palm. He let me see the size of him. Gigi shivered, then clenched tight.

I was still under the covers and planned to stay that way.

"You want to take off your—"

"Off," Adam said, dragging his boxers down his legs. I wiggled away, just a few inches, to get the right angle for my fingers to wrap around him. I watched my hand stroke his length and was mesmerized. I'd never had sex with a man this large. *And you never will*, I reminded myself.

"Mmm, that's good." Adam pushed his hand under the blanket and found my nipple. He circled the palm of his hand over my hard nub. I was suddenly aware of all the blood in my body and how it rushed to fill my lower nub, now equally hard. And when he took my nipple between his thumb and finger and squeezed, I squeezed his cock. Maybe a bit too enthusiastically.

"Easy." His hand jumped from my breast to my fingers. I released my grip.

"Sorry."

"Lube." He held out his hand.

I watched as he poured the liquid onto his fingertips. I thought he was going to show me how he liked to be stroked, but he reached under the blanket and, with a gentle but firm fist, nudged my legs apart.

"No, no, no," I said, but without a hint of hesitation, my traitorous legs opened, and my knees bent to make room for his hand.

"No?" He pulled away.

"Maybe?" My legs spread a little wider and I reached for his cock again.

"If you don't want this—"

"Shut up. New rules. No kissing. No sex." I lifted my hips in search of his hand. "All else, okay."

He vibrated a fingertip lightly on my clit. "Even orgasm?"

I tilted my hips and cupped his hand down and around my sex, pressing his fingertips against my opening. He slid inside and by the way he stroked and massaged my most intimate parts, I knew he understood my nonverbal answer.

I let go of his hard-on and gripped the sheets, closed my eyes, and tried to breathe through my nose since panting was drying out my mouth. I moaned. I sighed. I squirmed.

I was so close to coming and I wanted him inside me. Not his fingers. I wanted to be filled by Adam. My hand sought and found his cock, still engorged, but not as hard as when I'd let go. I stroked him to the same rhythm he was pumping me with his fingers. As he hardened, I tightened and then … I held my breath as the waves rolled through my core and squeezed his fingers. The contractions lasted several seconds, but not long enough.

I tapped his hand and pulled his fingers from inside my

body. I needed more. In silence we changed positions so he was behind me, his cock still firm in my hand. Then I pushed his tip against my shivering opening, desperate to have him. I pressed my ass back and … he pulled away.

"No! Wait!" My breathless plea was met by a grunt and a firm hand on my ass.

"Your rule. No sex," he growled. "And mine. No unprotected sex."

"I have an IUD. I'm clean." I arched my butt in search of him.

"Stop." He sat up and swung his legs off the bed, away from me.

I curled into a ball, embarrassed. Ashamed. "Sorry."

"Not your fault. I'm irresistible." He groaned and then chuckled.

"This is why I can't have nice things," I whimpered.

Adam turned to face me with serious, questioning eyes. "Because when you're given something nice, you stuff it in your vagina and Gigi squeezes it so hard it breaks?"

I laughed, then teared up, not able to say what I actually meant: What if I don't want to give you up when my turn is over?

We were silent for at least a minute. I was facing the door to the hallway, to Olivia's room. I thought about what she stood to lose if Brigitte was successful in gaining sole guardianship. About how awful it would be to take her from Adam and put her in a boarding school. About the fact she'd already lost two parents. She couldn't lose Adam and the whole Rhodes family. And if I had to put my own heart at risk to save hers, that was an easy decision.

"I'll do it," I said.

"Do what?"

"Anything I can, to help you keep Olivia. I'll be your fake wife."

Adam dropped his head and exhaled a long breath. He

got up and went to his dresser and pulled out a pair of boxer briefs and a T-shirt. He tossed the shirt to me. "Put this on." Then he put on the boxers and came back to bed. "Shove over, bed hog."

We lay side by side, not quite touching. My arms pressed the blanket down over me, creating a physical block from accidentally bumping into him. Adam lifted my hand and placed it on his chest, over his heart, so I could feel the beat. Then he slowly traced the length of my fingers with his, up and down, up and down. It was surprisingly calming.

"That feels nice," I said.

"It's something Olivia's counselor suggested I do to help her ground when she's feeling anxious. I thought it might help you relax." He closed his eyes and slowed his breath.

I watched as he fell into a relaxed state and realized my mind chatter, the horniness and fear, had stopped. He was a good man. A good father.

I broke the silence. "Did you know that kids whose parents hug them, hold their hand, and who generally have lots of safe, physical contact from people they trust, lose their virginity, on average, two years later than kids who crave connection?"

Adam opened his eyes but didn't change the rhythm of his soothing touch. "I did not know that. But good. Hopefully, Olivia will be twenty-five before she has sex."

"Right. Exactly—but only if *you* and everyone in your family keep her feeling as safe and loved as she does. Kids in boarding school are notoriously touch-starved. You can't let that happen. *We* can't let that happen," I said.

"No, we can't."

"Not that there's anything wrong with losing your virginity when you're on the younger end of the spectrum," I added, not wanting to sound judgmental. "Except that usually it's for the wrong reason."

"How old were you when you lost your virginity?" Adam asked.

I shook my head. "Let's just say I was a touch-starved kid and leave it there."

"I was sixteen," Adam offered.

We talked until well after midnight, everything from things we missed about being a kid to dreams we had once we finally felt grown up. I laughed more than I had in a year. And, I told Adam that I'd fake marry him and be a perfect fake wife for three months or however long it took. He thanked me but said he wanted to sleep on it since it wouldn't be a sure thing, and the risks if we screwed up weren't inconsequential.

I fell asleep wrapped in his arms, feeling both safe and loved, even though I was neither. But that's what I did; that was my pattern. I took attraction and affection and made them into something bigger. And because bigger was the last thing I wanted, for at least another five years, I blocked and ghosted every man I'd actually liked.

I knew it was messed up, but I took solace that with every month that passed I was one month closer to allowing myself to fall in love for real.

13

———

ADAM

Something poked my back, and I slowly became aware that the dream I was having was not a dream at all, that my semi was pressed against a woman's thigh. A woman who was wrapped tight in my arms.

Poke. Poke.

"Dadam, why is Auntie Lizzy sleeping in my spot?"

Auntie Lizzy? Lizzy! Realization dawned. We've been caught. This was the first time Olivia had ever seen a woman in my bed. I'd not planned for this. Not yet. Not ever.

I rolled toward Olivia, making sure the blankets covered me.

"Hi, sweetie." I checked the clock. Six thirty. "Um, last night it was late so Auntie Lizzy decided to sleep here."

Olivia nodded and yawned. Then she squinted at me. "But you and Auntie Lizzy aren't married yet. Nana said I wouldn't have a mom again until you got married."

Lizzy stirred. "Good morning, pumpkin. Do you always get up so early?" Lizzy's yawn started a chain reaction.

"Sometimes," she said with a shrug. "Are you and Dadam getting married today?"

Lizzy's look was clear: *You handle this.*

"No, sweetie, we're not."

"Oh." Olivia's brows pulled together and she dropped her head.

"Hey. What's wrong?" I put my thumb under her chin and tilted it so I could see her face.

That's when the tears started. "But, but, I want you to get married. Nana said I had to be patient. And I am, Dadam. I'm being very patient."

I looked from Olivia to Lizzy and mouthed, *Help me*.

"Olivia, your Dadam and I are talking about *maybe* getting married. But it's a big decision. It would change a lot of things."

"I know that," she said, scowling and wiping her eyes.

"What do you think will change?" Lizzy asked.

"I'll have a mom. And Dadam will have a wife. And we'll be a family. And, and"—she frowned as she thought —"and I think we'll get a dog."

I burst out a laugh. That was unexpected.

"A dog? Where in the world did that come from?" Lizzy asked.

"When Uncle Nick married Auntie Sophie, he got a dog. And when Uncle Josh and Auntie Paige got married, they got two dogs. So, can we? Can we please get a dog?"

"Uncle Dylan and Auntie Kama didn't get a dog," I pointed out.

"Because they're weird."

Lizzy, who'd been biting her lip to keep from laughing, lost the fight. "It's true. They are weird." She sat up and motioned for Olivia to jump in between us.

"Auntie Lizzy," Olivia said, serious, "why did Auntie Brigitte say you stole away Dadam?"

That was a full-force blow to my gut I did not see coming.

Lizzy answered with a question of her own. "When did she say that, sweetie?"

Olivia raised one shoulder. "When I had my sleep-over with her. Who did you steal Dadam away from?"

"Nobody, sweetie. I didn't steal Dadam. Auntie Brigitte made a mistake."

Damn right she did. My hands formed fists. My teeth ground against each other. My heart raced, and it took all my energy not to yell profanities. Real ones. I got out of bed and silently dressed in running shorts and a sleeveless T-shirt.

Lizzy watched in silence and was the first to speak. "What's going on? Where are you going?"

"For a run."

It was a good thing I didn't know where Brigitte was staying, or I'd have done something stupid.

I ran hard, pushed my body until I felt like puking. And when I got home ninety minutes later, I'd processed my rage and turned it into something more productive. I hoped.

Lizzy and Olivia were at the kitchen table; crayons and markers filled the space between them.

"Dadam, look what Lizzy drew. It's us! I'm coloring it to put on the fridge. Do you love it?"

Lizzy spoke before I could answer. "I understand bacon omelets are a fan favorite in these parts. You didn't have bacon so I made a salami omelet. A salamlet, right Olivia?"

"It's weird." Olivia scrunched her nose. "But pretty yummy."

"There's a plate keeping warm in the oven for you."

My heart clenched. I'd expected Lizzy to greet me with an admonishment of how immature I'd been to run off and leave her with Olivia, but she stood and walked toward me with open arms.

"I'm sweaty. And stinky." I crossed my arms to block her.

"Too bad, because Olivia and I agree that you need a hug."

Olivia jumped up from the table and threw herself at me.

I caught her, then Lizzy encircled us both, pressing Olivia between us. I freed one arm and wrapped it around Lizzy.

"Feel better now?" Olivia asked.

"Yes, pumpkin. I do." I kissed Olivia's forehead, then put her on her feet but didn't release Lizzy from the half hug. "And I feel clearer too."

Stepping back, my hand slid from Lizzy's waist to her hand. I inhaled a deep breath and, before I lost my nerve, asked the question we'd agreed to revisit in the morning, if it still made sense.

"Mona Elizabeth Sheila Hillhouse, will you marry me?"

She looked from me to Olivia before she answered.

"I thought you'd never ask."

Over the next week, Lizzy spent every day with me and Olivia. We'd agreed to not sleep in the same house before the wedding since there was no reason to torture ourselves unnecessarily. I'd also unwillingly agreed to a sexless marriage since our orgasm-only experiment left us both feeling more agitated than relaxed.

As for wedding planning, it was casual and basically stress-free since my whole family was already going to be at Nick and Sophie's for a big Canada Day party. Lizzy's only family was her mom, who lived on the East Coast, and who Lizzy said was not in a position to come. When I pushed, assuming she meant her mom didn't have the money to travel, Lizzy told me to drop it. So I did.

The only challenge was finding a marriage commissioner who was available to officiate on short notice and willing to work on the holiday. But where there's a will—and enough money—there's a way.

Lizzy wrote vows that promised just the right amount of commitment to make the wedding look legit, but not so much that either of us felt like flat-out liars. None of this "until death do us part" business, which, to be honest, even if I ever did get married again for real, I'd never, ever say to another person. My chest squeezed at the thought.

The only people who knew the truth about our fake relationship were Dylan and Kama. I hated not being honest with the rest of the family—for a second time—but we needed it that way in case I really did have to go to battle for Olivia so we wouldn't put anyone in a situation of having to choose between lying or ruining our marriage of convenience if they were called to testify about my suitability as a father.

I did my two-finger whistle to get everyone's attention, then wrapped my arm around Lizzy's shoulders.

"I know this wedding comes as a bit of a surprise to some of you—"

"Not to me!" Olivia interrupted with glee as she ran up and jumped into my free arm.

"And I'd be lying if I said I wasn't a little surprised myself to be tearing up my singles dance card—"

"Bro, who even says that?" Nick called from the back steps of his house.

I gave him the finger with the hand on Lizzy's shoulder. Subtle enough that neither Olivia nor Nana would see it.

"Lizzy has been family adjacent for over a year, and I thought it was time to, you know, make her family proper."

"Lizzy, how can you still be standing with all that swoon-worthy, romantic talk?" Dylan asked.

"Dude, you suck at speeches," Josh called over the laughs.

I felt Lizzy's shoulder shake. She was biting her lip again and trying not to laugh. "Sorry, but that was awful. You ready to do this, handsome?"

Am I ready? The blizzard in my gut said no. I swallowed the memory of the first woman who'd married into the illustrious Rhodes family—and then, who'd left me before anyone even knew what we'd done.

This is different, I told myself. Lizzy and I are on the same page. We have a shared expectation of where this is headed. And for how long. It's all good.

"Ready as I'll ever be."

I put Olivia on her feet then nodded at Lizzy and kissed her, as we'd planned. Our first public display of affection. As fake as our marriage was going to be, the kiss felt real. And lasted much longer than we'd agreed to. I squeezed my eyes closed, telling Belvedere to settle down, reminding him that there would be no wedding-night fun.

I nodded to the marriage commissioner. She raised her arms in a silent invitation to focus their attention on us.

Tapping the top of Olivia's head, I asked, "You have the rings?"

She shoved her hands into the deep pockets on her dress and showed me a ring in each of her small palms.

"Let's do this!" I called out.

The marriage commissioner said some stuff she told us was standard, prevow setup about the sanctity of marriage. I barely heard her over the thrum of my heart in my ears. I wondered if Lizzy was feeling the same way. I mouthed a silent question to her, "What could possibly go wrong?" It had become our inside joke over the week as we laid out plans and rules for our fake relationship.

Normally, Lizzy would smile or laugh, but she looked like she was trying to remember how to breathe.

"Adam," the marriage commissioner said, getting my attention. "Repeat after me."

I took Lizzy's hand in mine and said the words we'd agreed to.

"In the presence of my family and friends, I, Adam Jones Rhodes, promise to stand by your side, to share and support your hopes and your dreams.

"I vow to be there for you. To laugh with your joy, comfort you when you're sad, be your strength in times of need, and to catch you when you fall.

"I will be your partner in parenthood, your comrade in adventure, and your accomplice in mischief.

"For all that lies ahead of us, I accept that it will be a journey that can only be completed together.

"This I promise."

I reached for the ring that Olivia had been holding in her outstretched hand. I winked at my daughter, but when I tried to take it, she closed her hand around it, jumping up and down a few times.

"Can I put it on her? Please?" she asked.

Lizzy smiled and nodded.

"I promise too," Olivia said to Lizzy, breaking my heart. *What could possibly go wrong?*

The commissioner turned to Lizzy, who repeated the identical vows. Olivia put the ring on my finger and made her promise. And then I kissed Lizzy to whoops and hollers from the peanut gallery. I tasted salt and felt Lizzy shake under my hug. I gave her questioning eyes, silently asking if she was okay.

She gave a small smile and a nod, but her eyes weren't happy. And why should they be? Lizzy admitted that she was worried about becoming even more entrenched in my family and then losing that again. As the only child of a single mom, being part of a big family like mine was the wish she'd always made on birthdays and to Santa.

Her mom never delivered the dad and stepsisters, but the months she'd hung out with us had given her exactly what she knew she'd wanted all those years.

Her friendship with Josh was a mutually beneficial, platonic, plus-one to family events. She'd bonded with Sophie and was already Kama's BFF. She never expected to be so fully shut out once Paige came back into Josh's life.

That was entirely my fault. And we were both painfully aware that I had the power to do that to her again.

As my family organized to take photos, I whispered an unscripted, fake wedding oath to her, "No matter what, from this day forward, you will always be a member of this family, as the sister we brothers never had, but always needed. I promise."

Off script, Lizzy kissed me again. The way my body responded had nothing to do with brotherly love.

14

LIZZY

Being back in the Rhodes family was even better the second time around. Maybe because everyone believed I'd be a permanent fixture now. As surprised as some of the family had been with Adam's unexpected announcement, several commented on how well-matched they thought we were. Unfortunately, I could already tell it was going to be impossible to keep from believing it myself.

One of the unforeseen benefits of being Adam's wife? I didn't need to work, and for the first time since I was seventeen, I had a summer vacation. Being free in the evenings and on weekends meant more opportunities to hang out with my best friend and my new sisters-in-law.

On a mid-July Saturday, the brothers were all headed to a football game. We wives had been invited, but Paige had a better idea—a girls' night in with a few decks of tarot cards.

The gang came to Adam's house—our house—so Olivia could be part of the fun, at least until seven o'clock. Sophie and Nick drove down to the city from Lily Valley (and thus would be sleeping over), while Paige and Josh and Kama and Dylan arrived via Uber.

Everyone made themselves at home, and Olivia was in her element, a bundle of joyful energy.

"Hey, squirt," Josh said. "How about you get your favorite uncle a beer?"

She leapt from the floor where she'd been kneeling in front of a jigsaw puzzle, showing Paige how many pieces were already in place. "Don't do any without me!" She came back with an unopened bottle and walked right past Josh, handing it to Nick.

Josh grabbed her dress and pulled her into his lap. "Hey, that's my beer!"

"No, it's not. You said to give it to my *favorite* uncle, and that's Uncle Nick." Olivia looked conspiratorially over her shoulder. Adam winked from the kitchen. Josh tickled her until she screamed, "Uncle!"

"Tell me I'm your favorite uncle, or I won't let you go."

"You're my favorite uncle, Uncle Josh. Honest, you are. Dadam told me to give it to Uncle Nick."

"You little snitch," Adam said, lifting Olivia out of Josh's lap and resuming the tickling.

"Mona, help me! Tickle Dadam's ears. Help!"

Olivia had decided to call me Mona since, as she put it, "You're more special than just being Auntie Lizzy so you need a more special name now."

It was Adam who'd suggested Mona. At first it felt strange—no one had ever called me Mona before—but after a few days it made me feel like Superwoman with a secret identity. On the one hand, it was lovely to have a special name, on the other, it was a constant reminder of the real secret.

I jumped to save Olivia from Adam's fingers. I'd learned over the last two weeks that the fastest way to get him to cease and desist any kind of play was to blow hot air in his ear. It made him go weak in the knees. It might have been a dirty move, but so was setting up Olivia like that.

I inhaled deep into my belly and ever so slowly exhaled without blowing, to keep my breath as warm as possible. No words were needed, just my open lips positioned above his jaw.

With his arms full of a squirming Olivia, he had no way to block me and no choice but to put her down. She ran straight into Paige's protective hug. But then Adam was free to turn his attack on me, which he did without hesitation. Unfortunately, I'd admitted my vulnerable spot to him the night he told me his weakness. It seemed like a good idea at the time, some "getting to know each other" conversation while we lay in bed, half watching one of the *Fast and the Furious* movies.

He pinned my arms at my sides and bent his knees so he could push my chin up using the top of his head. I fought with all my might to keep him from getting access to the most ticklish part of my body. No surprise, he overpowered me and before I could beg for backup, his mouth and scratchy beard were all over my neck. I laughed so hard I couldn't speak, couldn't breathe. When I finally got an arm free, I did the only thing I could think of—I grabbed his balls and squeezed. That stopped him dead in his tracks.

But I hadn't considered the audience.

"Bro, there are innocents present," Nick said, leaning forward to cover Sophie's eyes.

"Take it upstairs. But be fast. Uber will be here in twenty minutes," Josh added.

"Yeah, take it upstairs," Olivia echoed. "We're trying to work on my puzzle in peace. Right, Auntie Paige?"

Adam and I collapsed on the couch, in the spot Josh had vacated to get himself a beer.

He came back with four and passed them to outstretched hands.

Olivia copied the adults and raised her hand too.

"Nope, nothing for the niece who just broke my heart. You can get your own drink," Josh said with a pout.

I leaned against Adam's arm and he wrapped it around my shoulders. I smiled at him, feeling like I'd won the family lottery. The smile he returned didn't reach his eyes, and *Bam!* I remembered this was all fake. Well, not the way Olivia loved her aunts and uncles and how much they all adored her, but my position in it.

We were only fourteen days into what Dylan expected would be two to three months of faking it, until Adam could make it as Olivia's primary legal guardian, a role that would give him the power to prevent Brigitte from taking Olivia to London and dumping her in boarding school. But I was already losing confidence that I could go the distance with the fraud.

The guys finished their beers and left for the game. Couples kissed, including Adam and me, since that's what newlyweds do. The public displays were the hardest because a chaste kiss on the cheek, the way we kissed good-night in front of Olivia, wouldn't cut it. No, he took my face in his hands and looked into my eyes before dropping his mouth to mine. The electricity between us was dangerous, a reminder to keep private kissing off our list of allowable fake-husband-and-wife activities. Adam didn't like it, but he didn't argue.

With the guys gone, Paige was the first to pull out her oracle cards. We'd each brought our favorite deck. I only had one, a gift from Kama a few years ago. I'd never used it on my own but enjoyed it when she came to my place and did a reading for me.

"Olivia, can we roll up your puzzle and do the readings on this table?"

She nodded but looked concerned.

"What's up, sweetie?" I asked.

"I don't have cards, so I can't play."

"Of course, you can," Kama said, picking up her deck and handing it to Olivia. "You want this deck?"

She held the box in the palm of her hand and made a serious face. "I hate to be rude, Auntie Kama, but I don't really like the picture on yours." She brightened as she placed the box back on the table and reached for mine. "I love the picture on Mona's, though. Can these be mine?"

"All yours."

"So this is what I was thinking," Kama said. "We take turns and each choose three cards from any decks we want. It can be three from one deck or one from three different decks. Two and one, whatever speaks to you. Then, you can ask one question of all three cards, and the first card you draw will be the answer as it relates to your past, the second one to your present, and the third to your future. Or it could be a situation, an obstacle, and then advice. Or mind, body, spirit. Or the first card could represent you, the second one your relationship, and the third one your partner. Figure out what you're curious about, and frame your questions accordingly. The questions can be anything, as long as they *don't* have a yes-or-no answer. Does that make sense?"

Sophie stood. "I'm going to need wine for this."

"Bring me a glass, too, please," Paige said with a laugh.

Kama pushed all four decks toward me. "Newlywed goes first. Which three do you want to use?"

I motioned for Olivia to come sit on my lap. "Should we do our reading together?"

She nodded.

"You pick."

Olivia pointed. "The fairies and the animals and the one with the moon face."

I followed Kama's reminder to knock on each deck, to clear it of the previous user's energy before shuffling. Then, I thought of my question: "What do I need to know right now?"

I decided to focus my cards on me, my relationship, and Adam, in that order and asking the same question for all three.

The first card came from the *Magical Messages from the Fairies* deck. It was 'Emotional Healing.' Since Sophie brought that deck, she read the message, which, in a nutshell, said my heart was in the process of breaking free from old emotional pain, and once I loved myself, I'd be open to be loved in new ways.

While Sophie and Paige made child-friendly comments with lewd subtext, Kama gave me a knowing look. I laughed at the jokes but felt the power of the message.

"Hey, can I take a picture of the pages from the book?"

"Go for it," Sophie said, handing it to me.

My next question was about the relationship. I let Olivia choose the deck for that message: *Wisdom of the Oracle.* I drew a card called 'Happy Happy.' It had a girl sitting crossed-legged on what looked like a giant Easter egg with rainbows flowing into and out of her.

"So pretty," Olivia said. "I want to draw that picture. Can I, Mona?"

"Of course. You know where your art box and sketchbook are?"

Olivia jumped and ran upstairs.

Paige read the message, which was shockingly accurate —or would have been for an actual newlywed. It read like a fairy-tale ending to me, a relationship dream, not reality. But I smiled and nodded and agreed that I was *almost* as lucky as each of them—only almost since they each believed they'd married the best of the Rhodes brothers.

The last card I drew was from the *Spirit Animal Oracle.* It was supposed to represent what I need to know in this moment about Adam. I drew the 'Wombat,' upside down— the protection message. Since I'd contributed that deck, I read my own card.

The girls were amazed at how accurate they thought the reversed wombat was as a representation of Adam. I didn't argue since, really, what did I know? I'd only spent four weeks with him, and he seemed pretty damned comfortable in his own skin, which the card challenged. It also said he was wearing a mask to keep from being hurt, but the only person being hurt was himself. If that applied to anyone, it was me, pretending to the world to be the happy wife of a truly kind man, but in private keeping him so far at a distance, I ached for his touch every waking minute.

Olivia dropped into my lap with her crayons and sketch pad to draw her own version of Happy Happy. While Sophie, then Paige, did readings, Olivia's picture started to look quite similar to the card she'd pulled—a frizzy-haired child sitting on an orb, emitting rainbows. Once Olivia was happy with her drawing of the girl, she added a man on his own orb, with connecting rainbows. Then a woman with the rainbow connection to the man and girl.

I told myself that the adults in Olivia's picture were representations of her biological parents. The only way to stop from being eaten alive by the guilt of the inevitable was to remind myself that the nuclear family was virtually every child's understanding of Happy Happy, because it's what society says is the ideal.

But when she labeled the man as Dadam, my stomach sank. I turned away, hoping that when I looked at the picture again, the woman would be left nameless.

"Mona, look." Olivia placed her hand on my cheek to turn my gaze back to her art. "This is you. And this is Dadam. And this is me. Instead of only two Happies, my picture is called Happy Happy Happy since there are three of us." Her smile communicated pride and joy and love.

"It's … perfect," I managed before lifting her off my lap. I feigned a sudden allergy attack and excused myself before a lightning bolt struck me dead for being yet another person to break her heart, ending any possibility of my morally bankrupt genetic line carrying on.

Miraculously, I made it to the upstairs bathroom before the egg-size lump in my throat choked me to death. I stared in the mirror and saw my mother's reflection, despite all the counseling, all the promises I'd made myself not to become her. I was just a different version, more modern and more in control, which made it even worse, made me more sociopathic than she ever was. At least she was honest about not wanting to be a mother. About not wanting to be *my* mother.

Me? I was lying right to Olivia's face, pretending to be giving her the family she'd wished for.

"You're such a bloody hypocrite," I said to my reflection, too disgusted to cry.

A knock on the door caught me by surprise.

"Just a second," I called with false cheer in my voice.

"It's me." Kama's voice floated through the wood, then the door slowly pushed open. "I'm so sorry. It's killing you, isn't it? It's not going to get easier, you know." She wrapped me in a tight hug.

Permission to grieve. I wept into her shoulder. My throat, so constricted I couldn't say the confusing thoughts fighting in my mind:

I'm too young to settle down. I'll resent them if I don't live my life first.

It's too late, you already love them.

But it's all fake.

So, why do I feel more loved now than I ever have?

Because Olivia's love is real.

That's not enough.

Kama released me and looked me in the eye. "You are allowed to end this. The Rhodes family is not your responsibility to keep together."

I nodded, still unable to force out words.

"I'll talk to Dylan. Tell him this isn't working. He'll figure out how to let you leave without hurting Adam's case. You want me to do that?"

I nodded, but as soon as I did, I wanted to change my answer. "No," I squeaked out.

I didn't need to end it early. At this moment, I didn't need to end it ever. But I knew how to change that, how to make sure I'd be able to walk away without feeling guilt or regret, a way to prove that my fake relationship was as real as fairy-tale love stories. If I embraced the situation and lived it fully until it reached its natural end date, our constant togetherness would no doubt get old in two to three months. That would mesh perfectly with the plans Adam and I had already agreed to.

And the best way to make sure we were both ready to resume our well-defined paths? My body relaxed as I realized that it would be for me to give in and allow Adam and myself to be a fake couple in private too. With all the benefits—and all the burdens—of being married with children.

My weeping morphed into semi-maniacal laughter.

"Honey, you're losing it," Kama said, rubbing my shoulder.

"Already fully lost," I said once I caught my breath. "Don't say anything to Dylan. Not yet. I know what I have to do."

What could possibly go wrong?

15

ADAM

The guys and I made our way back to my place after the game and a late dinner.

It was only eleven, but knowing Olivia would be asleep, I shushed the gang at the front door.

None of them bothered to take off their shoes—they went straight to their women for kisses.

"Where's Lizzy?" I asked.

"She never came down after putting Olivia to bed. Something about allergies," Sophie said.

"Why the air quotes?"

Kama answered, "It's nothing. She had an oracle reading that struck a chord. You know how powerful the messages from the cards can be."

I started to laugh, but Dylan caught my eye and gave me a warning—don't get her going.

"Yeah. I guess. I should check on her," I said, thinking that's what a new husband would do. "Nick, Sophie, see you in the morning. The rest of you? Safe trips home."

I looked in on Olivia first, stood and watched her sleep for a minute. I couldn't imagine life without her. Didn't want to even consider it—and being forced to, made me angry. I planted a kiss on her sleeping head. "I love you, pumpkin. No matter what happens, never forget that."

I opened my bedroom door and tiptoed to the bathroom to brush my teeth. I debated jerking off to reduce the time I'd have to spend with blue balls. This was the first night Lizzy and I would be sharing a bed as husband and wife. I'd given up my queen mattress for nights on the couch. As far as I was concerned, the whole ruse was an abysmal failure, and it couldn't end soon enough.

Since Lizzy didn't trust either herself or me to follow the rules of our stupid contract, we'd agreed to be in pajamas and keep to our own sides of the mattress.

With Lizzy's back facing my side, I slid in as quietly as possible, not sure if she'd want to talk and quite certain I didn't want to hear about some doomsday prediction made by tarot cards, interpreted by an amateur soothsayer.

She rolled to face me. *Dammit.*

"Hey, handsome. You have a good time?"

"Always fun with those guys. I hear you ...umm ..." I didn't know how to finish.

"Had a meltdown? Yeah."

"You know those cards are B.S., right?"

She gave me a small smile of agreement. "Yeah, but Kama believes them, and it can be fun."

"So, why'd you leave your own girls' night party?"

"Did you see the picture Olivia drew?"

I shook my head.

"You'll understand in the morning."

We lay in silence, close enough to touch.

"You don't have to stay if you're not tired. You can go down and tell them I'm better now that my knight in shining armor is home."

"Are you better, or are you actually worse now that I'm home?"

Her eyes got glassy. I was doing this to her. This fake relationship was ruining her, stealing her joy.

I reached out tentatively and placed my hand lightly on her shoulder. "I know we're not supposed to touch, but will you let me rub your back? Totally nonsexual. Therapeutic, to help you fall asleep."

Lizzy rolled to give me access.

"Um, so the only thing is, it needs to be skin on skin," I said.

She sighed so heavily, I thought she might be exhaling her last breath.

"About our agreement—"

"I'm sorry. I shouldn't have asked. You're right. I promised I wouldn't step outside the lines. And that's outside. Even though it really is relaxing and entirely nonsexual," I added, hoping to lessen the damage I may have done by proposing she break a rule put in place to protect her heart.

She turned to face me and I gazed into her deep blue eyes for a long minute before she spoke.

"Are you done?" she asked with the hint of a smile.

I was confused, but said, "Yes."

"What I was thinking, about our agreement, is that it's not helping. It's not doing what it's supposed to be doing. I don't feel less connected, and my heart isn't being protected at all. In fact, I think it's making things worse since I have all the sad feelings and nothing to balance them. Nothing to help me feel good during the in-between moments."

Again, we lay silently. I wondered if the patterns of her blinking was Morse code that I was meant to decipher. I wanted to read her mind since I didn't have a clue what she meant, but I was afraid to ask.

"Would you be willing to renegotiate?" she asked.

She's ending the agreement, and I'm going to lose Olivia. No, I'm not willing to renegotiate.

My body tensed. I shook my head, but I had to say yes. What I was doing to her wasn't fair. I had to let her go and face this on my own.

"I don't want to, but of course. If this isn't working for you …"

"Is it working for you?"

"Dylan thinks so. I have to trust—"

"I don't mean the custody battle. I mean this." She pulled at her T-shirt. "Us sleeping in different rooms and getting up before Olivia so she sees us together. The whole public displays of affection and private … nothing. Is that working for you?"

It was a trick question. It had to be. *Of course, it's not working for me. I think about you constantly and jerk off every day after you take Olivia down for breakfast. I want nothing more than to consummate this fake marriage.*

She filled the silence, thank god. "It's not working for me. I feel, I don't know, rejected and lonely all the time. So, I was hoping, if it's not too weird for you, that we could … that you wouldn't mind …"

"Are you putting sex on our allowable list? Is that what you're trying to say? Because that is a one hundred percent *hell yes* from me. And if you were to reach your hand down the blankets, you'd find that it's not empty words. Belvedere is ready for action."

She smiled and let me take her hand and guide it to the pajama bottoms constraining my fully engorged cock. Without breaking eye contact, she pulled her hand from my junk and guided mine under her own pajamas, shaping my fingers into a cup around her mound and pressing them against her sweet spot. Her very warm and very wet sweet spot. Without words, we stripped naked.

Lizzy lay on her back. I straddled her, held my weight above her, sitting up on my thighs. Even though our bodies were clearly ready to ride the slopes, I needed to show her that the sad and disconnected feelings she'd been having were misguided. I needed her to know she was more to me than just a new mountain to conquer.

"Can I kiss you?"

She licked her lips and nodded.

I placed my hand behind her head and tilted it so her face angled to match mine.

"Relax your neck. I've got you."

The weight in my palm increased as she exhaled and closed her eyes. I hated what I saw—a sadness, a pout that hadn't been there weeks ago. I questioned myself, not sure if I'd be helping or hurting her even more.

Lizzy opened her eyes. "Second thoughts?" Her eyebrows pinched together, and she tried to turn her face away. She must have truly believed that I didn't want her.

I had to show her how wrong she was.

"The opposite. Imprinting your beautiful face in my mind so I still see it when my eyes are closed."

I leaned forward and touched my partly open lips to hers. She lifted her chin to make tighter contact, but we maintained a soft connection, moved slowly with gentle pecks at the corners of each other's mouths.

Her tongue breached her teeth and tentatively explored the inside of my lower lip. I kept my mouth supple, a sharp contrast to the state of my cock. My heart raced, but my breathing slowed. Time was confused, like racing an unexpected avalanche. I couldn't decide if I wanted to stay in this safe, quiet moment or free-fall into an explosion of movement and tangled bodies, but I knew the choice was not mine to make. That nature was infinitely more powerful than my thoughts and it would take over whether we were ready for it or not.

I opened my eyes and met Lizzy's. I wanted to give her the full power of what came next, which meant taking momentary control of our positions. In one seamless move, I rolled off her and carried her with me. Now I was on my back, and she was on top.

She squeaked, then smiled, and her energy changed from questioning to commanding. Her mouth met mine again, this time with hunger. Our tongues connected then explored, pushing first one way, then the other, deep into my mouth then sliding into hers. She tasted like toothpaste, but sweeter.

Just as I was about to flip her over and take control again, unable to restrain from taking this to the next level, she pulled away and bit my neck.

"I need you inside me."

I tried to roll, but Lizzy held me in place, knees firmly pressed to the mattress on either side of my waist. She reached to the bedside table where I kept the lube and pulled open the drawer.

"I want to watch you stroke yourself."

She leaned forward and pressed her body flat against mine before pushing off and to my side where she lay on her arm, eyes intent on my cock.

That was so hot, I throbbed for her. I grasped my length close to the tip and moved my hand in small, quick motions, covering the head every few seconds.

"Slow down. I'm trying to learn how you like to be touched."

I watched Lizzy's face as she kept focused on my shaft. Her mouth was open and her tongue moved as if following the movement of my hand. It was getting to be too much.

"Lizzy," I moaned, "if you want this inside you, you need to let me put the condom on."

"Not yet." She pushed herself up, then lay on her stomach at an angle to my body with her face headed …

Oh, sweet Jesus … her mouth was wet and warm. Her lips wrapped tightly around my shaft, and her tongue … it did what my hand had been doing, but a hundred times better. When she cupped my balls and pressed a finger against my ass, I thrust. I didn't intend to. I was in the avalanche, body being tossed, out of control. I was not ready to die, so I gripped her hair and slowly but assertively pulled her head away from my cock.

She looked up and smiled. "Good?"

"Fuck me," I breathed. "Lizzy, let me fuck you."

I reached for a condom but she grabbed my hand.

"Are you clean? Because if we don't need this I want to feel you—*really* feel you."

I closed the drawer, empty-handed.

Lizzy got up on her hands and knees, facing the head of the bed, giving me full control of the next play. I was so hard, it was painful. I pushed my full length inside her in one swift thrust. Her walls squeezed tight, and she tilted her ass to take me deeper.

"Hard," she exhaled the word. I responded with a quick thrust. "Harder," she said with more voice. I pulled away slowly and rammed forward again. "Faster. Please."

Not yet. I wasn't ready to end this. I gripped her ass and slowed down. I pulled all the way out, and she moaned in disappointment. Before I entered her again, I placed my tip against her exposed butthole and gave a very gentle poke. She jerked, so I pulled back and pushed inside the proper target.

But she'd fingered my ass, which suggested she'd accept some tit for tat. My baby finger circled the puckered hole, and she pressed toward it. I only pushed in up to my first knuckle, but that was enough of a turn-on for me to lose it.

I came without warning. Hard and fast.

Once I'd stopped pumping, Lizzy fell to her stomach and shook out her legs. "Hard on the knees." She laughed.

"Hard-on is right. But not on my knees."

She rolled over and, for the first time in weeks, gave me her premarital smile. "Thank you."

I shook my head. "For?"

"Making me feel normal again. I guess I needed a hit of endorphins."

"But"—I lay beside her and traced a line from her forehead to her chin with my index finger—"did you come?"

She shrugged.

"Not on my watch. I can't leave a woman, let alone my wife, having to pleasure herself beside me while I sleep."

She giggled. "That would be kind of hot. Watching you sleep and getting off with a vibrator."

"It would be hotter if you let me show you what my tongue can do."

Her wide eyes and widening legs said a wordless yes.

As quiet as we were being, we weren't silent. And since the house was older than me, the walls weren't one hundred percent soundproof.

Someone tapped lightly on the bedroom door. Lizzy and I froze. Then Nick, in a stage whisper, said, "Sounds like he's trying to heat the bed with a stick of kindling. Poor Lizzy, having to live with a man whose log isn't big enough to light her fire."

Sophie's voice mimicked Nick's. "My firepit is hungry for some flames. You up for the job, big guy?"

Less than five minutes later, judging by the stifled moans coming from our shared wall, it was clear that Nick had accepted Sophie's challenge.

Lizzy climaxed and minutes later fell asleep in my arms. I had no desire to roll away or extricate myself from her. This was a first. Even when Brigitte and I were married, I was never into cuddling after sex.

I was too amped to sleep but didn't want to leave Lizzy. I rolled to make space for my hand between her back and my chest. Even though she was asleep, I still wanted skin-to-skin contact since it helped me relax too.

An unexpected side effect of learning how to calm Olivia

was learning that I had a form of synesthesia that ignited with touch.

When rubbing Olivia's back, I'd see colors in my head if I closed my eyes: pale shades of blue and green. There was movement in the color, but it was all very soft and gentle. Hypnotizing. An effective tool to put me in a sleep-ready state.

I placed a flat palm against Lizzy's spine. Gently, so as not to wake her. My hand covered almost the full space between her shoulders. I closed my eyes and drew my fingers lightly across her skin. The image was immediate and unexpected—a cacophony of color filled my mind's eye. A rainbow that swirled and pulsed. As I ran my fingers back and forth, back and forth, the colors intensified. It was hypnotic, but after five minutes was having the opposite effect I'd expected, and I was further from wanting to sleep. If anything, I was ready to have sex again.

My boner pressed into her tailbone and she stirred. Did I want to wake her? Was it fair to wake her? I should get up, go sleep on the couch. But what message would that send? The message I gave every woman. That once I achieved my physical release, and she received hers, we were done.

Lizzy had gotten what she needed. Not only did she show it the way her whole body shook but I could see it on her face, in her eyes.

And I'd gotten what I needed. We could make each other feel good—very good—for the next couple months. No point in having her think there was more to us than making the best of a ridiculous situation by cuddling up like some lovesick grommet.

I rolled away, pulled on pajama bottoms, and left without waking her.

∼

"Bro, did Lizzy kick you out after she heard the way a real man treats his wife?" Nick kicked my feet. Sun streamed in from the crack in the curtains.

"Bug off," I moaned. "What time is it?"

"Six thirty. I'm going for a run. I was going to go alone, but since you're up"—he kicked my feet again—"come with. I could use some competition."

"Sure. Give me five." I took the stairs two at a time, opened the bedroom door quietly. Lizzy was already up and in the shower. I sat on the bed and watched through the steamy glass doors. She was swaying and humming some song I couldn't make out. Soaping her body. Was it wrong to watch? To be getting hard? I mean, she's my wife, right?

I looked to the open bedroom door. Nick was stretching by the front door. Screw it. He could run alone. I covered my junk and whispered down the stairs. "Had a better offer. Coffee will be ready when you get home." Maybe.

"Chicken," he replied but gave me a thumbs-up.

I closed the door to the hall and stripped.

"Room for one more?" I asked, opening the shower door, no longer hiding my hard-on.

When she looked at me, I could tell she'd been crying. "You left. You regretted last night."

I stepped into the water and took her in my arms. "Bad assumption. I didn't want to wake you, and someone," I said, pointing at Belvedere, "was raring for round three, so I removed myself from the temptation." It was true, if not the whole story.

I felt her relax. I hated myself for how much I was going to hurt her when this was over. Even if I didn't force an end to the marriage once I had custody, she'd be begging for a divorce once she learned the full truth about how and why Olivia's parents died. A story I'd tell her after she no longer had to look at me every day because, god knows, she wouldn't be able to.

16

LIZZY

I t had only been four days—and four glorious nights—since Adam and I added kissing and sex to our allowable marital activities. I was feeling so much better. No more spontaneous tears. No more stress stomachaches. No more wondering what life would be like as Adam's real wife.

Life was as close to perfect as I could've ever imagined being in a twenty-four-hour-a-day relationship could be. Sure, Adam did things that bugged me, like leaving the rag he'd cleaned the toilet and floor with on the bathroom sink instead of tossing it into the hamper. Who puts a dirty towel near toothbrushes?

I mentioned it as a question. "What if I didn't know you'd just cleaned the toilet seat with that cloth, and I used it to wipe my hands?"

"Fair point," he answered. "Still not used to having another person in my bathroom."

I'd smiled and nodded, then wondered out loud what I was doing that might be bugging him.

"You wear too many clothes," he said.

"I what?"

"You're not naked often enough."

He made me laugh. And when we were naked, he made sure I felt adored. And when we were clothed, having adult time, he was attentive and interested in getting to know me and telling me about his rebellious and very lucrative life as a young snowboarder.

He also convinced me to stop feeling guilty about accepting the ridiculous amount of money he'd given me to live a dream life for a few months by helping me plan my trip. He'd done a ton of traveling in his twenties, sponsored to do stunts at ski hills all over the world and had ideas about places I might want to visit.

Dylan was certain the custody question would be settled by the end of August, so I was making plans to travel starting October 1. That gave us a month after the decision to give our fake marriage a good fake go of it, and then for me to suffer a breakdown and say I hadn't been prepared to be a full-time mother. So far that seemed like a stretch since Olivia was such an easy kid to parent. But it was early days, honeymoon phase for all three of us.

The one good thing my mom inadvertently taught me was to make sure I'd fulfilled all my own dreams before handing my life over to a man and child, or even just a child since, according to her, "Men are impossible to keep and children are impossible to get rid of. Like herpes," she said when I was no more than ten.

I had no idea what herpes was, and I'll never forget her look of disgust when I asked and she explained: "It has brown hair and blue eyes and is about this tall." She put her hand on my head and patted it. Even though I knew she meant that I was herpes, it still didn't make sense until I was thirteen.

By the time I was fifteen, the imperative to reach thirty before settling down and having kids had been drilled into me like a cult religion.

My bucket list had grown and shrunk and changed over the last ten years. In my teens, I only had two goals: to earn enough money to get my own place, and save to travel the world. Then, once I'd moved out on my own, my list included things like *get a cell phone* and *get my driver's license*.

I actually never put *earn a master's degree* on my list since it felt like that was less of a bucket list item and more of a thing to do to be able to afford other bucket list items. But in the last five years, that list had one original, albeit clarified, goal on it: take an extended trip around Europe.

And in less than two months, I'd be able to start that adventure. I was excited and counting down the days until I could get on a plane. At least, when I wasn't anxious and counting down the days until I *had* to give up this too-good-to-be-true, temporary life.

But if Adam was sincere—and I had no reason to doubt him—I'd still be welcomed with open hearts into the greater Rhodes family when my globe-trotting was done.

And because everything was apple pie and ice cream with Adam, it forced me to add one new rule to our marriage agreement.

"If I try to change my mind about Europe, I need you to say one thing to me," I'd said over this morning's coffee.

He put down his magazine. He always gave me his full attention when I spoke. "One thing?"

"I need you to say, 'So you can turn out like your mother?' Can you promise you'll say that?"

He shook his head. "You not going to Europe will never make you like your mother," he argued.

I returned the gesture. "You believing that doesn't matter. I believe it. And I don't ever want to be a mother like she was. So, in case I change my mind, I need you to say, 'So you can turn out like your mother.' Please."

He said he didn't like it, but he promised.

Olivia danced into the kitchen wearing her soccer cleats.

"I love how noisy these shoes are. Can I go to tap dancing camp next week?"

"Sorry. Already signed up for bike camp," Adam said. "But if you want to take tap classes, I bet we can find something once school starts again."

"Goody!" She clomped her feet with no discernible rhythm.

"Ladies, I'll be home from Nick's to make dinner. What do you think … wuh …wuh … wheat-free Wednesday?"

Olivia and I made matching faces.

"No?" Adam said. "Well, what *W* dinner can Wednesday be, then?"

"Watermelon!" Olivia said.

"Wine," I added.

"Watermelon and wine. I'll take that under advisement. But no promises."

Then he gave me a not-safe-for-work kiss, planted a G-rated one on Olivia's red head, and told us to have a great day.

I was a soccer mom in the morning, which was surprisingly fun. Olivia's camp was three hours long, so a few of the other parents and grandparents all went to a coffee shop nearby and filled a corner of the outdoor patio for ninety minutes on the last two days. I was the youngest person there—by a long shot. And the stories these parents and caregivers shared about all the time they spent waiting for their kids to finish activities greatly reinforced my commitment to not settle down until I'd lived a little more.

After soccer, Olivia and I had lunch and a visit with Nana, then playtime in the park. This was the kind of summer holiday I'd longed for as a kid, and I loved every minute of it.

"Hey." I tapped Olivia on the shoulder. "Time to put away the iPad. We're home."

"So soon? I was just getting to the good part."

"You say that no matter where you are in that movie." I laughed.

She shrugged. "Because I love all of it."

We got out of the Uber and were met by the sound of crying—lots of it. I looked around for the source of the caterwaul but saw nothing. It was Olivia's eagle eye that spotted the cardboard box on our front porch. A box with a smile logo, though the contents sounded anything but happy.

Mew. Mew. Mew. So much mewing.

Olivia dropped my hand and ran toward the house.

"Oh my gosh!" She peeked through the air holes. "Mona, it's a box of kittens. Is it for me? Ooh! I always wanted a kitten." She jumped up and down.

I approached the box. A hundred thoughts swirled in my head. Does Amazon deliver kittens now? Who would order kittens online? What was the return policy if you ordered the wrong size? What if the color or pattern of the fur wasn't what you expected?

"Can I open it? Can I, can I, can I? Please?" Olivia danced around the mewling parcel.

Where does one take a box of cats that's been delivered to the wrong house?

"Let's … um, let's make sure it's meant for us, okay?"

How could I let her down without ruining her day? Should we open the box? What if one was dead? What if they were undead zombie cats?

I couldn't think fast enough. At least, I couldn't think of helpful things fast enough.

"It is meant for me. I know it is. I wished for a kitten. I always wish for a kitten—well, a kitten and a puppy and a mom!" Her little hands were trying to pull apart the cardboard, but the box had been sealed with packing tape. It would require scissors or a knife to open.

I turned the box to lift it and saw an envelope taped to

the side. It had our address in big, black, block letters. Okay, then … not a shipping mistake.

Olivia was bouncing. I pulled the house key from my purse and handed it to her. She opened the door as I lifted the unbalanced, seesawing box and pressed it tight against my chest to keep it from tilting out of my grip.

Inside, I put it down on the living room floor and grabbed scissors from the kitchen. Once the lid was open, I have to admit, I oohed and cooed as much as Olivia did.

There was a healthy-looking mom cat and, as best as I could count, given how the kittens kept tumbling over each other, seven babies. Olivia zeroed in on an orange tabby.

"Look, she's a ginger like me! Can I hold her?"

"I guess so."

Olivia settled cross-legged on the floor and held the kitten high in two hands, letting it sniff her face.

I leaned against the couch and pulled the envelope from the side of the box. Should I open it? I wasn't sure. Even if the box was meant for this address, it certainly wasn't meant for me.

Olivia looked up and saw me staring at the paper in my hand.

"What does it say? Who's it from?"

Maybe it hadn't been addressed to me, but I was pretty sure Adam would let me read it, so … I opened the envelope. I tried to read ahead before I read out loud, in case there was something Olivia wasn't meant to hear.

"It says:

'Dear lovely family,

I hope you'll forgive me for leaving my cherished family with yours. I saw you painting the tree in your front yard a few weeks ago. I sat in my car and watched for several minutes. There was so much love, I could feel it from the road.

Eddie was a stray I took in four years ago. I've never been able to afford to have her fixed, so she's been an indoor cat. But as you can see, turns out Eddie is a female and she escaped when she was in heat—'"

"What's *in heat* mean?" Olivia asked.

"It means her body was telling her it was time to have kittens," I said.

"Yay, kittens." Olivia gave her little orange tabby a kiss and placed her back in the box, gently taking another out to cuddle.

I read the rest to myself since it was about the troubles this person was having, being forced to move and only finding places in her price range that didn't allow pets.

I thought of my apartment in a pet-friendly building, which would be sitting empty for at least six months, longer if I budgeted my travels well. I wondered if I was allowed to sublet it, then shook my head at the dumb idea.

I flipped the letter, looking for a name. Nothing.

Olivia cooed and cuddled a third kitten.

"You going to give them each a snuggle?" I asked.

She nodded and kissed the little ball of black fluff on the head. "Your name is Blackie," she whispered in its ear. The kitten mewed. "Here you go. Back to your mommy."

I texted Adam as a way to prepare him for the scene he'd be coming home to.

> What's cuter than a box full of kittens?

My phone pinged with a text message.

> ADAM
>
> You are.

I looked from my message to his, and my heart did a little double beat.

Thanks. I think you are too.

I held my breath and debated whether I should tell him via text about the real cuteness factor in his living room or wait until he got home.

ADAM

What? No, that was the answer to Olivia's riddle. It's "you are." Isn't that what you were asking?

Disappointment crept up my neck and weighed down my shoulders.

Yeah, I know. I was kidding. Home soon?

"Is that Dadam?" Olivia looked up, holding a black-and-white kitten against her chest. It was in perfect proportion to her size—two miniature models that personified precious.

I nodded.

"Take a video of me with my new kittens! Wait. I want to be holding Ginger One and Ginger Two." She gently placed the tiny cat in the box and scooped out the two orange kittens.

What's the best way to tell your fake husband that, under your watch, his daughter has just become the adoptive parent of eight cats?

"I'm ready," Olivia said, holding one kitten in her hands and the other in her lap. "Mona, video me and send it to Dadam."

"Why not?" I said, pointing my phone at her as she squealed with delight for her dad. She was basically incoherent with excitement, telling me to show him the box, pointing at kittens and giving them names between declarations of how adorable they all were. I hit Send and waited for a text reply from Adam. What I got was a phone call.

"I can explain. The box was here when we got home," I said as a way of answering.

Adam was silent.

"Don't be mad," I said.

"Mad? Why would you think I'm mad?"

"Because you're not saying anything?" I thought of my mother and how the quieter she was, the more dangerous her ultimate explosion would be.

"No, I'm just watching the video again. I'm amused, bemused, entertained, and confused all at once. Look at Olivia's face. I've never seen her so amped. All it took was a box full of kittens, eh? Never would have thought of that."

"You're not angry?"

"Lizzy, why would I be angry? What's there to be angry about? And who would I be mad at? Someone dropped a box of cats at our door … that's weird. And I'm not sure how we're going to convince Olivia that she can't keep them all. But anger is the furthest thing I'm feeling."

I couldn't explain it, but I felt like the reformed Grinch because my heart grew three sizes for this man. How could he be taking this so well?

"Did these cats come with food and all the things we'll need until we figure out what to do with them?"

"No. Nothing but a box full of cats."

He laughed. He laughed out loud, and it was the most heartbreaking sound I could imagine in this situation since never in my life had anyone laughed when I'd given them a new trouble to deal with.

"Mona, why are your eyes all shiny?"

"Lizzy, are you crying? Why are you crying, woman?"

"Allergies," I countered, standing to get away from Olivia and the cats.

"Nooo, you can't be allergic," Olivia wailed. Within seconds, she was crying, loud enough for Adam to hear.

"Oh, for goodness' sake, both of you are at it now? I'll be home in forty-five minutes. Be ready to go so we can get to the pet store and pick up food and whatever else we need for the night. Lizzy …"

"Yes?"

"There's no need to cry over spilled kittens."

I sputtered a laugh.

"And one more thing," he said. "As cute as that box of kittens is, you're way cuter."

I hung up before he could hear my sob. This man was going to be the death of me.

17

ADAM

As entertaining as it was to have eight cats, I was not ready to be labeled the Crazy Cat Dad. It was pretty easy to find the owner since the mom cat had a tattoo. The vet contacted the lady who'd dropped them off and then told us she'd shared the same story as written in her letter. They suggested we take the cats to the SPCA, but that idea was met with more crying than, well, a box full of kittens.

I gave the vet my number and asked them to pass it on to the owner, Bev. She called the following day, full of apologies. Lizzy wanted to meet her, to gauge whether she seemed responsible enough to sublet her place until she got home from Europe, hoping it would give Bev enough time to find a permanent home that accepted pets.

"Would you be willing to meet us for coffee?" I asked.

Bev asked if the next day would be convenient. We agreed on a time and dropped Olivia off with Nana for a few hours so we could talk without the input of Dr. Dolittle, who was so happy loving up eight cats, she thought we should get a dog with puppies too.

Bev seemed like a good person, the victim of a hot housing market that was hellish for renters.

"Have you considered moving to the Commercial Drive area?" Lizzy asked Bev.

"I've looked everywhere. The vacancy rate is non-existent."

"So, this is kind of a personal question, but do you have one of those credit score apps on your phone?"

Bev cocked her head and said a tentative, "Yes."

"If you'd be willing to let me see your score and contact your current landlord, I might have a short-term solution for you. Like six months or so to find another place that will let you keep Eddie."

Bev's credit rating showed she paid her bills and her landlord said she was a good tenant and he regretted his decision to sell meant she was losing her home.

We ended the conversation with a handshake agreement that I would pay to have Aurora, her mom cat, fixed and that we'd keep the two orange kittens, now named Apricot and Marmalade. Then Bev and Lizzy shook hands, agreeing that Bev would sublet Lizzy's place until January 1, but if she found a good home before then, she could leave early. Hugs sealed the deal.

We let Olivia say goodbye to Eddie and the five kittens we weren't keeping. She was not at all happy with the compromise of two cats and scowled at me between each cuddle she gave the departing kittens. Our two gingers settled in so easily, it was hard to believe we'd only had them for a few days.

My phone rang during dinner and though normally I'd ignore it, the 'Hell's Bells' ringtone told me it was Dylan.

"Hey, bro," I said, standing from the table to talk in private.

"So, I've got a good-news, bad-news scenario for you," he said. "Good news is that your brother is a lawyer and you won't have to break your piggy bank open to take your custody case to court. The bad news—"

"Brigitte is not backing down."

"Yeah. I just got the letter informing us we have a trial date set for August 24."

I did quick math in my head. "In four-ish weeks. Is that good or bad?" I was surprised at how calm I felt. I'd expected that if it came to this, I'd want to punch walls or throw rocks through windows.

"I'd say it works in our favor, since you and Lizzy will have been married long enough that it won't look so much like a setup. And Olivia clearly loves her, and she loves Olivia. So that's good."

"The judge isn't going to want to drag Olivia into this, is she?"

"Not immediately, but it's normal to have a child psychologist talk to the kid, ask her how happy she is and what she'd like."

"Olivia gets a say? Seriously?"

"Yeah, it'll be considered."

"But she's only five. If Brigitte promises her a box full of kittens, something her mean dad didn't let her keep …"

"She's not happy with Thing One and Thing Two?" Dylan asked.

"How to put this in terms a non-dad would understand … so, imagine you had a client who was so happy with your work, they left a box of a dozen different, high-end bottles of scotch at your door. Smoky, peaty, malty, nutty, woody, spicy. All a little different, and all delicious."

"Best. Client. Ever."

"Exactly. Now, your boss sees this box and says, 'Whoa! That's too much scotch for one man. One bottle is enough.' And he takes the other eleven bottles and returns them to the client."

"Bastard! I'd quit."

"Bro, you get the point? I'm the boss who took six of her cats away and only left her with two. I'm the meanie."

Dylan laughed. "You're overthinking. Stop. That's my job, and I'm confident the court-appointed psychologist will take into consideration bribes—which promising a box of kittens definitely qualifies as."

"Is there anything I need to do to be ready for this?" I asked.

"Still keeping all the texts from Brigitte? Letting her see Olivia whenever she wants?"

"All except last Friday. It was her time with Nana. Brigitte knew that but pushed, anyway. I didn't back down, though."

Dylan was quiet for several seconds. "Did you give Olivia a choice?"

"No. That's Nana time. Why would I give Olivia a choice?"

"If Brigitte pushes again, let Olivia decide. At best, it will show the court how important weekly visits with Nana are to Olivia. At worst, it shows the court you're flexible and giving Brigitte full access, something she's made clear *you* won't have if *she* gets custody."

"Got it. Hadn't thought of that," I admitted.

"That's why you're leaving me a crate of scotch when this is over," Dylan said, no hint of joking.

"That was not the point of my analogy, but sure … you keep our family together, and I'll sign you up for a lifetime membership in the Fine Scotch-o'-the-Month Club."

Back at the dinner table, Olivia gave me the stink eye. "No phones at the table, Dadam."

"It was your uncle Dylan. I had to make an exception. You know how he cries when I ignore him." I gave her a tickle.

Olivia giggled and squirmed away. "You know who else cries when you ignore them?"

"Apricot and Marmalade," I said, putting my fingers in my ears and making kitten crying sounds.

"No, Auntie Brigitte," Olivia said, pushing her bottom lip out.

My guts twisted. That manipulative wench.

Lizzy tapped the table in front of Olivia. "Did you know that human babies who are six weeks old cry for two and a half hours a day? And that by the time they're twelve weeks old, it's a little over an hour? Do you think Apricot and Marmalade cry more or less than human babies?"

"Way more," she said. "But I don't think they're crying because they're sad. They just don't know how to talk yet." She shrugged and raised her eyebrows. "That's how they tell us they want something. Right, Dadam?"

"That's right, sweetie."

"Did I cry a lot when I was a baby?"

How the heck to answer that? I had no idea. After Olivia was born, I didn't hang out with Dalton and Maggie nearly as much, with them doing the new-parent thing and me on the road, living the rock star, single-again snowboarder life.

What could I remember?

"You were a very happy baby. You probably cried a normal amount, but I think you laughed way more than other babies. I remember one video your dad sent me. You were like four months old. Your mom was filming, and your dad would go up to you wearing a dogface mask and then he'd take it off and you'd look startled—"

"Like this?" Olivia made wide eyes and her mouth formed a big, open O.

"Exactly like that! Your dad put the dog face mask on again and said, 'Hi, Olivia. Did you have a nice day with Mommy?' and you laughed and laughed. And then he took the mask off and said, 'Woof,' and you laughed more. He did it so many times, your mom told him he had to stop since she was worried you'd stop breathing. You were laughing *that* hard at your barking dad and the talking dog."

Even though Olivia and Lizzy were laughing and

reenacting the story I told, I couldn't laugh with them. All I felt was remorse. Guilt. Anger. Dalton and Maggie were amazing parents, and Olivia was the most loved baby. But because of me, she might grow up in a boarding school.

Lizzy caught my eye and mouthed, "You okay?"

I lifted one shoulder and started to shake my head, no, but changed my mind and nodded, quite unconvincingly, I'm sure.

"I have an idea," Lizzy said, tapping her lip with her index finger.

Olivia and I looked at each other and both said, "Oh no!" with equivalent drama.

"You're going to like this one," Lizzy said.

The truth is, Olivia and I loved all Lizzy's ideas, but we also loved ganging up on her.

"I thought of this a few days ago when I was looking at Olivia's drawing of us sitting on giant eggs and shooting rainbows at each other. I think we should make a collage of real photos of us and paint it the same way. What do you say? Is tonight a good night for a new family art project?"

"Yay! Can we put kittens on giant eggs too? Please?"

"Of course! Giant eggs and rainbow farts for everyone!"

Olivia and I cleared the table and cleaned up the kitchen while Lizzy prepared for our photo shoot in the backyard.

"I want to wear rainbow clothes. You too, Dadam. And Mona." Olivia changed out of her shorts into purple-and-red-striped leggings and a multicolored dress. Then we looked through my closet to find something that met her approval. It was a stretch, given my wardrobe was all athletic wear, jeans, and black T-shirts.

Lizzy came into the bedroom while Olivia and I were staring into my dresser drawers.

"Red shorts and a white tee. Looks like that's as rainbow as this guy gets."

"I figured you'd have trouble coming up with a suitable

outfit. So, I bought you something." She opened her own dresser drawer—the bottom drawer of my dresser—and handed me a plastic bag.

I pulled out a rainbow-patterned onesie and held it up. "It's beautiful," I sang, "but a bit too small, I think."

Olivia jumped off the bed and grabbed it from my hand.

"I love it! Can I have it? Please? It will never fit you, Dadam. Please?"

"Go put it on, sweetie," Lizzy said to the squealing five-year-old.

I pulled a second, identical onesie from the bag and held it up, looking at the tag. "Ladies' medium … I suppose I could squeeze into this." I tugged at the back of my shorts as if I was pulling out a wedgie.

"Hand it over, big guy. Yours is there too."

And so it was. All three of us, dressed in identical rainbow onesies with feet and hoods, posed on exercise balls in front of a white sheet Lizzy hung from the clothesline. She took pictures of Olivia holding her kittens, then of me, also holding the kittens. And I snapped a bunch of Lizzy with kittens. We sat together at Lizzy's laptop and each chose the one picture of ourselves we wanted to have in the collage and then printed them on photo paper Lizzy had bought.

"It's as if you expected we'd say yes." I put my arm around her shoulders.

"You haven't said no to me. Yet."

The subtext was clear: the day would come when I'd say no, and we'd go back to our old lives. Something I was less and less inclined to want to do.

18

LIZZY

The days flew by. If this is what summer vacation was, I wanted some every year.

It was the weekend, and we'd driven up to Lily Valley so Adam and Olivia could take me to their favorite tourist attraction: the mining museum. For some reason, as soon as we got to the village, Olivia changed her mind, said she didn't want to go now.

"You're sure you don't want to come with us?" I asked for the fifth time. "To hold my hand in case I get scared?"

"Mona," Olivia said, hands on her hips, "there's nothing to be scared of. And if there is, Dadam will protect you. Anyway, I want to play with Max."

I feigned heartbreak. "You're choosing to hang out with a dog instead of me?"

Olivia sighed and shook her head. "He's cuter." She jumped out of the van, slammed the door, and ran to Nick and Sophie's front door, opening it without knocking. We waited to get a wave from Nick.

"Thanks, bro. See you … when we see you," Adam called from his window. Then he turned to me and asked, "How long have you lived in Vancouver?"

"Six years."

"And you've never been to the Lily Valley Mine Museum. Tragic."

"I can't believe you were born here and you've never been to … the Vancouver Symphony," I guessed.

"Says who?"

"Am I wrong?"

"Quite. I took Olivia to see them do the Bugs Bunny songs and—"

"I was at that one! Did you go to the one where Chris Hadfield did all the patter between pop songs about space? That was amazing."

"I did. But that was before Olivia."

"Huh. You continue to surprise and delight me, Mr. Rhodes."

The mine museum was a two-minute drive from Nick and Sophie's place, out near the highway. Adam drove the van to the farthest corner of the parking lot, despite there being plenty of spaces closer to the entrance.

"Why?" I asked.

"Because way over here, nobody's going to park beside us and dent my doors with theirs."

I couldn't help but laugh. "A dent or two would give this beast some much-needed character."

"Why do you hate my van so much? What did it ever do to you?"

"It's just … boring. It doesn't look like something I'd expect a guy like you to drive."

"Oh yeah? What's a guy like me supposed to drive?"

"Something sporty, like you are. Something that stands out a bit, like you do. Something cool, you know?"

"Cool, like me?"

"No, because this van is proof that you're anything but cool!"

"Ouch. But being able to say you're my wife … I think

that makes up for the van and gives me serious cool-factor points, don't you?"

I couldn't tell if he was serious or just dishing back what I was serving him.

Adam paid the forty-dollar entry fee and signed us up for the underground tour that started thirty minutes later. We walked in the sun around the outdoor displays of giant machinery. Adam took my picture standing beside a dump truck that was so big it needed a train engine to operate. The info card said it was twenty-four feet wide, fifty-two feet long, thirty feet tall, and could carry 250 tons of rock.

I looked at the pictures Adam took of me. My strappy pink sundress and purple Keds were quite the contrast to the giant, black, ten-foot tall tire I stood beside.

"Remember in our vows when you said you'd be my accomplice in mischief?" Adam asked.

"I said no such thing," I lied.

"Roll video, please."

I started my camera's video and followed him as he walked to the same giant truck. He jumped up to grab the top of the tire and then climbed it. He got himself into the dumper on the huge truck and waved like an idiot until a staff person yelled for him to get down.

He pretended to be stuck and scared and begged the staff to call the fire department to help him. When she pulled out her phone, though, he swung over the edge of the dumper and let himself fall the twenty-plus feet to the ground, landing in a graceful roll and popping up with a goofy, "Ta-da!"

The museum staff person gave us both a dirty look but returned to her observation post without reprimanding Adam.

"Can you post that in our WhatsApp family group? Put a note to make sure Olivia does *not* see it, though. I've been wanting to climb that truck since the first time I saw it.

Didn't think it was appropriate example-setting to do it with Olivia here."

"Good call." I posted the video and took his hand. "Where to next?"

"Want to pan for gold? I'm feeling lucky today."

So was I. He didn't know it was my birthday since he never asked, and aside from my twentieth, when Kama insisted on celebrating, the day always rolled by like any other. Even as a kid, it was rare for me to get a present or for my mom to even remember. When I was a snarky teenager, I started to wish her a happy birthing day. She never wished me a happy birthday, but she did make sure to remind me how difficult my delivery was.

Still, I tortured myself for a good five years before giving up on the idea of birthdays altogether. And at twenty-five, birthdays seemed silly, anyway.

We walked to the water troughs and grabbed our pans. I dipped mine in and scooped up some sand. Before ten seconds had passed, a kid, not much older than Olivia, tapped my arm.

"You're doing it wrong," he said. "You have to swish, like this." He slowly rocked his pan in a pendulum motion, then looked at me. "Now you try."

I gave Adam big eyes. "How is it that all the elementary school kids are suddenly smarter than the woman with a master's degree?"

"I don't think it was sudden. I suspect you've been slipping for a while." He laughed.

"Laugh's on you," I said, swishing with a bit too much enthusiasm, accidentally on purpose splashing him with the icy water. Before he could retaliate, I ran toward the entrance to the mine tunnel. He caught me and threw me over his shoulder with ease, even though I was several times bigger than a five-year-old.

"I'm a little disappointed Olivia didn't want to come."

"She's been so many times, she knows all the lines. Now and then, a docent will skip over something another tour guide has shared, and she'll pipe up and say, 'You forgot to tell them about the time the film crew left all the dead bodies on the ceiling' or 'Don't forget the part about the washing machine' or whatever it is she thinks should be mentioned. It's pretty cute."

"She should get a job here," I said into his butt. Then I slapped it. "Down, please."

Adam dropped me to my feet, inches in front of him. I wanted to kiss him, but before I could decide whether it was appropriate, he stepped to the side and took my hand.

"She's already asked," he said, "but you have to be nineteen to lead tours. Something to do with the rules of working in a mine."

"Nineteen? For real? I got my first job with a taxable paycheck the weekend after I turned twelve."

We reached a giant bin filled with hard hats. Families with kids were already knocking each other's heads to test how well they worked. I put one on my head, and Adam adjusted the size dial until it squeezed my skull.

"There's your problem right there."

"My problem?"

"All these kids being as smart as or smarter than you— your brain hasn't grown to full size yet. I don't think I have to make Olivia's hard hat that small." He knocked me on the head the way all the kids were doing with their siblings. "What was your first job at twelve? And why were you working so young?"

"Sundays from noon to six, I worked at Tim Hortons selling coffee and doughnuts, heating up sandwiches, taking out garbage, cleaning tables. And then when summer came, I got to work full time."

"You *got* to work full time? You mean, you liked it enough to give up summer holidays?"

I didn't want to get into the whole "Mom is a narcissist who never wanted kids so I had to grow up fast" discussion. Instead, I shared the upside. "By the time I was eighteen and graduating from high school, I had enough money saved to move out and live in residence for my first year of university." I gave him a double thumbs-up, then asked, "How did you spend your summers as a kid?"

"At twelve, my only summer job was making sure my brothers didn't kill each other at bike camp and swim camp and computer camp and whatever other camps my folks could find to keep us all busy. I can't say I did a very good job at it, though. That summer Dylan broke his arm and Nick got a concussion. And Josh … now that I think about it, Josh was the reason Dylan broke his arm and Nick smacked his head."

"I can totally see that." I laughed. "Little Josh being the cause of the trouble. What did he do?"

"No, it's not what he did. I always figured that since he was the youngest and the smallest, he needed my protection from Dylan and Nick. I'm the one who accidentally broke Dylan's arm when I pushed him off his bike so he'd stop torturing Josh by riding around him like a shark, trying to make him fall off his bike. And Nick was goading Josh to do a jump he wasn't able to do yet. I told Nick to do it first, so he did. Apparently, he wasn't ready for that jump either."

"I wish I'd known you when I was twelve."

Adam scowled. "I was nineteen, twenty when you were twelve. I'm glad you didn't know me then. In fact, I'm glad you didn't know me when I was twenty-five. Or heck, thirty. You wouldn't recognize me. I'm not at all the same man I was then."

"Before Olivia," I said as a statement, not a question.

He raised, then dropped one shoulder. "Sure, let's go with that."

A docent jumped up on a platform and called us all to

attention. I didn't want to start the tour. I wanted to hear more about the man who came before the one I was getting to know, the man I was finding it far too easy to fall in love with despite common sense and decency. A series of if-only thoughts passed through my mind.

If only I were four years older, the age I promised myself I'd be before even thinking about settling down and starting a family.

If only I'd already done my world-traveling adventure.

If only Adam actually wanted someone to co-parent Olivia with.

We were directed to get into an open train. It was an authentic car and engine that actual miners used to ride to get to the depths of the mountain where they blasted and chipped away rocks, looking for copper. We sat in pairs in the small seats.

I was surprised at how cold it was underground. It was in the high eighties outside in the sun, but here, it felt like a brisk autumn night. I crossed my arms and squeezed them against my chest.

Adam put an arm around me and pulled me in tight. "It's always fifty-four degrees in the tunnel. Winter, summer, rain or shine. Sorry, forgot to mention that. You want to sit on my lap, soak up the heat from my chest?"

I thought he was joking. "If I say yes—"

He moved his arm quickly and scooped me onto his legs. I wiggled into a comfortable position.

"Careful there, Wife."

"Oh, double standard, eh? You get to break the mine museum rules but I don't?" I wiggled again.

Adam growled in my ear. "If you don't settle down—"

"Oh!" His hard-on completed his sentence, and I was suddenly flushed. But I didn't settle down. We quietly tortured each other for the entire dark trip underground.

We finished the tour, and Adam asked if I was ready for our next activity.

I leaned up and kissed him. "More accomplice-in-mischief stuff?"

"No way. My heart can't take any more of that. We're moving on to the comrade-in-adventure part of the program."

I was amazed he was able to repeat parts of our fake wedding vows, let alone the fact that he wanted to. We walked across the parking lot to the far side.

"Where's the van?" I said with urgency.

"I thought you'd be happy about it."

"What are you talking about? Where is it? Did Nick come and get it? We walking home?"

"Yes. And No. For our next adventure, I thought it would be more fun to drive a Mercedes SLS AMG."

Adam took me by the shoulders so I was facing the supercar where the van had been parked. "This is Van 2.0. Just go with it." He clicked a key fob and gull-wing doors swung skyward.

"You've got to be kidding."

"You want to drive?" he asked.

I shook my head so fast my vision blurred. "No. Not at all. I wouldn't know how."

"Sure you do. You drive stick."

I shook my head again, even though I could drive a manual transmission car and he knew it. But not a supercar.

"Let me know if you change your mind and I'll pull over and let you take the wheel. Hop in."

I did while Adam opened the trunk and ruffled around, muttering to himself.

"Let's roll," he said, sliding into the driver's seat and closing the gull wings.

We hit the highway, headed south toward the city. I was confused.

"Where are we going?"

"Birthday surprise." He winked.

"Wait. How did you know?"

"I'd like to say I figured it out on my own, but truth is that Kama told me. It was her idea to do something special for you. And she told me it would have to be a surprise. Otherwise, you'd argue. And when I told Nick and Sophie about my plan, they told me it was lame and offered to take Olivia for the night."

"Olivia knew about this?"

"Yeah, and I had to promise her two extra trips to the mine to make up for the one she missed today. I swear, she's going to grow up to be a heavy-duty mechanic. She loves the giant machines."

I watched Adam from the corner of my eye, his joy at driving this car, embracing a moment of Before Olivia life. I placed my hand on his leg. "Thank you," I said, but what I thought was, "I love you."

19

ADAM

We might have pushed the speed limit a touch, making the forty-five-minute trip to downtown Vancouver in under thirty. I pulled up to the valet stand at the Westbury Suites and winked at Lizzy.

She peered out her window at the white marble walls and chrome and glass double doors. "I feel like Dorothy. Or Alice. This is not home."

"Just act like you belong. 'Cause you do. Princess for a night. Right?" I clicked a button and the doors rose.

Lizzy's eyes dropped to the red carpet. "Adam, I can't go in there dressed like this."

"Trust me," I said, taking her hand and kissing her palm. Then I turned to the gentleman wearing a crispy white shirt, red tie, deep blue suit pants and vest. This was not a hotel where twenty-somethings learned to valet; it was a position that was earned through decades of experience. In a former time, these guys would have been right at home as butlers.

"Can you have our bags taken up and unpacked, please? Room for Adam Rhodes."

"No problem, Mr. Rhodes. Enjoy your evening."

Lizzy eyeballed me with a look like I'd just asked the guy

to do my laundry. I could have, except that all the clothes were brand new, tags still on. Another surprise, thanks to Kama's warnings. I let her handle the makeup and wardrobe for Lizzy and had one of my old clothing sponsors deliver a few new things for me, because why not celebrate along with my fake wife?

"What?" I said, trying to stifle a laugh.

"What are we doing?"

"We're staying in this hotel, and having dinner anywhere you want in the West End, and then we'll watch the Celebration of Light. We can watch from our room or the beach, as you wish."

She kept staring at me, like I was speaking a foreign language. And then I noticed the tears pooling in her eyes. She turned away. Kama had warned me about this possible reaction too.

"Hey, look at me." I walked around to stand in her line of sight. "If you'd rather, we can call this a delayed fake honeymoon night. You can be mad at me that it took this long to get it organized. But I don't want you to be sad. It's the Celebration of Light, and do you know how rock star I am to have pulled strings to have the event happen on your twenty-sixth birthday?"

That got the smile I was looking for.

"What country did you have to bribe?"

"All of them. But honestly, they were easier to negotiate with than Olivia was." I took her hand and led her into the luxury hotel's lobby.

The front desk staff treated us like royalty. For all they knew, we were. I'd rented the penthouse, a four-room suite with a private, rooftop infinity pool. If Lizzy wanted, we could watch the fireworks from the pool, which I'd asked to have heated to ninety degrees, a bit cooler than a hot tub, since we were more likely to sit back and have a couple of drinks than be swimming laps.

"Your key card, Mr. Rhodes. And one for you, Mrs. Rhodes. There is no button to your floor. Simply swipe the card and it will take you directly to your suite."

Lizzy looked at her cotton sundress. Down to her purple sneakers. Then at me. She held the card in her hand as if she wasn't sure she was actually supposed to have it. I could tell she was feeling underdressed and uncomfortable. I nodded at the desk clerk, "She broke a heel on her glass slipper last night at the ball."

The clerk raised her eyebrows and smiled politely. But Lizzy laughed, which was all I wanted—to help her relax.

Figuring the staff would need ten to fifteen minutes to unpack our bags, I suggested we have a drink at the bar. The hostess led us to a table with a view of the beach. It was packed with sunbathers. The Pacific Ocean never got warm enough to spend hours frolicking in, but there were a few brave people in the water.

Lizzy's eyes were wide as she scanned the room. I followed her gaze from the giant wall of windows that made us feel like we were seated right outside to the mirrored wall behind the bar. Her head tilted up.

"If you want a top-shelf drink, the bartender will need a ladder to get it," I said, pointing.

She turned to me. "Seriously?"

I fought to not laugh and smiled. "No. Those are empty. For show. Pretty impressive, though, eh?"

"I've never been in a place this nice. Is this the kind of bar you usually go to?"

I looked around, imagining it full on a Saturday night, what the clientele would look like, who they'd be. Rock stars and actors? Or venture capitalists and real estate agents? I figured the latter. "This place is a bit too formal for my taste. A bit too serious."

She nodded. "You've never brought a date here?"

"Never. It's a first for me too." In so many ways.

"Hmm. I saw a movie a few years ago." She faced me now. "It was about this woman who was trying to find herself after her husband died. The opening scene takes place in a bar that looks so much like this one."

"Maybe it was, given how many films are shot in Vancouver."

"I remember thinking, one day, I want to stay in a hotel with a bar that beautiful."

It struck me that she didn't say she *would* stay in a hotel like this, just that she *wanted* to. It was depressing, how easy it was to awe her; she seemed to have no expectation of ever having nice things—not that she was negative. Not at all. She seemed content with what she had, believing the best stuff was out of her reach.

"Do you remember the name of the movie?" I asked, pulling my phone from my pocket, typing in imdb.com. I crossed my fingers that this was indeed the place.

"It was called *Gin Gin Mule*. The main character was Ginger, but her husband called her GinGin. He dies of cancer and she finds out that he had all kinds of money she didn't know about. In the will he tells her to buy a new car and do the road trip of her dreams, the one she never got to do with him." Lizzy smiled. I imagined she was picturing herself in the character's shoes. "So she goes on this wild, cross-country adventure with a goal of having a Gin Gin Mule in fifty different hotels. That was her bucket list dream—to visit every state."

As Lizzy spoke, I looked up the film. "Bingo!" I turned the screen to her, opened to the page with filming locations. Vancouver was included on the long list. The bar itself wasn't named, but apparently that was enough to convince Lizzy this was the place she'd wanted to go.

She squealed. "I'm having a Gin Gin Mule!"

"So this bar was the first bar she went to before her big adventure. That's very cool."

"Actually, no. It was the opening scene in the movie, but it was the *last* place she went before deciding to go home. This was the hotel she stayed in when she realized how she wanted to live her new life. I love that movie."

She looked from the bar to the ceiling, around the room slowly, as if to memorize every detail.

"I can't believe I'm here," she said to the air.

"And now that you know where to find it, we can come back anytime you want." The words were out of my mouth before I realized what I'd suggested.

"I can," she said, closing her eyes and taking a long breath in.

We watched people on the beach while we had our drinks. Lizzy seemed lost in her thoughts and I didn't want to interrupt. But now I wanted to see the film that had made such an impression on her.

The sound of her straw sucking air told me she'd finished her drink. "Ready to see our room?"

We strode to the elevator because, Lizzy informed me, that's what sophisticated people do—they stride, they don't walk or bounce, no matter how giddy they are. Once inside, with the door closed, knowing the door would not open again until it reached the penthouse, I took her in my arms.

"I have a very important question that needs a serious answer," I said.

She looked concerned.

"Honeymoon or birthday celebration? What's your pleasure?"

Her laugh filled the car. "I have to choose?"

"Yup. Because if you say birthday, I'll implement Plan A, but if you say honeymoon, it's Plan B."

She tapped her lip with her finger. "But you said I get to choose where we eat and where we watch the fireworks. Where do Plans A and B come in?"

"All the before and after and in-between times. So, honeymoon or birthday?"

"What if I want to have my cake *and* eat it too?"

"A honeymoon birthday," I said, pulling her chin up to kiss my agreement with this idea. The funny thing was that if any other woman I'd known had asked for both, I'd have thought they were greedy, trying to get as much from me as they could in the short time I'd give them. But that wasn't how I felt about Lizzy or her request. I wanted to give her ten times more than she expected, and I wasn't sure why.

Was it because she'd sacrificed her entire normal life on a long shot to help me keep Olivia? Was it because when Olivia woke up every morning, she ran to Lizzy's side of the bed for a cuddle before she came to me? Or was it because Lizzy made me feel things I'd never felt before? With Lizzy, the impossible felt entirely within reach.

As a pro snowboarder doing stunts that could kill me, I worked from a place of acting on my gut because when an avalanche was chasing me down a mountain, there was no time to think, there was only time to feel the ground and move with it. And that worked great on the hill dealing with snow, but not always so well in real life, dealing with people. My gut reacts fast but doesn't take the time to consider consequences further than a nanosecond out.

I was getting better, having been forced to protect a toddler from acting on her own gut decisions, a toddler who'd inherited her parents' extreme sport, risk-taking ways. Keeping Olivia safe for the last three years had taught me to slow down and see the longer-term consequences of my actions. At least sometimes, and as I held Lizzy, a long-term consequence of this short-term, fake marriage was becoming clear: I might not get out of this in one piece, without a catastrophic injury.

The elevator door slid open, and Lizzy was still in my

hug with her back to what I saw. I'd slept in dozens of penthouse suites but never in this hotel. It stunned even me.

"Close your eyes," I said. "I want to carry you in."

She giggled against my chest and melted as I lifted her into my arms and stepped out of the elevator.

She trusts me, a voice in my head said.

Why shouldn't she? another asked.

Why should she? the first countered.

I scanned the giant living room, looking for the perfect spot to put her down. A wall of windows at the far end, overlooking the ocean, doors, half open on the two walls to the side. I carried her toward one and peeked around it— white granite counters and sparkling, stainless steel appliances awaited the personal chef who was on standby.

Behind the door beside it, a deep tub, giant mirrors, and a shower where I definitely wanted to have sex, but not yet. Crossing the room, Lizzy hugging my neck, eyes still closed and giggling with a joy I'd never heard from an adult before, I pushed open the last door—the bedroom. Bingo.

Fresh-cut flowers sat in a vase on a table by the window. I looked for a sign that our bags had been unpacked. A discreet card sat on the armoire. I didn't have to read it to know it was the name and direct number to our personal concierge. It was over the top, but the chef and butler were part of the room package, whether I wanted them or not. And since what I wanted was not relevant, I was happy to let Lizzy decide how much of their prepaid services we'd take advantage of.

"Keep your eyes closed. I'm putting you down but need to do one thing before you open them. Oh, and can you put your fingers in your ears and hum something, please?"

"What? You want me to—"

"Hum something to block the noise. I'll let you know when you can look."

Her smile was huge, her eyes squeezed tight. I stripped

naked and slid my legs under the duvet but sat with my back pressed against the leather headboard. Hoping to turn her smile into a full-on laugh, I called over her humming, "Welcome to your dream life, Cinderella. You can open your eyes now."

She did not disappoint. Except that she didn't strip naked and crawl into bed with me. She danced around the room looking from me to different items, pointing, saying their names, as if this was the first time she'd ever seen them in real life.

"Roses ... for me?" She spun "Look at that painting—it looks real. It is real, isn't it?" She ran her hand along the duvet. "So soft."

"The sheets are even softer," I said, patting the space beside me in the California king. "You should try them out..."

She shook her head and went out the door to the living room. "Did you see the view? Adam, this is ..."

I didn't hear what she said after that. She fell silent. I got out of bed, pulled a rose from the vase, and held it between my teeth. I grabbed a robe from the closet and pulled it around me—as much as I wanted her to see how much I desired her, I knew I needed to let her explore. I found her sitting in an oversized armchair with her head in her hands.

Dropping the rose on the table, I knelt in front of her. "Baby, what's wrong?" I tried to pry her hands away from her face, but she wouldn't let me.

20

LIZZY

hat's wrong? What's wrong is that you're perfect, and I'm not ready to meet perfect yet. And without even knowing it, in one day you've given me a lifetime of do-overs for birthdays either forgotten or gone bad. That's what's wrong. And I don't know if you're only being so nice because I'm doing you a huge favor, or if you really are like this. That's what's wrong.

"I don't deserve this," I whispered.

"Like hell you don't. Of course, you deserve this—one night to feel like a princess. And to make me feel like Prince Charming. I deserve it too. Fairy tales aren't just for five-year-olds."

He pulled my chin up and I let him see what I knew would be my blotchy face. That'll make him rethink this princess bullshit.

His brows knit together, and he shook his head wearing a pained look. "Do you remember the first time we met?"

I nodded. I was out with Kama, Dylan, and Josh.

"I knew you and Josh weren't dating and never would, that you were there as Kama's best friend and that Josh was Dylan's Mini Me. Josh never had a social life outside of

Paige, unless it was hanging out with Dylan and Nick. Sometimes with me. I was struck by you, your energy and how you laughed and the way you didn't give a care about embarrassing yourself singing karaoke."

"Embarrass myself?" I grabbed my heart and feigned hurt. Sort of.

"You've got a great voice, but you're an even better entertainer. Quirky and funny and, like I said, I admired how you were so at ease being a goof in public. And I had two competing thoughts that night—the first was that I wished Josh could see past his dedication to Paige, who none of us thought was coming back, because you were good for him. And the second was how glad I was that Josh couldn't see what was right in front of him because I wanted to steal you away and bring you home for myself."

I pictured that night and replayed the memory, with the adjustment of me leaving with Adam instead of in my own Uber.

"Why didn't you?"

"Because until I was forced to marry you—and I mean that in the most complimentary way—I had no interest in seeing any woman more than a couple times. And that wasn't me being an asshole player—not entirely, at least. I have Olivia to think about, and I didn't want her to be meeting and bonding with different women who more than likely would only be around for a few weeks, maybe a few months. And since Kama was now part of the family, and you seemed to come as part of that package deal being her BFF, I knew you'd eventually meet Olivia. I wanted it to be clean. And I'm glad I made the decision I did since it allowed you and Olivia to develop the bond you have."

I nodded but didn't feel like he'd answered the question of why he thought I deserved to be treated like a princess. Before I could ask, he continued.

"You know what she wished for when you were holding her and she caught Paige's bouquet, don't you?"

"I didn't then, but I do now."

"When she told me, it freaked me out. For one, I didn't want her to continue developing that relationship with you since I worried you'd keep getting closer to her and then you'd inevitably meet some guy, and we'd stop seeing you. And for two … Lizzy, you made it very hard to—"

"You said 'hard'," I muttered like a twelve-year-old, wanting to change the energy away from being so serious.

"That too. Let me rephrase: Mona Elizabeth Sheila Hillhouse, you are an easy woman to fall for and I found myself struggling to keep from acting on my—"

"Hardness?"

"Feelings, you goof." Adam shook his head but smiled.

"So to keep me from experiencing your hardness," I fanned my fingers in front of my face, "you preemptively hooked me up with an imaginary lover?"

"I knew it was only a matter of time before some worthy guy would scoop you up and you'd be gone from Olivia's life." He took my hands in his and pressed my palms to his lips, one then the other. "And mine."

"That's kind of sweet and *entirely* boneheaded since, if you'd asked I'd have told you what you know now: that my salad days are still ahead of me."

"Salad days?" Adam cocked his head. "Working in a restaurant again?"

"No, my fun, youthful times. Never mind. Just, next time you take it upon yourself to set me up, I'd appreciate if you'd imagine someone with a little more … I don't know, presence, maybe?"

Adam took my face in his hands. His expression was serious. "Here's the thing—even though it's only been about a month, I don't want to imagine you with anyone else."

My heart exploded and filled my body with rainbows.

"Shut up and kiss me, frog," I said. He pulled me up so we were both standing, and I fell into his strong arms.

It might have been the effect of the double Gin Gin Mule. It might have been that the air on the forty-eighth floor was thinner than at ground level. It might have been the off-gassing from 2,000 square feet of luxury carpeting. My vision blurred and the room spun, wild and wonderful, like a location change in a cheesy romantic comedy.

An ethereal voice, carried from far off in this magical land, whispered in my ear, "Breathe."

I blinked. Inhaled. Found my footing. It wasn't the alcohol, thin air, or off-gassing that spun my senses into sticky cotton candy. No, it was the kiss to end all kisses.

"Again?" My voice sounded hungry in my own ears.

Without a word, Adam took my hand and led me over to the giant bed. He pulled my sundress over my head as I stood, barely. My muscles were like al dente spaghetti—any more heat, any more humidity, and I'd collapse. He placed his hand on my lower back. That did it. The warmth of his touch softened the last of my bones. I fell on the bed with my bra and panties still on.

I pressed my hand to my chest to confirm my fear: my heart was no longer beating, it was vibrating. Adam didn't give me time to worry about whether the arrhythmia was life-threatening. He dropped his robe and swung his sword.

I thought I knew what to expect. We'd made love every day for the last six, and as good as it felt, nothing compared to the intensity of our first time. I was okay with that; having those level-ten sex emotions had been disorienting and exhausting. I was quite happy with level seven, the intensity rank I'd secretly assigned our passion time.

But the way Adam's eyes devoured my body as my heart triple-timed and I melted into the luxurious mattress, my passion-o-meter was already redlining.

So when his thumb hooked under the edge of my

panties, brushing against my skin, my hips arched toward him. Brazenly.

I moaned shamelessly.

And then … I begged. "Please."

"Please?" The roguish glint in his eye taunted me.

"Please."

Adam chuckled and the sound sent shivers down my spine straight to Gigi.

The look in his eyes turned wicked; instead of whipping my panties off, as the tilt of my hips was so obviously begging him to do, he dragged the black fabric down my legs—slow. As. Molasses. Even more torturous, he followed an inch behind with his mouth, pressing lingering kisses along my thighs, my knees, my shins.

With one final kiss on the instep of my right foot, he pushed up on his haunches, pressing his hands to the inside of my knees and spreading them apart so that I was fully open to his gaze.

I had never felt so vulnerable. Or so safe. The way he looked at me, from Gigi to my face and back again, felt like pure adoration. He saw me and he wanted me, but more than that, I could feel how much he wanted to make me happy. It was hard to believe.

A mistake. I was misinterpreting his lust for something else.

"Lizzy." He climbed up the bed and hovered over me, a question in his eyes. "Where'd you go?"

I pulled his mouth to mine. "I'm here."

"Stay with me," he whispered.

I opened my mouth to answer 'I will,' but Adam finished his sentence—"I can't make you come if you're thinking about laundry."

A sharp reality check, reminding me that we're living in the moment, not planning a future together.

Slowly, so slowly, he pushed against my opening, both of

us watching as his length sank deep into me. His thrusts started slow and shallow. Teasing.

I needed more.

Meeting his next downstroke with a quick lift of my hips, Adam groaned and his weight pushed me into the mattress. I wound a leg around him so he couldn't pull away.

He drew his lips down the side of my jaw, my neck, my shoulder until he held my nipple in his mouth, swirling the hard nub with his tongue.

My nails dug into his back, holding him close. His touches, from the gentle caresses to the powerful thrusts that left me breathless, felt bigger than any feeling I could name. Any reasonable feeling, at least.

"Adam. Please." I wanted to ask if he felt it too, but he squeezed his eyes shut. Blocked my question.

His hips crashed against mine, harder and harder, no longer holding back. Every surge of his cock taking him deeper, deeper, so deep I wondered if he was opening new space inside me and how I'd fill it once he was gone. My breath grew shallow. His grunts were almost pained.

We've been together a dozen times but this feels completely different. This doesn't feel temporary. This doesn't feel like a means to an ends. His lids spring open, his gaze almost pained. I flash on all the storybook endings we could have, if only …

21

———

ADAM

Adrenaline coursed through me, clouding my sight, clarifying my vision. There was nothing anyone could do to stop me from jumping out of this emotional chopper and into the free fall that had a very real risk of killing me. This was a woman I could see myself growing old with. My cock grew harder as a voice in my head chanted, "She's the one."

And that was it. With a forceful thrust, I planted myself as deep inside Lizzy as she'd take me. I held her body tight to mine. Our hips and lips completed an energy circuit that cracked with an explosion of passion and purpose. Rolling waves of pleasure and anticipation carried me deeper and deeper into a tsunami of feelings I didn't recognize, couldn't name, but wanted to hold on to.

Lizzy opened her eyes. I could see the questioning in them before she spoke.

"What … just happened?" She panted more than spoke.

And there it was. One word and one word only sat on my tongue. I opened my mouth to say it, but it caught in my throat, blocked by the pounding of my heart, which was still riding black diamond moguls. Or big waves. Or both.

It was dangerous.

"I think I love you," she whispered.

She was dangerous.

"I love you too."

This was dangerous.

I reminded myself that I thrived on danger. Made a living from living dangerously, taking risks no one in their right mind would take. And I was clearly not in my right mind telling her I loved her. But nothing had ever felt truer.

I pressed my hands against the headboard to give us space to breathe but didn't withdraw. She was still having aftershocks, milder and gentler contractions around my cock. I could stay here all day, filling her, having her squeeze me.

We held each other's gaze as our breathing calmed. Lizzy broke the silence.

"I think I'm done," she said with a shy smile.

Reluctantly, I took the hint and rolled off, but not away. Before she could break the connection, I pulled her against my stomach and wrapped her tight in my arms.

"Mine," I said with the same intonation the seagulls in *Finding Nemo* used.

She wrapped her arms over mine and squeezed even harder.

"That'll do, Pig," she countered, quoting the farmer in *Babe*.

"That'll do, indeed. Twice a day, every day, if I have my way." I let my lips fall against her salty neck. Not a kiss, more like breathing in her skin.

She squirmed. "Tickles."

I bit.

She moaned.

"Happy birthday, princess."

"Best birthday ever. I don't think you'll ever be able to top it."

She was thinking about a future with me, and I didn't just like it, I fucking loved it.

"And that was only the appetizer. You haven't seen half of what I have planned for the rest of the night."

"As long as nothing involves leaving this room. I never want to leave this room." She smiled, but her eyes glassed over.

I wanted to strangle the person or people who made her so sad to experience happiness.

"Why the tears?"

She dropped her gaze. "Because the fairytale will end at midnight when my birthday is over."

I sighed. "And what part of this fairytale do you not want to end? Is it being worshipped like a princess?"

She smiled and blinked. "Maybe."

"Or could it be the earth-shattering orgasms?"

Her smile grew.

"Or could it possibly be the experience of having sex on 10,000-thread-count sheets, made from 10,000-year-old Egyptian mummy wrappings? Extremely rare, you know. We'll probably be cursed for life—and afterlife—for what we did in this bed. And you know what? Since we've already desecrated these sacred sheets, I say we take them home with us since the power in them is stronger than the magical power of kittens to find forever homes."

That got the laugh I was looking for.

"Before I get out of this bed and show you what the concierge dragged in, I need you to repeat after me: I, Mona Elizabeth Sheila Hillhouse, deserve to be treated like a princess today and every day."

"I, Mona Elizabeth Sheila Hillhouse, deserve to be treated like a princess today and every day." She didn't sound convinced.

"I deserve this night," I said, giving her my best "listen to me, I'm your teacher" look.

She shook her head. I poked her in the ribs. She tried to squirm away.

"Say it. Mean it," I ordered.

"I deserve this night," she said.

"Damn right, you do. And so do I. Now, feast your eyes on this." I rolled from the bed and swung open the closet door like a game show host and dropped my voice two octaves. "Behind this door is an evening wardrobe for a night on the town. This is Evening Option A—the birthday evening." I moved the hangers so she could see the variety of dresses—six in different colors, styles, and lengths—then pointed to the floor to draw her attention to three pairs of shoes: new Keds, some flat sandals, and heels.

I moved to the dresser and pulled open the top drawer. "And inside this drawer, we have a small but sexy selection of steamy little somethings for a night in. This, of course, is Evening Option B—the honeymoon evening." I pulled out a black bustier and thong and held them up for her to see. My cock twitched, and her eyes went wide. I placed the items in the drawer and took out a feather boa, a silk scarf, and satin eye covers. She gasped.

"And since you already expressed your choice of experiencing both evening options, the only decision you need to make now is, which option are we starting with?"

"How did you—"

"Kama helped," I answered, predicting her question.

Her smile brightened and she jumped from the bed. "Are you starving? I'm starving."

"Famished."

"I vote that I try on every dress and let you choose which one I'll wear out to dinner. And we come back here to have dessert in the rooftop pool while we watch the fireworks. Then we see what damage we can do to everything in that drawer."

"I forgot to tell you, we have an on-call chef, twenty-four

hours a day. So if you can decide what you want as your birthday dessert now, he or she can be here making it while we're out having dinner."

Lizzy cupped her hands over her mouth and breathed into them like a paper bag. I heard her mumble, "Best birthday ever" before she pointed a finger to the sky. "Do you like cream-filled puff pastry?"

I nodded.

"Oh my god, really? Okay. Since this is a combination of my birthday *and* our honeymoon, I would like a cake that's also a combo—a *croquembouche*."

"A cock and what?"

"No!" Lizzy danced in place. "Croquembouche. Croquembouche! It's a French wedding cake. And it's perfect for eating in a pool. Bite-size cream puffs all stacked in a pyramid, drizzled with caramel. And maybe, if we get some on the sheets, the mummy we offended will be appeased with our offering. Win, win, win!"

"I'm going to let you order that, 'cause I still don't understand what you're saying. But first—shower, then fashion show, then food. Yes?"

Kama had done a perfect job choosing the perfect dresses for Lizzy's perfect birthday-honeymoon celebration. I couldn't decide which dress-and-shoe combination to suggest since she was a knockout no matter how she mixed and matched the outfits.

"I have one question: Do you want to feel like yourself tonight or like someone else?"

She nibbled her cuticle. "Good question. I'm going to say … a new-and-improved version of me."

I shook my head. "Not what I meant. I don't want a new-

and-improved Lizzy. I want to take you out as *you*. What I want to know is if you want to push yourself out of your fashion comfort zone."

"Push me," she said without hesitation.

"Then you'll be wearing the shortest dress with the highest heels."

She squealed. "I was hoping you'd say that!"

While Lizzy put on makeup, I dressed and made sure the pool setting was to my liking. I ran my hand through the water and barely felt it. Like everything else about this day so far, it was perfect. A temperature warm enough to sit in for an hour but not so warm we'd overheat. Overheating would come later. Back in the sheets.

Since she didn't know the restaurants at this end of town, I suggested three that I thought had the nicest atmosphere for an intimate meal. She chose based on name.

"The Steakhouse sounds too bloody, and Clove sounds too much like the place will have the stench of East Coast hippies."

I gave her a questioning look.

"All-natural cigarettes. Patchouli. And week-old sweat."

I shook my head in awe of her creative conclusions.

"Clink Bar and Bistro sounds like the perfect place to be accomplices in mischief."

She had no idea what kinds of mischief I had in mind for her. For us.

It was four blocks to Clink. Lizzy took my hand and interlocked her fingers with mine. I never held hands in public, except with a specific five-year-old. But not only did this feel okay, it felt right. I rubbed my thumb against her palm, and she shivered beside me. The power of my touch made her smile. I felt like a god.

My stomach lurched as my DNA reorganized itself, sending waves of changes into my limbs, my lungs, my heart, my brain. She did that to me. I inhaled, expanding my chest and tilting my chin in a walking power pose. *My woman*, my energy projected to the men on the street looking her way. Mine.

22

LIZZY

As ravenous as I'd been when we left the hotel, I was too giddy to eat. I poked at my appetizers—two brie, cranberry, and pecan pinwheels and two pancetta, pear, and pecan puffs.

Adam said I was nuts, ordering fruit and pastry when I could have steak and bacon bites or crab and bleu cheese bruschetta, which is what he ordered and ate in four ravenous swallows.

"Do you not like them?" he asked, pointing to the remaining pinwheel and puff.

"I love them. They're delicious. It's just that my …" I hesitated, trying to find words to describe the sensation. "Everything from my throat down feels so expanded, so amped, so energized, it feels like there's no room for food to push by, even though my stomach is craving more. I'm hungry, but I feel full. I know it doesn't make any sense."

Adam reached across the white linen tablecloth, carefully weaving between our wine glasses, and picked up the cranberry appetizer in his fingers. He brushed my cheek with the back of his hand and gently touched the pastry to my lips, which parted, not so I could eat but so I could inhale a shaky breath.

"That's not helping," I whispered as I exhaled. My heart did a double beat and heat rose in my cheeks. I felt light-headed.

Adam pressed the pastry against my teeth, not forcing, but teasing, taunting. My tongue reached out to guide it in, but brushed against his finger instead. I tasted the salt of his skin and pushed my tongue past my teeth, beside the appetizer, to the inside of his finger. I dragged my tongue along his sensitive skin.

Now he looked as flushed as I felt. I slipped off my shoe and pressed my foot between his legs, my toes finding what I hoped they would. His free hand dove under the tablecloth, onto my foot, pressing it down against his hard-on. We held eye contact while my tongue danced with his finger and my toes massaged his cock.

I gave the brie bite a gentle push and it fell from Adam's delicious digit, bounced off the table to the floor. My breathing was ragged, depriving my body and brain of oxygen. I closed my eyes and saw stars, fireworks, an explosion of intense colors, my feelings, both overwhelming and soothing at the same time. My very own personal Celebration of Light.

I opened my eyes to find his were closed.

"Home," he growled, squeezing my foot one last time before nudging it off his lap.

I assume he dropped money on the table. I was too busy trying to remember how to breathe to focus on anything more than my own feet, now back in my heels.

Adam grabbed my hand and pulled me out the door with more force than I expected. I wobbled and twisted my ankle. He yanked me up before I fell.

"I'm carrying you," he said. Not a question. He lifted me

easily and cradled me sideways, my arms around his neck and his under my knees and behind my shoulders. His hard-on filled the space under my ribs, above my hip. I looked up at his face, serious, focused, intense. I wondered if this was how he looked when he was flying down mountains, being chased by walls of snow and death. People stared.

"Mine," he said with conviction, looking straight ahead. He was no longer a cartoon seagull protecting a fish, he was a god claiming a woman. Claiming *me*.

My grip tightened. "Yours," I assured him.

We reached the hotel, and he still didn't put me down. Inside the elevator, he kept me in his arms. Standing in the middle of the penthouse living room, he said, "Don't move," as he lowered me to my feet.

I stood and watched as he moved around the space. First, he looked in the kitchen.

Then he locked the elevator door. When he faced me again, I didn't recognize him.

The man who stood before me did not drive a gray minivan; he rode a chariot. He didn't watch Saturday morning cartoons with a five-year-old in matching Scooby Doo pajamas; he owned Saturday night and all the pleasures that it demanded. This god stripped out of his jeans, T-shirt, boxers, and socks and stood naked, staring at me in silence.

As my blood pulsed through my heart and around my lungs, my organs melted and flowed into my stomach, swirling together in a red and pink version of Vincent van Gogh's *Starry Night*.

Adam spun me and unzipped my dress. He pulled it over my head in a fluid motion, then undid my bra before the dress hit the ground. His hand grabbed my ass and his fingers hooked inside my panties, pulling them down my thighs as far as my knees. He turned me again, facing him now with my naked ass reflecting in the floor-to-ceiling mirror beside the elevator. His hand touched the top of my head and the meaning was one hundred percent clear.

I knelt in front of him and took him in my mouth.

Each time I opened my eyes to look at him, his gaze was intent on the mirror behind me. He was staring at my ass while I sucked him off. I knew what he was thinking because I was thinking it too.

He moaned and forced his hips forward. I worried I'd take him too far, so I pulled away, keeping my hand on his balls but removing my mouth from his cock.

"Don't stop." It wasn't a request.

I ignored him and stood, taking the risk I'd anger this god by disobeying him.

"My birthday. My choice," I said.

He growled, a sound somewhere between disappointment and frustration.

"Did you pack lube?" I asked, praying he had.

He cracked his neck and walked toward the bathroom, returning with a small container. Adam reached out to hand it to me. I shook my head and took his free hand in mine, wrapping his fingers around my butt cheek.

"It's for you."

I bent forward, hands on the wall, and gave him access to the most protected part of my body. He'd already claimed every other part of me. I wanted to give him my most intimate space.

"Fuuuck," he exhaled.

I'd never had anal sex before but I'd read how to make the entry as comfortable as possible. I focused on the instructions in my mind and after the initial shock, was surprised how quickly my body relaxed once he was inside me. He took me with force but also with a gentleness that communicated with my heart as he drove himself home. I didn't orgasm, but I still felt complete when he withdrew, spent, panting, and glistening with sweat.

I turned to face him, and he showed yet another side. No longer the god who owned me, I could see myself reflected in his eyes. I was a goddess who could rescue myself, no longer a princess who needed to be saved.

We moved to the bed, and without words, we collapsed. It was only eight o'clock, but I was exhausted—physically, emotionally, spiritually.

I woke to the sound of fireworks and cheers.

"Hey," I said, rubbing Adam's arm, which was resting over me. "It's 9:55. The birthday fireworks you organized start in five minutes. You getting up?"

"Mmm … quick shower before we drop into the pool," he said, sounding still half-asleep.

We kept the shower focused on cleaning bodily fluids off us, not starting the process of getting more on us, then slid into the pool as the first of the main-event explosions filled the sky with a dazzling display of red, orange and white bursts of glitter.

From our rooftop pool, five hundred feet above ground, we looked out and down on the Celebration of Light. Music, timed to the fireworks, played over loudspeakers at the beach less than a block away at ground level. The addition of another two blocks in height made the instruments sound ethereal under the *pows* and *bangs* of the explosions.

It was a perspective of the sky I'd never considered. Familiar, but so very different.

We sat, fully submerged in the water with as much of our bodies touching as was possible without my climbing into his lap. My arm rested on his thigh. His hand squeezed around my shoulder, holding me so tight I could feel his heartbeat against my side rib. My own heart matched his rhythm. We were in sync.

It was a perspective of life with another person I'd never allowed myself to consider. And there was nothing familiar in this feeling.

"Sad really," he said, "how bright they burn and how fast they die. Guess that's life, though."

The sweet, swirling lava in my belly paused, hearing a warning in his tone. I tensed, trying to tamp down the sensation that rose from the pit of my gut.

It touched my heart. I felt it crack. A fracture. Still in one piece, but the fragility was palpable.

"Happy fake honeymoon," I whispered to myself.

Adam kissed my temple. "Happy real birthday."

Crowds of people cheered as the sky below us exploded in a cacophony of color.

"Kind of blows your mind, doesn't it?" I asked.

Adam nodded then threw his head back and groaned. "Your blowjob cake. We totally forgot about it."

The tension evaporated as I chuckled, "My what?"

"That cock in *bouche* cake. We totally forgot. I bet the chef tried to deliver it but couldn't get up."

I smacked the water, splashing us. "Rats. I was really looking forward to that chocolatey, caramelly, whipped cream, puff pastry, body painting you promised." My bottom lip pushed out as a joke, though I was truly disappointed. "I guess it's true what they say—that you can't have your cake and eat it too."

"Are you forgetting who you're with? What day this is? I am Adam Hot Shit Rhodes and your birthday-anniversary blowjob cake wish is my command." He jumped from the pool and went into our suite. I could hear him on the phone. Then he dropped back into the water with a giant splash. "The tower of edible body paint will be delivered before the last rocket fizzles. That will give us a solid ninety minutes to finish celebrating you and your special day."

"You said 'solid'."

"Let me show you solid." Adam pulled me through the water from his side and clutched me tight against his chest. He possessed me.

My feet didn't touch the floor of the pool so I was anchored but floating. Floating in the sky above the firework explosions, warm, safe, and utterly terrified of the impact that the inevitable return to the ground would bring.

23

———

ADAM

It had been a full week since Lizzy's birthday-honeymoon weekend, and things between us were stupendous.

In fact, life all-round was better than I could have hoped—and that was freaking me right the eff out. Communication and dealings with Brigitte had been uneventful. She hadn't forced us to live by her heinous calendar. She was respectful of asking when Olivia was free, not imposing her schedule upon us. I felt like I must be missing something, not seeing a sign or a warning. I'd been lulled into what I knew was a false sense of safety, so I was on high alert for hidden dangers. It was exhausting.

What wasn't exhausting was Lizzy. Everything about time with her was rejuvenating. We were one full month into our arrangement, which meant in the best-case scenario, Olivia and I would be saying goodbye to her in two months, a fact I tried not to think about. Carpe-diem and all that jazz.

I lay in bed, listening to her sing in the shower, and checked my phone, remembering someone had texted while we'd been making love this morning. Probably phishing since nobody texted before nine on a Saturday.

I was wrong.

DYLAN

We need to deal with this today.

And then a link. I clicked it. It was to a local, online sports magazine. I'd made the home page.

Former stunt snowboarder, Adam Rhodes, setting a bad example. Again.

Adam Rhodes, former lead member of the Triple Extreme snowboarding stunt team, was filmed last weekend at the Lily Valley Mine Museum climbing, and apparently getting stuck, atop the thirty-foot tall WABCO haul truck, one of the site's attractions.

Never one to turn down an opportunity for attention—especially of the female variety—Rhodes is seen scaling it while an unnamed woman films him, despite clear signage that explicitly forbids climbing on the truck.

Rhodes, who was one of a three-person stunt team, has been out of the spotlight for three years since the deaths of his two partners, Dalton Blain and Maggie Jackson, during a stunt that went terribly wrong.

Blain and Jackson had left the sport two years prior, after marrying and conceiving a child. When asked why he was leaving the sport, Blain said, "There are old stunt snowboarders and there are bold stunt snowboarders, but there are no old, bold stunt snowboarders. My focus is on my family now, and I'm ready to leave the extreme sport to the next generation."

Blain and Jackson's daughter, Olivia, was two years old when the couple were enticed back to the sport by Rhodes, who'd been invited by the Frozen Frontier Ski Resort in Alaska to resume his death-defying stunts as a marketing boost for the hill that had recently landed on a list of twenty ski resorts families should avoid. Having seen a significant income decline, the resort decided to push their extreme sport hills with Rhodes as the draw.

But Rhodes, seeing an opportunity for an even bigger media splash, coaxed Blain and Jackson out of retirement to join him in a never-before-filmed trick with the three of them simultaneously jumping from a plane, parachuting to dropping distance of the hill, and then boarding the triple black diamond run.

Disaster struck when Blain's and Jackson's chutes collided, entangling the cords and leading to their untimely deaths. Rhodes, who jumped seconds after the pair, survived the stunt, though he has not been seen on the slopes since.

It is rumored that Rhodes, who was named as a joint guardian to Blain and Jackson's daughter, is currently embroiled in an ugly legal battle with Jackson's sister, Brigitte Jackson, for the little girl's exclusive guardianship.

Rage exploded like a high-altitude blizzard in my gut. I threw my phone across the room, narrowly missing Lizzy, who'd just stepped out of the bathroom.

"What the hell?" she said, picking up the device and dropping it on the bed by my feet. "It's—"

"Who did you send the video of me climbing the truck at the mine to?" I said the words through clenched teeth to control my volume, because I was on the verge of yelling.

"Last weekend? Our WhatsApp group, like you asked," she said, giving me a questioning look.

"There's no way my brothers would've shared it. So if it wasn't you, who did?"

"Um, I don't know what you're talking about."

"Check your phone. There's a link in our group chat." I banged my head against the headboard.

Lizzy rounded the bed, plucked her phone from the night table, and dropped down beside me. My muscles weren't sure if they wanted to move away or press closer to her. I stiffened. I watched the rise and fall of my own chest as

Lizzy read the article, gasping and swearing under her breath.

And now she knew. Not the way I'd planned to tell her about my role in my best friends' deaths. I tried to check in with how I was feeling, another trick I'd learned from the counselor to help Olivia stay grounded, but there were too many emotions. Humiliation. Anger with myself. Regret. Shame. Hurt. Betrayal.

I heard my voice calling to Lizzy, laughing. She was watching the video. She turned her phone to me. "See? It's not the video I shot. I'm in the frame with you."

I hit my head harder for having blamed her without bothering to look at the video myself. Humiliation. Anger with myself. Regret. Shame. Hurt. Betrayal.

"I'm sorry," she said, turning to face me, cross-legged at my hip.

"I'm the one who's sorry."

"You know I'd never, ever do anything to hurt you or Olivia. Right?"

"I'm know. Misdirected anger."

"I'm sorry that you can't be yourself without someone challenging it and finding fault with you."

I was confused. I expected she'd have a hundred questions about my role in Dalton's and Maggie's deaths. That she'd judge me. Her reaction didn't make sense.

"You're not angry or disgusted or—I don't know? Like it says, if it weren't for me, Olivia would have real parents."

"Jesus, Adam, you *are* a real parent. And everyone in this family is real family to Olivia. Yeah, it sucks that her birth parents died, but you didn't kill them. And she's not suffering. I don't know what kind of life she'd have had with Dalton and Maggie, but she'll have nothing to complain about if she spends the next fifteen years being raised by you and the Rhodes gang."

"Which is further and further from becoming a reality because of this."

"Dylan will fix it," she said, so sincerely, I laughed.

"What?" She gave me a gentle punch.

"I think it's funny how differently we see Dylan. You seem to see him as this smart guy your best friend married. And despite knowing better, I can only see him as a pain-in-the-ass younger brother. Even when he's lawyering me, he's still my kid brother first, barely a legit adult."

"Hm. And how do you think your brothers see you?"

"As a fuckup," I said. "No question."

Lizzy shook her head with eyes cast down, breathed in a sigh that was reminiscent of a disappointed parent, then straddled my legs. She took my face in her hands. "You're— what I like to call—wrong. In the last year-and-a-half, I've spent more time with both Dylan and Josh than you have, and I can tell you they don't think of you as a fuckup. They look up to you—"

"Ha!" My tone was cynical. I tried to lift her off me but she hooked her hands together under my armpits. Immovable object meet unstoppable force. I let her win. "Whatever. It doesn't matter what they think. All that matters is the court of public opinion. Did you scan any of the comments under the article?"

She nodded and shrugged. "People are judgy assholes. Anyone who knows you knows better than to believe the rotten tomatoes thrown at you from that story."

"Wait, you don't believe the story?"

"Of course not."

"But it's all true, Lizzy. Every word of it. I loved the spotlight. I enjoyed the attention I got from women. I did convince Dalton and Maggie to come out of retirement. And yeah, I jumped two seconds after them. Not a word of a lie in the piece."

Dylan's ringtone interrupted me. I didn't want to talk to

him, but I knew there was no point putting it off. Lizzy leaned to grab my phone from my feet and I took the opportunity to escape. She handed me a buzzing, shattered screen with a kiss.

"I'll start breakfast," she said, leaving the room.

I answered. "You going to tell me I'm fucked? That it's time to give up guardianship of Olivia?"

I could tell Dylan was pissed because he was silent. All I could hear was the sound of his noisy yoga breathing. I listened and mimicked him since the deep, controlled inhalations and exhalations helped calm me.

Finally, he spoke. "You're going to quit that easy? I think you're an idiot if you do, but hey, you're the client. If you're not up for the fight …"

"Fuck you, Dylan. You don't know what it's like to carry this guilt," I said, making a fist, knowing if he was here in front of me, I'd use it.

"Maybe not, but you don't know what's it's like watching you quit every time things get a bit hard for you."

"Seriously, fuck you. I didn't earn a million-plus a jump by quitting when things got hard, asshole."

"I'm talking about emotional risks, bro."

"Whatever."

"We have about twenty-four hours to reply and turn this story around. I'd like to think this isn't going to impact the judge's consideration, but it will. I need you to drop Olivia at Nana's or Dad's and for you and Lizzy to come over for a strategy meeting so we can figure out how we're going to handle this."

"I don't know—"

"I want you here an hour ago. And drop the victim bullshit. I need you on your game. This is going to be your Kilimanjaro jump. Do or die, and dying is not an option. If you're not willing to do this for Olivia, you'll damn well do it for me since my reputation is on the line."

"Asshole." I hung up and called down the stairs, "Ladies, I need you ready to be out the door in ten minutes. Olivia, you're going to Nana's. Lizzy, you're seeing Kama today. Understood?"

I didn't wait for an answer and headed to the shower. Adrenaline pounded through me. My arms needed to punch it out. I should have been heading to the gym, not planning to sit around a table drinking coffee. My blood beat loud in my ears, an avalanche descending on me. My vision blurred, and I knew if I tried too hard to bring things into focus, I'd die. I couldn't see through the whiteout inside me.

I made the water as hot as it would go. Not nearly hot enough. I cursed the temperature limiter I'd put on the hot water tank to make sure I never burned Olivia in a bath. I cursed all the accommodations I'd made over the last three years to be the best father I could to a little girl who deserved better.

London. Boarding school. Maybe that's what would be best for her now that she was school-age. Lots of kids are raised that way. Better than being in homes with incompetent parents. Better than being raised by Brigitte. And maybe by me too.

"Pack your sketchbook and the new paint markers," Lizzy called, obviously back in the bedroom. Boarding school could never be better than Lizzy as her mom.

I punched the wall, not hard enough to break the tile or my knuckles, but with enough force to feel.

Lizzy popped her head in and called over the sound of the water, "You want me to warm up the van?"

She didn't sound mad or upset about being ordered to get ready without any explanation. I swiped my hand over the shower glass, gave her a wan smile and a thumbs-up. She smiled and returned it. A wave of guilt crashed over me. I may not be worthy of Lizzy's love, but Olivia was, and the only way she'd keep getting it, even if only on weekends once our deal ended, was if I was willing to fight for her.

I resolved to do whatever Dylan told me. Not for myself. I'd do it for the little girl who'd had her heart more brutally broken in her first two years of life than I'd had in thirty-two years. And still, she had room to trust and love again. I'd be damned if I'd be the one to break that trust.

24

LIZZY

Dylan was brilliant.

Using the video that I'd shot, he framed a new narrative about why Adam had climbed the giant truck and sent it to the local search and rescue organization. They posted the goofy antics as a way to draw people to their website with a quiz about backcountry preparation and safety.

Adam also issued a public apology to the mine museum for not having followed proper protocol to get permission to climb the truck. And he made a donation to the museum in Olivia's name so she'd get a plaque on the wall with all the other significant supporters. Win, win, win.

As for Brigitte's reaction, she just rolled her eyes and made some comment about how ridiculous Adam was.

Olivia's soccer camp had ended, and I was now a Bike Camp Mom. Adam dropped her off and headed up to Lily Valley, where he was helping Nick cut trees for firewood. Since this camp didn't let parents hang around, I was free until 3:00 p.m.

I was enjoying one of the first days on my own since joining this family a little more than a month ago.

My phone rang. Unknown number. I debated letting it go to voicemail, but curiosity got the better of me. Would it be the police threatening to arrest me for tax evasion or a vacation company telling me I'd won a round-the-world trip?

"Hello?" I fully expected a click and an automated message.

"Ms. Hillhouse?"

"That's me," I said tentatively.

"Ms. Hillhouse, Olivia's taken a fall—"

I gasped. "What happened? How is she?"

"She's fine. Or will be. She's broken her arm and is on her way to Children's Hospital. Are you—"

"I'll be there as soon as I can." I ran to the front door to put on my shoes.

"We've tried to reach Mr. Rhodes."

"He's not in town today. I'll let him know. I'm his wife." I was surprised at how naturally it slipped out.

"Olivia will be in the emergency department."

"Emergency at Children's. Got it." I hung up and debated whether it would be faster to call an Uber or a cab. Unsure, I called both. While I waited impatiently for one to arrive, I sent a message to the family WhatsApp group.

Olivia broke her arm at bike camp. At Children's Hospital. Anyone able to meet me there?

The Uber arrived first. It was a miracle I remembered to cancel the cab while we were en route, given my brain felt like it was filled with cold air. I'm the worst in emergency situations. I freeze up.

It's okay, I tell myself. I don't need to handle anything. All I have to do is be there to pick up Olivia, who will be fine. Olivia, who is fine. It's a broken arm. A rite of passage for every kid with daredevil parents. I can handle a broken arm that's already in a cast.

The Uber dropped me off at the emergency door. The ER

was packed with a dozen people in line. To hell with waiting my turn.

"Excuse me. I'm sorry to barge in line… pardon me. Excuse me. Do you mind?" As politely as I could, I nudged by all the people waiting until I was at the front. "My daughter is in Emergency. I'm sorry. I'll be fast," I said to the people closest to me. What little calm I was grasping escaped in a whoosh of panic as soon as the intake nurse was free. I dropped into the chair at her desk.

"I'm looking for Olivia Rhodes. She was brought in with a broken arm."

The lady smiled and typed in her name. She then shook her head.

"How do you spell the last name?"

"R-H-O-D-E-S."

"Not coming up. Date of birth?"

I was confused. My brain felt freeze-dried again. I blinked to clear my vision. "It's in September. She's five. I can't think of the date. I'm embarrassed."

The woman looked at me. "What's your relationship to the child?"

"I'm her … stepmother. I'm married to her dad. I know I should know. I do know. I just, I can't think."

She stared over her glasses at me and then typed some more. Someone in line sighed loudly and said, "Seriously?"

"Olivia Jackson-Blain was admitted—"

"That's her. Sorry. I forgot she doesn't have her dad's name … never mind. Can you tell me where she is?"

"What's your name?"

"Lizzy Hillhouse."

The woman dialed. "Hi, Darlene. Can you do me a favor? Can you ask Olivia Jackson-Blain, the little girl with the broken arm, if she knows a Lizzy—"

"Mona—" I interrupted.

"Mona Hillhouse?" The woman at the desk nodded. "Okay. Yup." She turned to me. "Apparently, she's been asking for you."

Relief ballooned in my chest and I stood before she told me where to go. A door automatically opened behind me. "Ask at the nurses' station inside. They'll take you to her."

Three steps in the door, I caught the eye of a nurse. "I'm looking for Olivia—"

"Mona," Olivia's voice called. I could hear the fear in it. "I'm over here, Mona."

I didn't wait to be escorted. I followed the sound and pushed open a curtain. An older woman wearing a red vest that said 'volunteer' on the chest was sitting with her. She stood and said, "She's been anxious for you to get here."

"Thank you for staying with her." I reached to take her hands in mine. "Thank you. Thank you."

"She's a brave young lady. Get better soon, Olivia," she said as she waved and left us in the curtained room.

"Sweetie pie, they said you broke your arm. Where's the cast? Is it hurting? What happened?"

Olivia broke down in tears. "Dadam is going to be mad."

I dropped into the vacated seat and took her free hand. Her other was hidden in a sling.

"He's not going to be mad, pumpkin. Do you know how many bones Dadam has broken? Basically all of them."

She shook her head. "Not about my arm. I ran over a boy with my bike."

I tried to keep emotion from my face as anxious laughter and concern for this other child's well-being rose within me. "It's okay. Accidents happen."

She scowled. "I did it on purpose." Before I could ask why, she continued, "He said Dadam killed my mom and dad and that you were nothing but a, but a, I don't remember, but it wasn't nice."

My stomach twisted and my worry about the other kid's well-being dissolved as I flashed on an image of tire tracks across his flattened belly.

"Dadam isn't going to be mad at you, sweetie, I promise. He's going to be mad at that boy, though. And what he said about your parents? It's not true. None of what he said is true."

"Why did he say it?"

"Because some people are about as smart as a grilled cheese sandwich. Because some people read stories in the newspaper and believe the baloney they read. But you have to believe that Dadam didn't have anything to do with your mom and dad dying."

"But he was there. And he's strong. Why didn't he save them?"

My mind raced. This wasn't a conversation I ever expected to have. I wasn't sure it was even right for me to be having it. But here I was. And better me than Brigitte, I figured.

"He wanted to save them. He wanted to so badly. They were his very best friends in the world. But their parachute was broken, and there was nothing he could do."

She nodded. "Why did that boy call you a bad name?"

I raised my shoulders and held them near my ears for several seconds. "I don't know what bad name he called me, but he doesn't know me, does he? He can call me all the bad names he wants and it won't change the truth that I love Dadam and I love you. For the record, the only name I think I should have is *fruitcake* because you and Dadam are nutty as fruitcakes and you're making me nutty too. But being a nutty fruitcake isn't a bad thing, right?"

"No it's a delicious thing." She smiled, then winced. "It hurts."

"Have you had an X-ray yet?"

She nodded. My phone pinged with a new message.

"Guess what?" I tapped Olivia's nose. "We're having a cast-signing party at Nana's house tonight. Everyone's going to be there. Uncle Dylan will pick us up and take us over once you're all done."

"Where's Dadam? I want Dadam." Her bottom lip trembled and I could tell she was trying not to cry.

"He and Uncle Nick are out in the forest cutting trees, so he probably hasn't heard his phone ringing off the hook. But you know that as soon as he gets the message he'll be here as fast as … as fast as … what?"

"As fast as Marmalade trying to catch a fly."

"Exactly!"

We played a puzzle game on my phone for close to an hour before being moved into a small room where they applied Olivia's cast. I paid the extra fee to have the colored bandages. The doctor was amazing and offered to use two colors since Olivia couldn't decide between the pink and the orange—her new favorite color since getting Ginger and Marmalade. It was a work of art.

As directed, I went to the nurses' station to have Olivia discharged.

"I'm sorry," the nurse said. "I can't release her to you. You're not her legal guardian."

"I'm her stepmother. How much more legal do I need to be?"

"You're not on her guardian list. I have Adam Rhodes and Brigitte Jackson. They're the only—"

"But I'm her stepmother. I'm married to Adam Rhodes."

"You have to appreciate I'm just following the law here."

"Well, you have to appreciate that Adam is out of town and god only knows where Brigitte is."

As if magicked into appearance, there she was, coming through the same automatic doors I'd come through over two hours earlier.

"I'm Brigitte Jackson. Olivia is my niece and my legal

charge." She motioned for Olivia to go to her, but she held my hand even more tightly.

"I don't want to. I'm going to Nana's. Where's Uncle Dylan?"

"He's in the waiting room. But he can't take you either. Only me or Adam. And I don't see Adam." Brigitte shook her head and addressed me. "Could he not bother to show up?"

I saw red.

"Since Ms. Jackson is here, you can all leave together and figure out where Olivia will be going outside." The nurse gave me a stoic grin.

The doors opened, and we exited with Brigitte leading, Olivia holding on to my hand for dear life until she saw Dylan standing by the door.

"Uncle Dylan." She ran to him and he scooped her up.

Once in the parking lot, the veneer of warm and fuzzy that Brigitte had managed to maintain in front of the nursing staff blew off in the brisk afternoon wind.

"Olivia, enough stalling. You're coming with me."

Olivia's face contorted and she started to sob. "I want my dad."

"Unfortunately, he's dead—"

"For god's sake, Brigitte." Dylan kissed Olivia's head and put her on her feet beside me. Then he took Brigitte by the shoulder and spun her away from us, pushing her to walk away.

Olivia held my leg. I reached down and carefully lifted her into my arms so we could bury our faces into each other's shoulders. My heart pushed passed my throat and squeezed itself behind my eye sockets, leaving no room for the tears that had, until a second ago, been collecting there.

I whispered in Olivia's ear. "I'll stand in this parking lot until Dadam comes. I won't let her take you if you don't want to go with her."

Dylan and Brigitte were having words halfway across the parking lot. They were too muffled to make out, except for the tone. Neither was happy.

When they came back, Dylan did the talking.

"So Brigitte has *graciously* agreed to let Olivia come to the party at Nana's. And since it didn't occur to her to bring a car seat, I'm *graciously* letting her borrow mine." He growled the word *graciously* each time.

"I want to go with you, Uncle Dylan," Olivia begged.

Brigitte glowered and started to speak, but Dylan put his hand in front of her face, stopping her.

"Lizzy, would you be gracious enough to ride with Brigitte and Olivia? To remind her where Nana lives?"

"Of course. I'd be delighted to."

"Great," Brigitte drawled, sounding like this idea was as far from great as possible.

"And Sophie just texted that Nick and Adam are on their way back to Lily Valley so they'll all be at Nana's before the pizza's gone."

I gently jiggled Olivia in my arms. "Woo-hoo! Ham and pineapple pizza! Our favorite!"

An hour later, the door to Nana's house flew open. "Where's my little daredevil?" Adam called.

Olivia, Nana, Kama, Paige, and I were all sitting at the puzzle table working on a rainbow-colored cat. Age-appropriate, with about 100 pieces.

Dylan and Josh were in the backyard. And Brigitte? She was sitting in her car, apparently having to make a very important phone call. In private.

We'd learned that both she and Adam had been called as soon as Olivia arrived at the hospital. And even though I was named on the bike camp's emergency contact list, I hadn't been given official, government emergency contact status.

Brigitte came into the house close on Adam's heels, not even giving him time to hug Olivia before starting in on him. "Nice of you to show up. I'm sure the judge will be very interested in how long it took you to get here, leaving Olivia in the care of strangers. What would have happened if I weren't here? She'd still be at the hospital."

"Not the time," Adam said, his smile at odds with the tone of his voice.

"What judge?" Olivia asked.

"The judge that's—"

"Brigitte!" Every voice in the house cut her off.

"What? She knows about the guardianship challenge. I don't see any reason to keep her in the dark. I'm not clear why you all do. Keeping secrets isn't very nice."

Olivia was now in Adam's arms. Nobody spoke.

"Adam," Brigitte said his name like he was a kid in trouble, "your grandmother would not let me take my niece for our scheduled auntie bonding time until you got home to see her. You've seen her, and I'd like to go now."

"I want to stay with Dadam." Olivia started to cry.

Dylan and Josh came in the back door, laughing. All eyes turned to them.

"What's going on?" Dylan asked.

"What's going on is I've been sitting in my car for over an hour, waiting for Adam to get home so I could take *my niece* to a movie. And now she doesn't want to go."

"In all fairness, Brigitte," Dylan said, using what I assumed was his lawyer voice since I'd never heard him speak with so much condescension, "nobody expelled you from the house. You could have been inside working on the cat puzzle, having your auntie-niece bonding time with the rest of the family."

I wanted to high-five him. To do a *whoop-whoop*.

"But for the small fact that I'm not family. And neither is Olivia, in case you've forgotten." Brigitte glared at Adam, then turned toward the door and left without another word.

"That was uncomfortable," Kama said, breaking the silence after we all watched Brigitte's car peel away.

Adam carried Olivia to the couch and winked at me to join them. Olivia told Adam the story of why and how she'd hit another kid on her bike. I watched Adam's face, his jaw tensing at first, then relaxing as he held back a smile when she said she'd run over him on purpose. Olivia looked up with big eyes. I hoped I was right, that he wouldn't be mad.

"Well," he said, "you've just learned your first lesson in stunt riding. You have to work up to the hard tricks. I suggest you start by perfecting riding over mice, and then move on to medium-size animals before you try to ride over a boy again." He was smiling and gave her a tickle. "Promise me, no more human obstacle stunts until you've perfected jumping Apricot and Marmalade?"

Olivia's eyes were wide and her mouth hung open. "I'll never use Apricot or Marmalade in stunts! Ever."

"Then no more little-boy moguls either. Promise?"

"I promise, Dadam."

"Now, where did you leave room on that princess-perfect plaster for me to sign?"

It was still early, not even six, when Olivia fell asleep on Nana's couch while the rest of us gabbed. Adam and I took her home and put her to bed, then collapsed in front of the TV. I was finally able to voice the question that had been playing on repeat in my brain since I was told I couldn't take Olivia home from the hospital.

"Will you add me to Olivia's official caregiver list for emergencies?"

Adam choked on his soda.

I choked on a piece of my heart that broke off and lodged in my windpipe.

25

—————

ADAM

Did she understand what she was asking? Being a child's legal emergency contact wasn't as easy as adding a name—and removing it again—on a whim. The reality was it would probably take longer to get her added than our fake marriage was going to last, and with her in Europe for nine months, it made no sense at all.

But what today's events taught me was that it would be a good idea to have another person on that list. Someone I could count on to be in town, to be sober, and who made Olivia feel safe.

"Nana," I accidentally said out loud.

"Nana what?" Lizzy asked.

"She'd be the best secondary contact in case of another emergency."

Lizzy pulled up her legs and wrapped her arms around them. In the six weeks we'd been living together, I'd learned this was her tell that she was upset and trying not to show it. I sighed. Did I have the fortitude to tease out what was bothering her? Between worrying about Olivia and restraining my rage against Brigitte, I was tapped out.

Growing up with brothers, having had only one serious

relationship with a woman whose sole emotion was demanding, I had no training in how to navigate the softer emotional lives of women. But having a career that required me to see what was coming before it happened, I was pretty good at reading environmental signs. And the sign Lizzy was waving screamed, "I need to vent."

I touched her leg. "Something's bothering you."

She pinched her lips together and gave a small shrug.

"I can't read your mind, Lizzy. And I'm exhausted. Please talk to me. Don't make me play twenty questions."

She held my gaze for several long seconds and mouthed words without sounds. I tilted my head and raised my eyebrows, the universal body language for "Spit it out, woman!"

"I want to be one of Olivia's official emergency contacts." Her tone was clear: this wasn't a request.

"It's not that easy. I can't just name random people. There's an expectation that those contacts are family."

She bit her lower lip, her nostrils flared, and her breathing got loud. I watched her chest rise and fall, fast and hard, like we'd just had sex. But unlike postcoital heavy breathing, her eyes were angry. I didn't understand why she was having such a strong reaction to something out of our control.

"What's going on? Why the death glare?"

She whispered, barely loud enough for me to hear, "You promised. You promised I'd still be family after …"

Dammit. "That's not what I meant. Of course, you're family. Where it counts the most, in Olivia's heart. But on paper, where it counts for government officials"—I shook my head and made a sad face—"you're not family."

Her scowl intensified. She blinked. The daggers in her eyes replaced by flamethrowers. "On paper," she poked my chest, "specifically, on a provincially recognized *marriage certificate*, I believe I actually *am* family." She poked me hard on the sternum with each syllable.

"Lizzy." I tried to take her hand but she jerked and twisted out of my grasp.

"Forget it. I'm going to take a bath." She slipped away quietly and went upstairs without making a sound. I heard the bathroom door gently close and then water running.

I flopped against the couch and closed my eyes. Two months ago, I could never have believed I'd be spending my summer holiday as a married man. It was a crazy thought. I imagined myself sitting in this same spot virtually every night after Olivia was in bed, watching some crap on TV while I worked whatever muscle set the day called for, until I was tired enough to sleep.

My free weights were in the basement now, barely touched since Lizzy moved in. Not quite. Well used those first two weeks we were fake husband and wife, and doing much better at the fake part than the husband-and-wife part. Those weights helped me work out more sexual frustration than I'd had since I was fifteen and too freaked out about accidental pregnancy to have sex like all the other guys were.

But in the last month, cardio workouts had been exceptional and at least once a day. Holding up my own weight while I straddled Lizzy was giving my biceps and triceps attention. My low back and core were taken care of every time she rode me. And my thighs experienced a regular burn … my breath hitched and my cock began its rise to attention as I imagined Lizzy kneeling before me.

I looked toward the stairs. The water was still running. Would there be room in the tub for me? I bounded up three at a time and burst into the bathroom, startling her. Her eyes were red.

I don't know how often this woman cried before she met

me, but now it seemed a weekly occurrence. My hard-on retreated. Good lad.

"Can I join you?"

She blinked twice and turned off the water, nodded, and pulled her legs up to make room for me at the tap end.

"I've never shared a bath before, but I think if I sit where you are, and then you lean against me, that would be the most comfortable."

Lizzy nodded and scooted forward. I dropped my clothes on the floor and slid in behind her. With my knees bent, she fit between my thighs quite nicely. She sat upright, so I pulled her against my chest and wrapped my arms around her ribs, under her breasts. Although my original intent had been sexual, seeing her looking so sad, I didn't want to trigger any kind of movement in my groin.

"I'm sorry," I said. I wasn't prepared for what to say next, so I let the silence hold us. The weight of her torso, pressed against me, increased as she finally relaxed.

"I'm sorry too. I overstepped. It's not my place to demand that level of responsibility for Olivia. I wasn't thinking. You're right. In two months, I won't even be here. Also, what if the call had been something worse, and we'd needed to make a serious decision about—" She gasped then released a single sob.

I held her shaking body. Once her breathing returned to normal, I tilted my head. "Hey, look at me."

She wiggled into a position where she could meet my eyes.

"I trust your decision-making with Olivia, implicitly, no matter what situation. Hell, I trust you more than I even trust myself."

She scoffed.

"I'm not kidding. You're the most compassionate person I've ever met. I've never known anyone who listens the way you do, who hears subtext. It's like you listen with your heart, which sounds ridiculous and I don't even know what that means, but that's how it feels. So yeah, if Olivia was ever in need of an important decision to be made on her behalf, you'd be the person I'd want at my side to make it."

From all that, what was her takeaway?

"Why don't you trust yourself to make the best decisions for Olivia?"

My biceps tightened. "I don't have a great track record, you know, protecting the people I care about. Let's just leave it there, okay?" I moved to get out of the tub, but she pressed to hold me down. "I'm getting too hot," I said, trying again. Being thwarted again.

"Dylan's broken arm and Josh's concussion weren't your fault, you know. And seriously, you were how old when your parents put you in charge of keeping the peace? That wasn't fair."

"It's not them."

"Adam, you cannot claim responsibility for Dalton and Maggie. Did you design the tandem parachute? Did you test it? Did you pack the one they were wearing? No. And given the insurance company had to admit the accident was not an 'Act of God,' even the law has said that the blame falls squarely on that parachute company."

"Fact is, though, they'd still be alive and Olivia wouldn't have a broken arm if it weren't for me. I'm the one who convinced them to jump, ergo, their deaths are on my head. And this conversation is over."

I leveraged myself out from under and behind her and stepped from the tub.

"But you know what?" I added as I dried myself. "I'm going to talk to Dylan about starting the process to have both you and Nana added to Olivia's official emergency contacts. I should have added Nana years ago. And I'm sorry I suggested you weren't family. Regardless of how long our agreement lasts, you're now and always will be part of Olivia's mixed-up family unit. She's lucky to have you."

Before Lizzy could respond, I was out the door, clicking it closed. I pulled my running gear from my dresser. "I'm going for a run," I called. "You want me to bring home doughnuts?"

She didn't answer, so I opened the door to find her totally submerged but for her nostrils. Her eyes were closed and if it weren't for the rise and fall of her chest, I'd have thought she'd drowned. I left without disturbing her.

26

LIZZY

W hen Adam got home from his run—with six gourmet doughnuts—we pretended like the bath conversation never happened. I didn't want to press about when he'd add me to Olivia's official list, and it was obvious he didn't want to talk about the past. So we ate doughnuts and watched *Sweet Tooth* until we were both yawning.

The next morning, I was in the kitchen having coffee, and he said he was going to pick up a new phone since the one with the smashed screen still worked for incoming calls, but it was impossible to type on. He'd swapped his SIM card into his old phone and had been using it for the last few days.

"Would you be willing to let me have your old phone? It's like three generations newer than mine."

Adam looked from the phone on the table to me. He picked it up and rolled it over in his hands a few times, then stuffed it in his pocket.

"Let's get you a new one at the same time. We can have matching phones, if you want," he teased, "as long as you're willing to get a proper device, not a froufrou phone."

Of course, it was a generous offer, but after the ridiculous amount of money he'd already given me, there was no way I was going to accept a phone from him. And I didn't want to waste any of mine on something I didn't really need since my shoestring, bucket list European adventure had become quite a bit more upscale given the windfall. For the first time in my life, I found myself justifying upgrades from economy tickets to more comfortable seats and more central hotels. *If I have legroom on the flight, I'll sleep better and won't miss a day of being a tourist. If I'm staying in the center of the action I won't waste time and money on transit so I'll get to see more sights.*

"I don't need brand new. I just thought your old one still had some life in it, so why not use it. How come you don't want to give it up?"

He turned his back to me and cracked his neck from one side to the other. He took his time pouring his coffee. I could tell by the rapid expansion and contraction of his back muscles that I'd upset him and he was trying to find his calm voice.

"Never mind. You don't have to—"

He turned and leveled serious eyes at me. "It was the phone I had before."

"Before?"

"The accident."

"Oh." I didn't understand why that made it special.

Adam pulled out a chair beside me, sat and spun my chair toward him, taking my knees in his hands so I had to give him my full attention.

"The phone is basically brand new. I only used it for a few months. And I couldn't keep using it after since it was painful to see the WhatsApp group I shared with Dalton and Maggie. And I couldn't delete it since—it felt wrong. I know it's weird, but it's not a phone anymore. It's … I don't know what it is."

"It's like a shrine to their memory," I said. "And to your

connection to two of the most important people in your life. I get it. I'm sorry. I didn't mean to press."

"No, it's okay. I'm actually glad to tell you. Nobody else knows about it. It's too morbid."

He mindlessly squeezed my thighs a bit too hard. I lifted his hands and wove our fingers together. "I don't think it's morbid at all. I think it's the opposite. You're keeping part of them alive. You're keeping their voices alive. One day Olivia might want to read the conversations. It might be a nice connection for her too."

He shook his head.

"Too many adult-only conversations?" I smiled and poked at his ribs. He didn't return my playful expression.

"No, I'll never let her read it because then she'd see how I convinced her dad to do the stunt with me. I know she'll have to learn about all the details one day, but I …"

"It's all good. You don't have to explain. I get it."

We sat in comfortable quiet—comfortable for me, at least—for several minutes, drinking our coffee. I broke the silence.

"During my master's studies, I did a semester on treating trauma. One of the traumas we covered was survivor's guilt. I was wondering if you've done any counseling for that."

"I don't have survivor's guilt," he growled. "I have asshole-friend guilt. And let's drop it." Adam stood and put his coffee cup in the dishwasher. When he turned to face me he was smiling, as if this was a normal Sunday morning coffee conversation. "Did you want to come with me? Can I change your mind about a new phone? I'm happy to get you a new one. Really."

"Nah, I'm good. And I think I hear my favorite cartoon about to start. Go do your thing. Take your time. Olivia and I will hang out. I had an idea about an art project we can do that won't require her to use her right hand."

~

Adam was gone a couple of hours and when he got home, he was in his usual good mood.

"Are there any ice cream monsters in the house?" he called from the front door. Olivia jumped up from the kitchen table—currently the painting table—and ran to him.

"I am! I want ice cream," she barked.

"Mona Elizabeth Sheila? How's your inner ice cream fiend today? Nana accidentally bought more than will fit in her freezer. We need all scalawags on deck to help her out of this sticky situation."

Olivia giggled. "You're silly, Dadam."

"No, you go and have fun with Nana. I'm going to clean up, make a cup of tea, and sit in the sun with my journal. That okay with you?"

He winked and nodded. "I hope you're prepared to eat until you puke, Olivia. The job lands on the two of us."

"Gross!"

"Get your sneakers on, scamp. I'll be right down." Adam went upstairs and was back in thirty seconds.

"What? You're still tying that shoe? Here, let me help."

Adam's approach to helping was to take off her shoe and tickle her feet until she called him King Fergus, the hero of *Brave*, one of her favorite animations. Then he helped her make the dog chase the rabbit through the loops while she complained that slip-ons were way easier, especially with her cast.

Once Olivia was ready, the best dad and husband ever sauntered over to where I was leaning against the doorjamb between the front hall and the living room, took my chin in between his thumb and fingers, and tilted my head until our mouths were an inch apart. "You sure you don't want to come?"

I'm not sure if he meant the double entendre, but the way

my body heard what he'd asked made me shiver and then laugh. "For ice cream? No. You go have fun. For after ice cream? I'll be waiting." I sealed my promise with a kiss that lasted long enough for Olivia to interrupt with an impatient "Come on, Dadam. The ice cream is melting."

~

It was nice to have time in the house on my own. As much as I loved being part of this family, the switch from living by myself to living with an energetic five-year-old, a seemingly always horny thirty-two-year-old, and two kittens was sometimes a little overwhelming.

After journaling in the backyard for a luxurious ninety minutes without any interruption, I took my notebook upstairs to put away. Adam's old phone sat on top of his bedside table. I glared at it as if it was responsible for my thoughts. Moved to pick it up. Backed away.

It was calling to me like an evil witch offering delicious but dangerous sweets.

I took a step toward it. My heart beat thumped in my ears as my blood pressure shot up and the acrid scent of anxious sweat rose from my body as I considered the risk, as if I'd already taken it.

I wanted to resist, but I also wanted to know how bad the coercion for Dalton and Maggie to do the stunt had been. I told myself I was snooping as a professional, as a counselor who wanted to help a patient heal. Even though my body was clearly communicating a different truth—that I was being a nosy fake wife—it didn't stop me.

I touched the screen and was met by a password request. I punched in the four digits every Rhodes brother admitted they used for everything. The trust they had with each other —and Nana, whose phone number it was—had been given to me when I joined their WhatsApp family group. It hadn't been intentional or entrusted to me with a solemn promise not to use or share it. It had been stated in a flippant exchange between Josh and Nick while telling me secret stories about Adam they thought I should know.

My stomach tensed when the phone unlocked, showing me Adam's home screen—a photo of himself, Dalton and Maggie standing on a mountaintop. I paused but couldn't stop myself from tapping the WhatsApp icon. I stared at the conversation list for a long minute before convincing myself to scroll and find the group with Maggie and Dalton. It was pretty easy to recognize—it was called "Utter MADness."

My breathing shallowed. *What will you do with the information once you know?*

I shrugged in answer.

I scrolled backward in time, reading messages about planning the jump. All three people were equally engaged, and all three sounded equally committed to the stunt. I scrolled until months before the stunt was even mentioned. There was nothing there that even hinted that Adam had coerced his former teammates into this.

I leaned against the headboard, wiped my slick hands on the duvet, and closed the chat.

That's when I saw another group. This one with Dalton only. Steeling myself for another stinky adrenaline rush, I tapped it open. And there it was—the conversation that had been plaguing Adam's conscience for three years. It wasn't that long, maybe thirty exchanges. But it was right there in black-and-white: Adam coercing Dalton with one-liners like, "You know you want to," and "Don't be a pussy." I shook my head. I hated that insult.

Backwards, backwards, backwards, I scrolled quickly, landing on a message from Dalton to Adam.

Dude, M won't stop harping on about us doing this jump with you. She wants to do it so bad. The full-time mom thing is killing her. But I'm not willing to go there. Old + bold = dead, ya know?

No disrespect, but if you die, I'll cry, but you won't be leaving a kid behind.

And Adam's reply,

I know, man. She's been hounding me to harass your ass until you give in. Don't do it. Stand your ground. And fuck you—for all you know, I have a dozen little secret babies in the world, waiting to meet their famous dad.

Dalton: *Your nightmare, bro.*

So what happened?

My anxiety about snooping evaporated as I looked for a conversation with Maggie. It was lower on the list. When I found it, I scrolled as far up the conversation thread as I could go and read from oldest message to newest. And it was one hundred percent clear that Maggie was the force behind her and Dalton joining Adam's jump. She'd found her own sponsor—the company that made the tandem parachute. She'd negotiated an even better sponsorship deal than Adam got with the mountain that was paying him to jump from a plane and board down their slopes.

Adam tried to talk Maggie out of it, using all the same reasons Dalton had argued to him.

Wait a minute … I switched from the conversation with Maggie over to the one with Dalton. There was a long section that was identical. The only difference was that in the one with Maggie, Adam argued to *not* take the risk, and Maggie threw insults at Adam. It looked to me like Adam was reporting to Dalton what Maggie's arguments were and Dalton was feeding Adam reasons to give to Maggie that this was a bad idea.

Shit. This was a game changer, not only to help Adam heal from what I'm certain was survivor's guilt but to be able to attack Brigitte and her assertions that Adam was an unsuitable father due to his thrill-seeking lack of common sense.

Brigitte needed to see these exchanges, too, since she

blamed Adam for her sister's death. As hard as it would be to hear or accept, Brigitte had to know that Maggie had driven that bus over the cliff, despite both Dalton's and Adam's pleas to not risk her life.

And Dylan needed to see this, too, since he'd said the biggest strike against Adam in the guardianship battle was his lack of acting in a manner befitting a parent due to his apparent role in coercing Olivia's parents to jump with him. This would have to help with his case.

I opened my phone and figured out how to transfer WhatsApp chats to another phone. I sent all three conversations to my cloud account so I could have a better look from the desktop app. And so I could create a timeline that proved Adam was a responsible parent and had been thinking about Olivia's future even more than her own mother had been.

Now I just had to figure how to tell Adam that he'd created a false history of the events that led us to becoming fake husband and wife. I made a wish to the universe: please let one false history plus one fake marriage equal one real happily ever after for Adam and Olivia.

When my inner voice added *And me*, I broke into yet another stinky anxiety sweat.

27

ADAM

"**D**arlin', I'm home!" I called as Olivia and I burst through the front door, hyped up on way too much sugar.

"Darlin', I'm home!" Olivia mimicked.

"Darlin's, I'm making dinner!" Lizzy's voice floated in from the kitchen.

"I'm too full for dinner," Olivia moaned, grabbing her stomach, then flopping onto the couch.

I carried two tubs of ice cream to the kitchen.

"I come bearing the fruits of my hunting and gathering."

Lizzy put down her chopping knife and opened the bag with the ice cream.

"Sour cherry chocolate and moose tracks! These are two of my favorites."

"Nana forced us to bring them home. Olivia chose the chocolate moose poops, and I picked the more sophisticated flavor. Glad you like them."

"So, Nana really did have more than she could keep?" Lizzy asked.

"She had space in her deep freeze, but you should've seen what she set up. It was pretty crazy. She had twelve different flavors, and we did blind tastings of them all. We missed you. Nana said we'll have to do it again next week and that you have to come. No excuses."

Actually, it was my idea to do it again since I knew Lizzy would love a dessert tasting the way Nana surprised us. Nana agreed to do it again—next week pairing a variety of pies with vanilla ice cream. That would be the surprise part for Lizzy.

She poked her head out of the kitchen and checked on Olivia, who had turned on the Disney Channel and was cuddling her kittens. She was wearing the noise-canceling headphones I'd set her up with a week ago when Lizzy and I wanted time to ourselves and didn't want to be overheard. I told Olivia these headphones were the best way to watch movies with singing since she'd be able to really hear the lyrics. She was a convert; and I was going to have to get her her own pair now.

"I have something I need to talk to you about," Lizzy said, squinting like the light was too bright but only in one eye.

"Oh no, not the dread pirate talk!"

She gave me a half smile. "You may not be far off. You might want to make me walk the plank after I tell you what I did … but then you'll be happy."

"Oka-ay." I moved to sit down, but she took my hand and pulled herself into my arms for a hug. "That's nice." I sighed and kissed the top of her head.

"So-o-o, I did something that I know was wrong," she spoke into my chest.

I tried to take a step out of her grasp so I could see her face, but she held fast around my hips.

"Just let me say what I need to before I see your expression. And then you can glower at me."

I felt a wave of something uncomfortable in my gut, that feeling you get when you're watching a movie and you know there's something bad hiding around the corner, but the hero doesn't know it's there. Except I wasn't sure if I was the hero or the observer. "What did you do?" I asked, trying to sound light, not quite sure I nailed it.

"I snooped."

She snooped? I couldn't imagine what she'd snooped at. I had nothing snoop-worthy in the house. Hell, I had nothing snoop-worthy in my life. No secret gambling or porn addictions. No hidden bottles in the garage.

"And what did you find?" I asked, more curious than upset.

"Ilookedatyouroldphone." She said a jumbled word so quickly, it took me a second to understand.

"You looked at my old phone? The one upstairs."

She nodded.

"Did you decide you *do* want me to buy you a new one after all?"

She shook her head.

"So you looked at my old phone. Not a crime punishable by hanging and quartering."

She released her grip on me, and I let her out of my hug.

"I downloaded the chats you had with Dalton and Maggie." She pointed to her laptop, sitting at the end of the kitchen table.

"You what? Why would you do that?" I wasn't sure if I was angry, but I did feel like she'd violated something … my privacy? My trust?

"I need to show you something I found." She sat and touched the chair beside her. "Look at this and tell me what you see."

What did I see? I saw a spreadsheet with dates in the first column, and rows labeled with my name, Dalton's, and Maggie's.

I looked at the words in the fields and tried to make sense of them. The columns looked like conversations that felt vaguely familiar. But I didn't understand the empty boxes or the color coding.

"Do you see it?" Lizzy asked.

"Explain it."

She did. With great enthusiasm. Full of smiles and positive exclamations about how great this was. For me. For Olivia. For all the Rhodes family.

I heard what she was saying; maybe I even saw what she was seeing. But I didn't feel what she was feeling.

I was confused, that feeling you have when you know you left your car on Level B near the elevators, but you're standing there looking at the space where your boring family van should be and the vehicle in the space is a shiny new sports car. You want to feel amped and happy, but in your gut you know something's off.

Her interpretation of the exchanges between me, Dalton, and Maggie was backward.

I closed my eyes and was in a free fall. Fear and exhilaration swirled together like a snow tornado in my chest and stomach.

Lizzy touched my arm. It felt like an electric shock. Standing too quickly, I knocked over the chair. Didn't bother to pick it up. I pointed to the laptop. Felt a pain in my chest and bent over to catch my breath.

Lizzy touched me again, and I swatted her hand away.

"You crossed a line," I said. "Those conversations were not yours to look at."

"I know. And I'm disgusted with myself for snooping. But do the ends not justify the means in this case?" Her face contorted.

"What ends do you see, Lizzy? You want to know what I see?" I clenched my jaw. "I see a little girl finding out that her mom loved living a life of danger more than she loved her daughter. I see a little girl finding out that her dad loved his wife more than he loved his daughter. And I see that same little girl finding out that the man she accepted as her surrogate dad was responsible for tearing her life apart."

"That's not what I see," she whispered.

"Frankly, I don't think you have a very good track record for seeing what's right in front of you, so that doesn't surprise me." It was a low blow that I *almost* regretted.

She swiped a hand across her eyes. "If you don't trust my judgment, let Dylan have a look and tell you what he sees."

"This is none of Dylan's business."

"Are you crazy? Of course, it is. This could be the information he needs to get Brigitte to back off. Or have the judge rule in your favor."

"You don't get it, Lizzy. This"—I hit her laptop and accidentally knocked it off the table—"means nothing. It's one blip in a lifetime of bad decisions that have hurt everyone I've ever cared about. Dylan will look at this, and what he'll see is exactly the same thing I see because he knows that when it comes to taking care of people who are important, I'm shit at it."

"You're not," she argued.

"Yeah. I am. Drop it."

"Dadam, what are you and Mona fighting about?" Olivia stood in the door, her bottom lip trembling.

"Come here, pumpkin," Lizzy and I said simultaneously.

She looked from me to Lizzy and ran full speed into my open arms. I picked her up and held her tight.

"You're not shit at taking care of me," Olivia said in a small voice.

I held her closer. *Not yet.*

"Will you watch *Aladdin* with me? I'm at the part where you need to sing the new world song with me or it sounds bad."

"We can't have that."

I looked over at Lizzy who was retrieving her laptop from the floor.

"I'll replace it," I said without emotion.

She shook her head then looked up at me. Expressionless.

Olivia wiggled in my arms. "Come on, Aladdin's probably already singing. We'll have to rewind it to where they kiss."

Lizzy made a noise, a sarcastic little laugh. "When in doubt, just rewind to the first kiss."

It seemed clear she was referring to us, our first kiss. But which one? In my mind, we had three. The first time our lips touched: the challenge kiss. Our first kiss as fake husband and wife: the lie kiss. And the one that shook my world and, for one devastating minute, made me forget who I was and believe in happily ever after, goddess-princess style: the fool's kiss.

I turned to ask, but the back door clunked closed with Lizzy on the other side.

28

LIZZY

"Hey, it's me," I said, trying to make my voice sound normal.

"What's wrong?" Kama asked.

"Where are you? Work or home? Can I come over?"

"At work for another twenty minutes. What's going on?"

"Can I come over? I can pick up food," I offered. "Sushi? Indian?"

"Of course. We're good for food, though. Did something happen with Brigitte?"

"Not really, but it's about that. I'll tell you when I get there. Will Dylan be home?"

"Do you want him to be? I could suggest he go hang out with Josh or send him over to Adam's—sorry, your place."

"No, I think I want him to hear this, even though it's going to end my fake marriage early."

"Lizzy? What's going on?" Kama's concern was clear.

"I'll fill you in in person. Thanks, Kama."

I ordered an Uber pickup for thirty minutes and quietly went back inside. I covered the bowl with the chopped onions and peppers and put it in the fridge; Adam could finish making the pasta sauce. He watched me go up the stairs but didn't stop singing his part in Prince Aladdin and Princess Jasmine's falling-in-love song.

I debated what to toss in my bag since I wasn't sure if I'd spend the night at Kama's or come back here. Better to overpack than not, I decided, putting my toothbrush in its travel case. I changed into a clean sundress so I wouldn't need to pack a full change of clothes. Fresh undies, face cream, and a light sweater fit easily in my oversize purse with my wallet, sunglasses, and laptop.

I was ready to go in under five minutes and sat on my side of the bed, dangling my feet over the edge. Now what?

I felt inexplicably calm. Too calm. Calm before a category 5 hurricane calm.

Plodding downstairs, I dropped my bag at the front door. Olivia looked up from her movie.

"Perfect timing, Mona! You can sing the princess's part. I want to be the birds." She squished closer to Adam to make room for me.

"I don't know the words to this one," I admitted.

"That's okay. Dadam, turn on the sing-along."

Adam gave her the look.

"Please!"

"Better," he said. "Even princesses need to use manners."

Olivia rolled her eyes. "I'm being the birds now, and birds don't have manners. They can be very rude, especially when I'm trying to sleep in the morning."

My heart swelled. God, I loved this child.

Although I didn't know the song I was supposed to sing, the tune was easy enough to follow. I intentionally messed up to make Olivia giggle.

By the end of the sing-along, Adam was laughing too. I felt bad about leaving but steeled myself. I couldn't ignore this conflict the way I'd been ignoring the subtle change in his energy at the hotel after he'd given me the best night of my life.

"I'm heading to Kama's for a visit. I've got an Uber on the way."

"No, stay. The best part's coming." Olivia crawled up on my lap and pressed my shoulders against the couch. "You're my prisoner. You can't leave until I let you go."

"But I have a secret weapon. Prince Adam, help me escape the evil bird prison!"

"And suffer the raucous wrath of the wretched robins? Sorry, tonight you need to be a self-rescuing princess, I'm afraid."

"Tweet, tweet, tweet, tweet. You're mine forever."

"Princess powers, activate! Strength of a thousand butterflies," I said, wrapping my arms around Olivia and easily lifting her off my lap, depositing her into Adam's.

"No fair." Olivia pouted.

"Why don't we all go? You want to visit Uncle Dylan and Auntie Kama? You can watch the rest of the movie there. Uncle Dylan would make a very good singing snake, don't you think?"

I gave Adam a look, a small head shake to say, "I need to talk to my best friend. Alone."

He returned a questioning look.

"My Uber will be here in less than five minutes."

"Scads of time to pack a few toys, right, little chickadee?"

"Tweet, tweet, tweet." Olivia jumped from Adam's lap and ran up the stairs.

"Seriously, Adam, I need to talk to Kama. Girl stuff."

"I'm sorry I yelled at you. I overreacted." He stood and pulled me into a hug. "I know you're trying to help. And I appreciate it. But …" He inhaled a long breath, then pushed my shoulders away from his body so I had to step backward. "Those messages aren't yours to share."

"But why? Why won't you—"

"Lizzy, I'm serious. Drop it. Dylan's doing his job. I trust him."

"But—"

"I don't need to raise the dead, okay? I have you as my ace in the hole. Best mom ever. Brigitte won't stand a chance against the Wonder Twin parent power we've got happening. Right?"

My phone beeped. "Uber's here."

"Olivia, time to roll!" Adam yelled over my head.

She bounced down the stairs, talking a mile a minute about the toys she'd packed and how we could each have one to act out the characters in the movie we'd been watching.

"You going to give Dylan a heads-up that you and Olivia are coming?"

"Nah. As long as I show up with scotch, no warning is required." He opened the liquor cabinet and pulled out a bottle, checked to see how full it was, then swapped it for another. "Hey, Olivia. Have room in your bag for a present for Uncle Dylan?"

She looked from the bottle to her small backpack and shook her head.

I took it from his hand and dropped it in my own bag.

Adam grabbed his new phone, wallet, and keys from the coffee table, and we headed out.

Olivia took my hand. Adam went toward his van, saying, "Car seat. Safety first."

We pulled up to Dylan and Kama's condo just as Kama was walking up the street.

"Perfect timing!" Olivia yelled, running to meet her.

"Oh! I thought …" She didn't finish her sentence.

"Yeah," I said, grabbing my phone and one credit card from my purse, then handing the bag to Adam. "Take this inside for me? Kama and I are going to pick up food for dinner. Right, Kama?"

"Right," she said, looking from me to Adam. "Hey, pumpkin." She ruffled Olivia's red hair.

"I don't think Dylan's home yet, but let yourselves in. We'll be back ..." She looked at me.

"When we're back," I answered, looping my arm through Kama's and basically pulling her with me down the sidewalk.

Dylan and Kama's downtown condo wasn't close to any grocery store in comfortable walking distance—at least, not comfortable with bags of groceries. But they were near lots of restaurants. And it was still early, just after 5 p.m.

"Are you okay to leave Dylan with Adam and Olivia? Will he be upset if you and I go out for dinner without him?" I asked my best friend.

"Not if we bring back something already cooked. Will Adam?"

"Don't care. He's already mad at me, and if I do what I know I'm going to do, I expect he'll be furious enough to ..." I shook my head as the thoughts and words tangled in my throat.

"But ... I thought ... after the birthday night ... What the hell is going on?"

"First, where can we go that's quiet enough to talk and has cheap drinks? Then I'll fill you in on everything."

Bar None was basically dead, so we got our pick of tables. Kama ordered a ten-ounce glass of house red. I was about to order the same but was struck by a wave of sadness and regret. "Can the bartender make a Gin Gin Mule?" I asked.

Kama looked quizzical and then said, "Uh-oh. You're planning your escape."

That made me smile. "You remember that movie?"

"We only watched it like a hundred times."

"Four, maybe five," I corrected.

"The way you talked about it for months, it felt like it was a hundred."

"It made an impact."

"Apparently. But why are you thinking of it again now?"

I filled Kama in on the details of my birthday night and how I told Adam I loved him and he said it back but then pulled away after the firework display ended.

"He was mostly normal again in the morning, but it's been weird since," I said. "We're still having sex—oh my god, Kama, if Dylan is anything like Adam ..." I fanned myself as my belly flip-flopped and my lady parts shuddered their agreement.

"Full-body massage, am I right?" Kama asked.

I shook my head.

"Oh!" She sounded surprised. "Then sorry to tell you, but your man pales in comparison to mine." She blushed. "Okay, so sex is great. He got weird after 'I love you' was spoken. To be expected. And"—she raised her eyebrows—"I bet you got weird too."

I raised one shoulder. "Maybe? I don't know. But that's not the problem. I went snooping. I found something."

I told Kama the whole story. She listened with rapt attention, holding her wine glass pressed to her lips, taking regular small sips until the glass was empty. I hadn't touched my mule yet.

"What do you think? Should I tell Dylan and risk Adam's wrath, or should I let it go, like he told me?"

Now it was my turn to drink. I sipped three long pulls from the copper cup and emptied it to the last bit of ice. The drink was cold going down but quickly warmed my stomach.

"I don't know. If you tell Dylan, you know he'll tell Adam that you did."

"Of course! He'd use it as evidence that Adam is a totally

responsible parent. It would kill all the arguments that Brigitte is making against him. I don't understand why he can't see that."

I caught the waitress's eye and waved for a second round.

"What should I do?" I asked again.

"I think you're right. If you tell Dylan, you'll basically be handing Adam early divorce papers. He'll be furious. And even though I don't understand why he doesn't want anyone to know about the exchanges with Dalton and Maggie, that is his decision."

"But—"

"If you broke a trust like that with me, I'd be pissed too. Put yourself in his shoes." Kama tilted her head forward and looked down her nose in a very mom-like way.

"But you have to agree that it could help him win." I tapped under her chin to make her stop mom-glaring me.

Kama moved her head side to side as if considering. "Yes?"

"So it's worth it, right?"

She did the head waggle again. "No."

"No! Why no?"

Our second round of drinks arrived, and Kama held her glass to her lips, breathing in and sighing before taking a sip.

"Dylan seems relatively confident that Adam can win without that information. He gave up everything to take Olivia in when Brigitte wouldn't. He did all the right things, taking her to counseling, doing everything the child psychologist recommended. He quit stunts. She's part of a huge extended family that loves her. And he's married to a woman Olivia adores."

"But—"

"So here's what I see," Kama said, putting her glass down. "Don't be mad, and don't interrupt."

I scowled. "What?"

"You've never been this interested in a guy. In all the years we've been friends, you have never once told a guy you loved him—"

"I've thought it before—"

"Don't interrupt. I can't remember anyone you dated for more than a few weeks before ghosting him—"

"Not true, I—"

"Shut up. You've been forced to stay in this fake marriage, even after allowing yourself to have deep feelings. And we both know you liked Adam long before you married him."

"As a friend—"

"Uh-huh. Because anything more would be too risky. That's why Josh was such a perfect distraction—there was zero risk it would *ever* become anything more than friends."

I wanted to tell her she was wrong, but in my heart I knew she wasn't.

"What you have with Adam? I know the marriage part is fake, but the relationship part? For god's sake, Lizzy, that part is as real as it gets. And I think you're scared shitless. You're leaving for Europe in less than two months, at which point you know this relationship will end. No matter how much he loves you. He's not going to wait for you to come home the way Josh waited for Paige. And I think that's why you want to share the messages with Dylan, because you know it will ruin everything you have with Adam, which will make breaking up that much easier."

"That's not why," I whispered into my copper cup.

"He's ruined your perfect plan, Little Miss 'I'm Not Getting into a Serious Relationship until I'm At Least Thirty and Mature Enough to Be a Mom' Hillhouse."

I raised my middle finger and swallowed two fluid ounces of gin and ginger beer.

"You're nothing like your mother, okay? I'd think that six

years of psych courses would have gotten that through your thick skull. Olivia adores you—"

"She adores everyone," I argued.

"You're not a narcissist. You're not your mother. You're not living a life ruled by other people's wants and needs. Stop sabotaging yourself. You make me crazy."

"Yeah, well, even if I did believe I could be a good mom for Olivia for longer than a summer, the deal ends as soon as Adam gets full legal guardianship, so what difference if I tell Dylan and give Adam one more nail to hammer into Brigitte's coffin—"

Kama cringed.

"Sorry, bad metaphor. This marriage has an expiry date. All the extra weeks of fake wedded bliss will make the whole having to move out and back to my lonely single life even harder."

Dammit. My eyes flooded.

"Thank the goddess you can actually see that. But it doesn't have to end, you know."

I scoffed.

"Lizzy, he loves you. You know he does."

"He's grateful to me—"

"Shut up!" Kama leaned back in her chair and gazed up at the ceiling, then sighed and looked me right in the eye. "I'm going to tell you something, but you have to promise not to tell Adam that I told you, or he'll kick Dylan's ass."

"Tell me what?"

"Promise." Kama pointed with both index fingers.

"I promise. I won't say a word. What?"

"When Dylan and I were dating and you and Josh were doing your BFF ride-along, Adam used to ask Dylan if you'd be coming to different events. It was pretty much guaranteed he'd be there if Dylan said you would be, but hit-and-miss when he said you weren't."

"That's probably because I hung out with Olivia and gave him a break from full-time dad duties."

"Right, because that's exactly what used to happen; he'd drop Olivia in your lap and bugger off to get drunk with his brothers. No. As I recall, he stayed pretty darn close to you."

"He was making sure Olivia was safe. Stranger danger and all that."

"Do you hear yourself? You're talking out of both sides of your ass."

"Now who's using terrible metaphors?"

"You can't argue. And now you're thinking about doing the one thing that would give Adam a legit reason to break up with you. Those messages are not yours to share. And you know damn well that's true."

"It would be worth it if it guaranteed Olivia got to stay in the Rhodes family."

"And if it guaranteed you wouldn't," Kama said. "You know who *would* tell Dylan about the messages? Your mother. Because that's the selfish thing to do. Think about *that* before you make your decision."

29

ADAM

Lizzy and Kama showed up two hours later.

If I believed in telepathy, I'd have high-fived Olivia for the way she greeted them. She slid out of the oversized armchair she'd been curled up in, walked to the breakfast bar where the girls were unpacking bags of burgers and fries, and with her hand on her hip and her cast arm in the air, said in a very Nana-like tone, "And where have you two been?"

By Lizzy's stagger, I could make an educated guess. And I was pretty confident I knew what she and Kama had been talking about. Hunger and anger battled for dominance in my gut.

"Getting dinner, of course," Lizzy said with a distinct slur. "Come and get 'em. They're from this great place Kama took me. No Holds Barred, right?"

"Bar None, actually. But good guess," Kama said, sounding not quite as gooned.

Kama plated the food, and Lizzy handed it out.

"Two hamburgers and double fries for Kama's brilliant husband. Same for my handsome man. Single for Kama.

And Olivia, you get a choice. Would you like a chicken patty or a hamburger?"

"Chicken, please." Olivia licked her lips.

Lizzy carried her plate to the table and joined us. She enunciated every word and spoke a bit too loud for how close we were all seated. "Can someone please explain to me why hamburgers are called *ham* burgers? There's no ham in them. No pig. I mean, a chicken patty is made of what?"

"Chicken, of course," Olivia answered with enthusiasm.

"Correct." Lizzy slurred, pointing at her. "And pork chops are made of …?"

"Pork!" Olivia called.

"Yup. Salmon burgers and tuna steaks," she stopped and examined her hands for five seconds then continued, "those names make sense. But what doesn't make sense is why we call this"—she waved her burger in the air—"a *hamburger* when it's a cow patty. Am I right?"

I almost choked on my cow patty, and Dylan looked like he was struggling to swallow too.

"Technically, I think you're mistaken," I said, holding in a laugh.

"Technically …" Lizzy looked like she was trying to glare at me but couldn't quite focus her eyes. "I think you're very handsome. Did you know *that*?"

Not what I was expecting. "And you're very cute when you're … inebriated." I hoped Olivia hadn't yet learned what inebriated meant. The last thing I needed was for her to talk about her drunk stepmother in the upcoming interview with the court-assigned psychologist.

We ate more than we chatted and got through the meal quickly. It was almost seven.

"I hate to be a party pooper, but we have a pumpkin who will turn into a princess if she's not in bed soon. Time to pack up your coloring things, Olivia."

"No! I don't want to leave now."

"Oh dear, we're too late. The demanding princess has already taken over the body of my sweet pumpkin. This calls for drastic measures."

Olivia squealed and ran to hide behind Lizzy. "Don't let him get me. You have to protect me!" she begged.

Lizzy wrapped her arms around Olivia to keep me from tickling her. "I'm trying," she whispered, "but he won't let me."

I backed off. "Dylan, you good to drive, or should I call a cab?"

"Load 'em up." Dylan scooped Olivia into his arms and put her on his shoulders, then grabbed her car seat. "Let's get you home so you can rest up to princess another day."

As we walked to the parking garage, Kama grabbed my arm, letting Olivia, Lizzy, and Dylan get far enough ahead to not overhear.

"She told me. About the messages," Kama said.

Fists formed without intention. I closed my eyes and inhaled a long breath through my nose.

"I'm not telling Dylan. And I warned her not to tell him either."

My eyes popped open. That was a surprise, Kama not supporting Lizzy's decision.

"Why?"

"Because it's not her place to share your secret. I admit, I really don't understand why you don't want Dylan to know, but"—she held up her hand to stop me from speaking—"it's none of my business either. I trust you know what you're doing and have a good reason for it. So, you can trust that this secret is safe with me. And I'll do whatever I can to keep Little Miss Nosy from oversharing."

I reached out to hug her.

"Don't be a weirdo," she said. Then she laughed and hugged me. "You're a great dad, Adam. Anyone can see how happy and well-adjusted Olivia is. Now you just have to work your magic on Lizzy."

My muscles constricted—lungs and all. It felt like I'd already used some kind of black magic on her since she had such a skewed idea of who I was, as if when I said I'd been careless, she heard cautious; when I told her a story of me being untrustworthy, her takeaway was that I was reliable. And when she saw evidence that I put the people I loved at risk for selfish reasons—evidence in the form of a child now in my care—she spun that proof on its head and reflected it as the opposite.

But Lizzy's witchcraft was more powerful than my magic, and I was about to say so to Kama when Olivia called from the back seat of Dylan's car, "You can't blame me if I'm cranky in the morning since I was ready to leave ages ago."

Releasing Kama from the hug, I jogged to the car. Lizzy was in the front passenger seat, so I folded myself in beside Olivia.

Dylan turned to face me. "I know it's a tight squeeze back there, but I wanted to keep my eye on burpy so I could make a quick stop, if needed."

"I'm fine," Lizzy drawled. "Just ate too fast, that's all."

"In case your cow patty decides to voice its opinion about being called a cow patty, I want you up here."

"You keep saying cow patty and you'll be pulling over for me, bro." I gave Dylan's seat a nudge.

We made it to the house without incident. I released Olivia from her car seat, and she ran to the front door yelling, "Good night, Uncle Dylan. I love you!"

Dylan got out of the car. "Can I talk to you for a minute?"

I handed Lizzy my house key and watched her take very intentional steps up the front path.

"What's up?"

"While you and Kama were having a heart-to-heart, Lizzy said she'd found something that could help with

Olivia's case. I think. She seemed to be talking in code, I assume so Olivia wouldn't understand."

My teeth clenched so hard my jaw popped. An old injury. One I didn't appreciate being reminded of.

"What exactly did she say?"

"In essence, she said, '*They were texting. That woman, the bad one, you know who I mean, she's wrong. You have to know. She's wrong. I have proof.*'"

"Curious." I opened my mouth wide to pop my jaw back into place.

"You have any idea what she's talking about?" Dylan asked.

"Ramblings of a drunk girl. If I figure it out, I'll let you know." I slapped him on his shoulder. "Thanks for the lift. And the spontaneous hangout time. And bring that scotch with you next time you come over."

"If you want the recycling fee"—he dug into his pocket and pulled out a quarter—"consider us even."

"You're a jerk." I laughed, catching the coin.

I should have left with Dylan.

I should have slept on the couch.

I should have avoided Lizzy.

But I waved as Dylan drove away, tucked Olivia into bed after making sure she'd brushed her teeth, then sat on the edge of the bed where Lizzy was lying on her back, staring up.

"When I was a kid, I used to wish for those glow-in-the-dark stars and planets you stick on the ceiling. We should get some, don't you think? Then we could make love under the stars without worrying about being arrested." She laughed and added in a quiet, faraway voice, "That would be so cool."

I was angry, and I needed to tell her she'd overstepped a line that I didn't think she could recover from. Before I'd put my thoughts into words, she started rambling again.

"My mom told me she didn't want me. She said when she found out she was pregnant, she went to her doctor to ask for an abortion. But he refused. Can you believe it? All she had to do was go to a walk-in closet to get one."

"You mean clinic? A walk-in clinic." I was trying to process what she was saying. "You think your mother should have aborted the baby that ended up being you?" My anger toward Lizzy took a jarring redirect. Who tells their kid they tried to end them?

"Yeah." She sighed. "She didn't want kids. She wanted to have a life, you know? 'Kids ruin everything.' That's what she always said. But she only had me, so really, she should've said, 'Lizzy ruins everything,' but I never argued with her. She got really mad when I talked back."

"I'd like to meet your mother," I said, massaging my jaw to keep from jamming it again.

"I know I never met Maggie, but I think she was a bit like my mom."

"She was nothing like your mother," I said, a little too loud.

Lizzy rolled onto her side to face me. She stared, unblinking, for a long minute. I didn't speak, since nothing in my head fell into the productive-conversation column.

It was Lizzy who spoke again. "I wish my mother had died and someone like you had raised me. I didn't even have godparents. Maybe that's the trick—if you have kids and want to live until they're adults, don't have a Plan B for them." Again she laughed at her comment, which was as far from funny as I could imagine.

"Can I tell you a secret?" she asked.

"Mmm ..." I wasn't sure I wanted to know.

"I don't want to get a divorce. I love you, even when we're not having sex, you know. I don't even want to go to Europe anymore."

My guts twisted. Ten minutes ago, I'd been ready to tell

her this fake marriage was done. I'd been ready to take my chances with a system that erred to awarding guardianship to blood relations. I'd been ready to risk Olivia's happiness to protect … what? I wasn't sure now. But I did know I was still angry that she'd shared something of mine that wasn't hers to give away. That she'd gone behind my back and broken my trust.

Lizzy pulled off her sundress and yanked me down on the bed with her. She tried to get my T-shirt off. I didn't help her. She gave up and tugged at my shorts, but I held them in place.

She kissed me, but my jaw was still locked and my lips were too tight to return the affection.

"You're drunk," I said, pushing myself to sitting.

Her eyes glistened. "I was drunk on my birthday and it didn't stop you then."

"Yeah, well I was drunk too," I said, perhaps a little too harshly, judging by her pained look.

"I should go. You don't want me here." She turned away.

I do want you here, I thought. *But we can't sex our way through this. We need to talk.*

"Stay," I said. But only after she'd rolled out of bed with a loud thump as her feet hit the floor.

I should have said, "Come back to bed," but instead I asked, "Where are you going?"

She dropped her sundress over her shoulders again, zipped a hoodie on over top, and left without another word.

The bottom step creaked and then the plank by the couch. Would she lie down, turn on the TV? The plank creaked again. She bumped into something and swore. The back door opened and then quietly clicked closed.

I probably should have gone after her, tried to talk. But I didn't. I leaned against my headboard and closed my eyes.

30

LIZZY

Would somebody please shoot the robins?

I tried to cover my head but realized I had no pillow. Blinking into the still-dark sky, I started to put things together. I'd slept in a hammock in the backyard. With a blanket from the couch. *You should've grabbed a pillow,* I chastised. *And a shotgun.*

"Shut up," I whined at the wailing birds, realizing halfway through the word that at some point while I slept, homicidal construction workers had attacked me with nail guns. I squeezed my eyes closed on reflex, afraid to touch my forehead for fear of driving the roofing nails deeper into my brain.

My teeth and tongue were dry. My throat constricted but had nothing to swallow. I coughed and my brain nails screamed hello over the sound of the jackhammer sound coming from my chest.

First, water. Then ibuprofen. Then a mattress.

Swinging my legs to the ground, I forgot that the hammock had an aggressive auto-eject function. I pitched to the dewy grass and lay there long enough to feel fresh cold seep into my skin.

I am never drinking again.

Never.

Ever.

I climbed the back stairs carefully, concentrating on making sure my feet were well and truly on each riser before taking my next step. I sighed in relief that I'd made it to the top of the stairs without tripping. The screen door squeaked so loud I closed my eyes to buffer the sound. I floundered forward, toward water. Ibuprofen. A mattress.

The house was blissfully quiet once the door closed, muffling the raucous, predawn robin song. Water from the kitchen sink. Ibuprofen from the upstairs bathroom.

I can make it to the bed.

Please let Olivia sleep in this morning.

I made a wish that Adam would take pity on me and whisk her away when she crawled in to cuddle.

I tried to avoid the squeaky stairs but obviously misremembered which ones they were since I announced my impending arrival three times. I hoped Adam had slept with earbuds in so I didn't wake him.

The bedroom door was ajar, the room dark. I headed to the bathroom medicine cabinet and found the bottle of painkillers. I took two, not sure if they were normal or extra strength, and not willing to turn on a light. I didn't care whose toothbrush I grabbed or if I over-squeezed the toothpaste. Clean teeth felt heavenly. But I hadn't considered where I placed the glass on the counter, and bumped it when I reached to place the toothbrush back in its cup. It tumbled into the sink with a loud clatter.

"Worst thief ever," a voice from the bed mumbled.

I dropped my damp clothes on the floor and slid naked under the duvet. I tried to press my chilly body against Adam's warm one, but he blocked me. Pulled away.

"Too cold?"

He sighed. I couldn't make out his expression.

"How you feeling?" He asked. His tone was flat.

"Like I made some very bad life decisions last night."

He sighed again. "Yup."

I reached out to touch his chest but he rolled away and sat to get out of bed. "I'm awake now. You can sleep."

"No, stay." I grabbed his arm and pulled him down. "I'm awake too. We can be awake together."

I could tell he was looking at me as he inhaled long and slow, then forced the air out of his lungs in a quick, hard burst.

"No. I'm mad at you. But I'm not ready to talk. And you're too hungover. So, yeah. You sleep it off, and maybe by then, I'll have figured out … I don't know, just figured things out by the time you get up."

Acid pushed up from my stomach into my esophagus, forming a wall that blocked my throat so I couldn't swallow. Rubbing my neck, I moaned.

"Don't puke in the bed." Adam pulled on clothes and left me to die alone.

I silently counted the throbs in my head—one, two, three, four, five. The focus seemed to reduce the pain. Twenty-six. Twenty-seven. A replay of Adam's voice and tone—disappointment and anger—rose above the pounding. I silently counted louder. Forty-one. Forty-two. And then I must have dozed.

～

Clunk.

I awoke with a start.

"Coffee. When you're ready."

The room had lightened enough that I could see Adam's expression, his mouth a straight line, no hint of a smile. His eyes looked through me, not at me.

"Thanks. Do you have one too?"

"Already had mine." He turned to leave.

"Can we talk now?"

He stopped by the door but didn't face me.

"I'm feeling a lot better," I said, pressing my thumbs against my temples. I hoped the coffee would dissolve the small finishing nails that still occupied my brain cage.

His open-mouth sigh told me he didn't want to talk, but he moved toward the bed, lips taut, eyes avoiding mine. He sat on top of the duvet and leaned against the headboard.

Still under the blanket, I pulled myself to sitting and held the coffee between both hands. The mug wasn't much warmer than room temperature. I took a swig—the coffee was cold. But it had caffeine, so I took a longer draw and then put it down.

"You're mad," I said.

"No shit, Sherlock."

"I'm sorry. But Kama won't tell Dylan. I know she won't."

"And she doesn't have to because you already did."

I inhaled in surprise and choked on my spit. "No. I didn't. I haven't. I swear."

"Drunk is not an excuse for breaking a trust."

I tried to think. I didn't remember talking to Dylan.

"What did he say?" I asked. I knew it was wrong, but I hoped he agreed that Adam should use the messages in his argument.

"He told me to find out what the hell you were babbling about." He finally turned around. "Lucky for you, you were basically incoherent."

"Oh." I wondered if the disappointment showed on my face. "Will you tell him?"

"Lizzy, forget what you *think* you saw. Drop it."

It had been better than a month living this fake life, and even though there were so many reasons I should not be personally invested in the outcome, I was. It was becoming more and more difficult to remember that my role was temporary. As much as I did not want a daily reminder from Adam, I did need something to keep me focused on the only part of this adventure that I had control over.

Olivia came in quietly, handed me a kitten, and kept one for herself.

"Dadam said you don't feel good and that we have to be quiet. Apricot doesn't purr as loud as Marmalade, so you can cuddle her. She'll make you feel better."

I held the kitten in front of my face and snuggled into her soft fur while my wants and needs mounted a mighty battle in my mind. Once I'd calmed my emotions, I placed the kitten on the bed to roll around with her sister. I had an idea.

"Feel like making a vision board today, Olivia?"

"I don't know what that is." Her shoulders, hands, and eyebrows lifted in sync.

"It's like a poster with all the things you wish for. We find pictures that look like the things we want and glue them onto a poster. Then you hang it in your room so you can look at it every day and remind the universe what you want."

Olivia started bouncing and nodding as I spoke.

"Do you want to do one too?" I asked Adam.

He shook his head.

"You have to," Olivia whined, a little too loud for my head. I drank the rest of the cold coffee.

"I already have everything I've ever wished for." Adam picked up a kitten and wiggled his fingers in the furry belly.

Olivia's eyes widened. "Did you want kittens too?"

He smiled and said with so much sincerity, "All I want is what makes you happy."

"All I want is what makes you happy, too, Dadam. And you too, Mona."

I choked down a lump of guilt since my plan for the day was to make a poster of what would make *me* happy, with no concern for anyone else.

"What would make me happy right now is a long, hot shower. And once I'm done, we can go to the thrift store and find a stack of magazines to cut up. Sound good?"

"Great!" Olivia shrieked.

At least it felt like a shriek to my inflamed brain. I winced.

She whispered, "Sorry," and Adam scooped her off the bed and hung her by her feet as he carried her, this time actually shrieking, "Kittens! I need my kittens!" out the door.

I placed the small cats on the floor, and they bounded off after their loving leader.

By the time I got downstairs, the double dose of acetaminophen and ibuprofen had done their job and my head felt almost normal. I was surprised at how quiet the house was. A note on the kitchen table explained it:

Couldn't wait. Picking up magazines. Home soon.

Adam's writing.

At the very bottom was a row of *x*'s and *o*'s from Olivia.

I was starting to doubt my education and all that I'd been led to believe about the resilience of children after divorce. Or maybe I doubted my own resilience to bounce back. For sure, I doubted the odds that I'd ever have as perfect a real relationship as this temporary one.

Yup, I needed this new vision board. I thought about the last one I'd made—only seven months earlier. Among the images it had a beautiful, two-story, West Coast modern home and two kids. A little girl with red hair who looked about six and a baby of undefined gender.

I shuddered at the similarities between the house I was now living in and the little girl whose crusts I cut and left for the birds. I tried to remember what I was feeling when I made it. I'd been with Kama and Paige. We'd laughed a ton. But was I subconsciously imagining and telling the universe that I wanted a life with Adam and Olivia, or were those the

only pictures I could find that looked like a reasonable way
to be Future Lizzy?

I texted my bestie.

> Hey. Do you remember making vision
> boards with me and Paige last December?

KAMA

Of course.

> Did I mention Olivia specifically when I put
> the redhead little girl on my board?

KAMA

Yup.

My heart stopped and my vision clouded with the
sensation that I was going to faint.

KAMA

Why?

I gasped in a breath, realizing I'd stopped breathing.

> I'm an idiot.

KAMA

Sometimes ... Why?

> Making a new vision board with Olivia
> today.

KAMA

Careful what you wish for! Your witch
powers are enviable.

> Apparently. Love you.

Over an hour later, Adam and Olivia came home carrying two bags filled with magazines.

"We had to go to three places." Olivia dropped down beside me on the couch with great drama.

"The thrift store didn't have what I thought either of you would be looking for—mostly old fashion and celebrity gossip mags. So we went to a pet store where Olivia found six magazines with pictures she could imagine on her poster."

"Then we had to go to a weird place to get some for you. It was so boring." Olivia sighed.

"Travel agency," Adam added.

My smile was involuntary. "How did you know?"

"I had an inkling."

"And the third place?"

"Olivia convinced me to play too. So we dropped by that tourist kiosk in Gastown that has all the brochures for activities to do in and around Vancouver. I grabbed a bunch of outdoor-type tours and stuff."

And that's how we spent the rest of the day—cutting, gluing, and listening to Adam tell stories about all the crazy things he and his brothers did as kids.

The intention for my board was to picture being in all the places I'd wanted to visit, with a time frame. I added numbers to each location, a subtle way to suggest which month I wanted to be in that place—Big Ben with a 10 for October glued to the street below, the *Arc de Triomphe* with an 11 for November, and so on—since my error with my last vision board was not including the number 30.

Olivia's board was covered in pictures of bunnies, puppies, kittens, and birds.

"Looks like you want to be a vet when you grow up," Adam said.

"Nope. I just want more friends for Apricot and Marmalade."

I mouthed, "Good luck with that," to Adam, then asked, "What about yours? Is that a vision board or a memory board?"

It was covered with images of mountain biking, snowboarding, zip lining, hiking … all the outdoor activities.

He stuck it to the fridge with a magnet and stood back to look at it. "A bit of both, I guess."

It struck me that his vision and mine had no overlap. Mine no longer had a redheaded little girl on it. No baby. In fact, as I gave it a final look, I became aware that there wasn't a single person on my whole collage. Not. One.

I looked at the poster on the fridge. There were several pictures of kids. On Adam's memory-vision board, every image had people in it. Every. Single. One.

The difference was striking and sobering.

31

ADAM

It only took a couple days for Lizzy and me to reestablish the comfortable energy we'd had before the day she overstepped, snooped, and snitched. Although I couldn't forget that she'd betrayed my trust, we didn't speak of it again. Although I couldn't stop thinking about what she believed she'd seen in those messages, wondering how she'd gotten it so wrong, and hoping she was right.

Seeing the truth, that it really was Maggie who'd pushed to do the stunt, lightened the rock of guilt I'd been carrying, but the space that opened filled with anger at Maggie. How could she have put herself ahead of Olivia like that? How could she have risked not just her life but Dalton's, all for a three-minute adrenaline rush?

Even with this new knowledge, I held my ground with Lizzy and kept her at arm's length to make my point about promises before I gave in to my baser desires and we had sex.

On top of obsessing about the messages from Maggie wasn't enough stress, I battled with myself every day about my fraud of a relationship with Lizzy that felt like it had the potential to be something more than a temporary fix to a problem with a very clear end date. And even though I knew the ends would justify the means, I couldn't help worry that Olivia would be as—or more—heartbroken than I knew I was going to be about Lizzy leaving.

If I was awarded full legal guardianship, Dylan said it would be best if Lizzy continued to live with us for at least a month after the decision, so that it didn't look so blatantly like I'd gamed the system.

But if I lost, Lizzy's status as a fake wife and mom could end within a few days.

Dylan was even more confident in his ability to win my case. I was less so after meeting with the court-appointed psychiatrist. All of us had to meet with her one-on-one—me, Lizzy, Brigitte, and Olivia.

I wasn't worried about what Lizzy said or how she was rated, which I assume was being done. Nor was I concerned about what Olivia said since she was just as skippy-happy leaving the meeting as she was when she bounced into the office with her backpack full of "evidence," as she called it, that she should stay with me. There was a tense moment when I refused to let her take the kittens and she asked for my phone so she could call and tell the psychiatrist I was being unreasonable.

I only barely worried about my own interview. I mean, I didn't feel I ever had to stretch the truth or outright lie to look like I was doing a solid job. Even the story about how Olivia broke her arm didn't phase the psychiatrist.

What had me waking up in the night was the about-face Brigitte had made in the last weeks. It was like she was under some kind of spell, hypnotized to be an entirely different person after she left her meeting. It wigged me right out.

Since Brigitte had taken steps to better understand the needs of a five-year-old, Olivia had gone from begging me to go with her on her auntie playdates to looking forward to the time alone with Brigitte. She'd had several sleepovers and had come home looking rested enough for me to know Brigitte was, in fact, treating her like a little girl, not a miniature version of herself.

Lizzy threw a leg over my belly and pulled me back to the moment.

"What are you distracted by while I'm trying to be the only thing on your mind?"

"The normal."

"I don't like this new normal," she said, kissing my throat. She kissed down my chest, then stopped.

"Let's invite Brigitte over to talk. Maybe we can convince her to move back to Vancouver now that she's been here the whole summer and seems to be enjoying herself. You don't even know why she's so hell-bent on suddenly having Olivia in her life. If we knew that, it might help figure out a way you can both get what you want." She kissed a few inches lower.

I knew where she was headed and as much as it pained me, I stopped her.

"I know why." I needed to tell her so she'd understand why Brigitte couldn't be reasoned with. And I fully expected this would be the last time Lizzy would spend a night in my bed.

She sat up. If cocks could talk, mine would have screamed obscenities at me.

"The short version is that a long time ago in a place far, far away, Brigitte and I were together. As in, married."

"What?" Lizzy's shock ricocheted off my body and crashed around the room.

I placed my hand on her sternum to help calm both of our hearts.

"Married? Like, officially? For real not … like you and me?"

"Kind of? It was before Olivia, when Dalton and Maggie

were only dating. And … so were Brigitte and me. Those two were serious and got engaged. Brigitte and I weren't. At least, I wasn't.

"But Brigitte always wanted to be like Maggie—she just never quite made it. And the fact that the three of us had this cool stunt snowboarding thing happening together, she always felt left out. And she was. It was a fact."

Lizzy didn't speak. She didn't pull away. She didn't look disgusted, but she did look concerned.

"So, things were good with Brigitte. I was twenty-four, making a shit ton of money, had a pretty girlfriend who worshipped me." I winced. "Sorry. But she did. Dalton and Maggie were getting married, and I guess I got caught up in all the crazy, stupid love energy. So I thought, *what the hell*, and I proposed to Brigitte."

"Oh. Wow." Lizzy looked somewhat shell-shocked.

"Do you want to know more?"

She winced but nodded.

My arms crossed in front of my chest, a protective posture, expecting and deserving a punch of disgust. "We planned a double ceremony. And the day before the wedding"—I paused, not for effect, but to prepare myself for the onslaught of judgment—"I bailed."

"You didn't!" Lizzy's eyes bugged out but she didn't move otherwise. "No wonder she hates you."

"It gets worse," I said, steeling myself for the best part of the story. "She actually didn't hate me. She said she understood. And we kept dating. But we never talked about it. It was like nothing ever happened. So a year later, we'd been together at that point for three years, and things were fine. I was on the road for a month at a time, but always happy to come home to see her. For whatever reason, she asked me to marry her. And I said sure."

I paused to see if I could read what Lizzy was thinking. She looked curious, not enraged, so I kept talking.

"But after the fiasco of the first wedding, we just did paperwork. Maggie and Dalton were our witnesses."

"No ceremony? How did Nana and your family feel about that?"

"Aside from Dylan, who only found out a few months ago, none of them ever knew. We were in Switzerland working. Brigitte was just hanging out, but the rest of us were there doing stunts for a film. So the wedding was like a spontaneous Vegas thing, but in snow.

"The plan was to keep it quiet and do the whole real thing with the family in the summer and pretend like it was new."

"What happened?" Lizzy pushed her hand under my crossed arms and rubbed the area over my heart.

I was having a hard time understanding her reaction, which was as much a non-reaction as anything. I'd dreaded her knowing this. I covered her hand with mine, raised it to my lips, and kissed it before putting it back.

"Literally, as soon as we were legally married, it was like Brigitte became a different person. Maggie and Dalton had been trying to get pregnant. Brigitte always wanted what her sister had, and … it was not fun. At all. I think we lasted three weeks before Brigitte came home to Vancouver and I stayed in Europe, a few months longer than I needed to. Maggie got pregnant, so she and Dalton stopped stunt work. And I was like, that is not the life I want. I did not want kids. Not then, not ever. That's what I thought. Brigitte gave me an ultimatum, which I did not respond very well to."

"What ultimatum?"

"To quit. To be an adult and start a family. Or lose her."

"Ouch."

"Obviously I didn't quit. That's when she decided to move to London and do graduate studies. We were still married, and Maggie was sure we'd work things out once I met hers and Dalton's kid. And when Olivia was born, they made Brigitte and me her legal guardians. It made sense, I guess."

"Who ended it?" Lizzy asked. "And when?"

"This was more than six years ago. And it was a mutual agreement that we were done. The thing is, she sent me divorce papers before we did the stunt that ..." My throat strangled the words before I could say them. I suddenly felt very tired.

Lizzy didn't press for more. "That must have been such a hard time for you."

"Brigitte came home for the funeral. It was the first time we'd seen each other in about a year. I assumed we'd do the co-parent thing."

"But?"

"She wished me luck and flew back to the UK."

"What a bitch," Lizzy whispered into my neck.

I looked at her, confused. Was she actually siding with me?

"Well, I was the one who didn't ever want kids and let that ruin our marriage, so I guess it was her way of saying, 'Fuck you, asshole.'"

Lizzy shook her head. "Wait a minute. If you and Brigitte never officially divorced, then ..." She stopped midsentence.

I inhaled. Held my breath. Exhaled. "I signed the divorce documents in April. You should have seen Dylan's face."

"Surprised?"

"No, furious—on so many levels. And he's convinced that's what triggered her to start this fight. From what she gleaned from Olivia's overactive imagination and me finally giving her what she'd wanted for the last five years. I guess she assumed I was ready to move on and that's pissed her off."

Lizzy nodded, considering. "Do you think she actually wants to be Olivia's primary caregiver, her mom, or is this just tit for tat retaliation for breaking her heart?"

"You got me."

"Pretty shitty, either way."

"Come here." I pulled Lizzy into my lap, facing me. "I'm not understanding your reaction. You seem ... I don't know. Like you don't think I'm a total bastard."

She kissed me. She kissed me?

"Why would I think you're a bastard for not being bullied into being a parent when you didn't want to be? I think you were brave to stand your ground. Did you love her?"

I nodded. "I did."

"It's heartbreaking." Lizzy squinted at me. "Do you still love her?"

"No. Not at all. It's been years since I felt anything positive for her."

"Do you think she still loves you?"

"No. I can't imagine."

"I don't know. She's kind of acting like she still does. Fine line between love and hate and all that."

"That would be inconvenient." I leaned forward and kissed Lizzy's neck. She moaned and tilted her head to give me more access. Minutes later, I was deep inside Lizzy, and Brigitte was as far from my mind as London to Vancouver.

While we were showering the next morning, Lizzy proposed an idea.

"We should invite Brigitte over and have a social evening with her. Take Olivia to Nana's so we can speak freely."

"So I can swear freely, you mean."

"No! No, not at all. No swearing. I'm wondering, if you were to give Brigitte the space to express how she's feeling, to listen and not argue, if she might back off, at the very least tell you why she suddenly wants Olivia—but doesn't really want Olivia, given her boarding school plans."

"Play nice for a night," I said.

"Play nice for a night. Like *really* nice. Like *let her vent six years' worth of hurt* kind of nice."

"I don't think I can do that." It was the truth. Brigitte triggered me beyond reason.

"I'll be there as a buffer, a conversation director, a mediator if needed. But I don't think you will. I have faith in you. You're so good at putting yourself in my shoes and empathizing with me. Just do the same for her. Try to remember that you loved her once."

I buried my face in the spray of water and considered. Tilting my head to the side, I said, "What could possibly go wrong?"

Lizzy laughed but answered with a serious tone, "Nothing worse than going to court and having a conservative judge give guardianship to Brigitte. So, yes? Shall we do this? Tonight? Maybe, if we're lucky, avoid the whole court fiasco altogether?"

"Do you think Dylan should be here?" I wondered aloud.

"I think Dylan should definitely *not* be here! This isn't about lawyers, it's about healing a broken heart."

I texted Brigitte as soon as I was out of the shower. Proposed she come by at seven, after dinner. She replied within an hour. Said she'd be here at four. I almost sniped that four wasn't the offer, but Lizzy told me the meeting time was not a hill worth dying on.

Lizzy made a shopping list with supplies for what was turning into an intimate dinner with the two women I'd made love to more times than all the others combined: the woman I'd loved enough to marry who I now wished I'd never met, and the woman who was kind enough to marry me, who I might have started to wish would change her mind and give me a chance to be a real husband. It was emotional whiplash.

Nana, as always, was more than happy to have Olivia spend the night. Olivia, on the other hand, complained the whole drive over that it wasn't fair that I got to have dinner with Mona and Auntie Brigitte.

"You're one hundred percent right, pumpkin. It's not fair at all. But I don't get to decide this one. Mona's in charge tonight."

"Humph. She bosses you around too much."

"What?" I almost drove into a parked car since my head swung around to see who was sitting in my kid's car seat. "Why would you say that?"

"Auntie Brigitte said that Mona is bossy and is pushing you over."

I had to swallow my rage. "And what do you think? Do you think Mona is bossy?"

"Well, she does tell us to do a lot of things. But ..." She shrugged her small shoulders. "They're always fun or delicious things, so I don't mind."

After I left Olivia with Nana, I drove around the corner and sat in the van for a solid ten minutes, calming down. How dare she? Lizzy was not bossy, and I was not a pushover.

By the time I got home, Lizzy had made a damned impressive charcuterie platter. There was a bit of fruit, but it was virtually all meat, cheese, and vegetables to accommodate Brigitte's ketogenic diet. When I pointed out that the bubbly blush she'd asked for the last time I let her sit in my house was not ketogenic, Lizzy scowled and told me not to judge.

"You're not the boss of me." I scowled back.

"Just play nice. This isn't about being right, it's about giving Brigitte the floor and figuring out what she needs to hear from you that will keep her from taking Olivia away."

~

An hour and one full bottle of prosecco into Lizzy's "Give Brigitte the Floor" tour, Brigitte's tone had softened. Her anger seemed dulled by an emotion I'd never experienced with her: regret?

"Maggie always did what she wanted, and I did what I should. She was happy, and I was … doing what I should. I wanted what she had. Being pregnant made her so happy." She was facing Lizzy, answering Lizzy's questions about her childhood. "And then after she was born? It was painful to look at her social feeds. Her life was so perfect."

Lizzy gave me a look, the "tell her the truth, you idiot" glare.

I scowled my silent but loud and clear reply.

"I'm sure Maggie had regrets too," Lizzy said. "Big decisions often have consequences we may not have considered. And I'm sure your sister had days and weeks when life wasn't exactly what she wanted."

"Lizzy," I warned.

Brigitte shook her head. "You didn't know her. Her socials were—"

"Her social media feed was exactly like everyone else's—painting a picture of the life she wanted, the way she wanted to feel and look all the time."

"Elizabeth," I warned. "You didn't know her."

"Probably," Lizzy added. "I assume she was like most normal people. Don't you do that, Brigitte, just share the highlight reel of your life?"

Brigitte scoffed. "I'm not on social media anymore."

"Oh." Lizzy sat back in her chair, looking defeated.

"Lizzy's got a master's in psychology so she likes to psychoanalyze everything." I smiled to make my voice sound lighter than my mood felt.

"I don't have a highlight reel. That's why I got off. Because you're right. And I had nothing to share that made me feel good about my life."

"I'm sorry," Lizzy said. Then she looked at me and made the face with the laser eyes.

"Me too," I added.

"So, Adam told me you're as good as married. Is he British?"

"The man who thinks he knows it all is wrong again. You don't see him here, do you?"

I looked at Lizzy and returned the death glare, since she was the one now making the conversation difficult.

Brigitte continued. "It looks like married life is treating you two well."

Lizzy and I looked at each other and answered simultaneously.

"Yes," she said.

"No," I said.

"What?" Brigitte and Lizzy said in unison with identical expressions of surprise.

32

LIZZY

Adam took a huge risk. He spilled the beans. Told Brigitte that our marriage was fake. Legal but not legitimate. If Dylan had been here, I'm sure Adam would have ended up in the hospital, having his arm torn off as his lawyer brother dragged him from the room.

Brigitte listened with polite silence.

Once it was clear that Adam had finished his strip tease of our secret, Brigitte appeared to soften. She tilted her head and asked, "To be one hundred percent clear, this relationship you have with Lizzy is just for show?"

The pause between her question and Adam's answer felt like an eternity. I bit my tongue to keep from filling the dead air. I stared hard at my cuticles to avoid catching either of their eyes. My body buzzed with the need to jump from my chair and into Adam's arms and say, "No! It's more than that."

"The marriage was strategic." He said the word with conviction.

"Strategic," Brigitte repeated. "What was the plan? Stay together until I left?"

"Basically."

Again, silence hung between them. I wondered if they were still aware that I was in the room. I dared not move. My breathing was shallow and slow. Silent as a broken refrigerator.

"So," Brigitte finally said, "what would happen if I decided to stay in Vancouver? To not return to London?"

"Is that a pain-in-the-ass rhetorical question, or are you seriously considering staying?" Adam asked.

I cringed at his tone, raised my eyes without moving my head and caught Brigitte raising her open palms in the air, an expression of "What difference does it make?"

"What the hell does that mean?" I could hear the anger rising in Adam's voice. I was impressed he'd kept calm for as long as he had, but I knew he wouldn't be able to hear the subtext of her question.

"Brigitte," I said in a quiet voice, "what might make you decide to stay?"

"A second chance," she said, looking directly at Adam.

Suddenly, the air was alive with the sound of a thousand squealing dental drills. My hands flew to my head. I pressed my index fingers hard against my ears to block the attack. I looked up, expecting Brigitte and Adam to be reacting to the sound too. They gawked at me like I was insane.

"You don't hear that?" My voice didn't sound like my own.

"Hear what?"

"That high-pitched whine. It's … it's so loud."

"Sounds like you have a migraine coming on," Brigitte offered. "Probably the prosecco. The lower quality ones can do that."

I registered the insult but didn't have the ability to respond. "Going to take a painkiller. Lie down." I stood on wobbly legs and made my way up the stairs to the bedroom.

It took at least a half hour for the sound to dissipate, but eventually it did. As I lay on the bed, looking at the vision boards Adam and I had made almost three weeks earlier, I knew that the feeling of possession I had over this man—of his attention, his heart, his family—was not mine to feel.

Strategic. That's what he'd said. That's what we had. A strategic relationship that served us both. At least it served me. In under a month, I'd be standing in front of Big Ben, doing the Harry Potter guided walking tour and taking a river cruise down the Thames.

But as I looked from my vision of a dream future to Adam's, the two images blended, and I saw myself taking pictures of happy couples in front of all the attractions I was going to see. I dropped into the scene. Newlyweds, still in their wedding clothes, approached. "Excuse me," the woman said, "you don't look busy. Can you please take our picture?"

I watched myself take photos of a dozen different couples and families and groups of friends. And when they were gone, I tried to take a selfie. I stood with my back to St. Paul's Cathedral and extended my arm, but couldn't get myself and the whole landmark into a shot. I looked around to find someone to ask. I was alone. All alone.

Was this really my dream, to travel around the world on my own?

You won't be on your own, I told myself. *You'll meet other people on their gap-year adventures.*

I saw myself again, sitting alone in a restaurant. A group of young people with accents from all over the world sat nearby, laughing and sharing stories. Somehow I knew they'd met at the hostel. But I was staying in a hotel. A room with one bed and no way to meet new travel friends.

I spent at least an hour immersed in my vision board, replaying my imagined, solitary tourist experiences in front of every landmark, in every city, in every country I was planning to visit.

Then I tried to imagine myself inside Adam's vision

board, where every picture was focused around family and friends. Sure, they were skiing and doing outdoor activities, but it wasn't the locations that he'd chosen pictures of—empty slopes or beautiful forests—it was the experience of doing things he loved with people, presumably future people, he'd love.

I didn't need that kind of image on my future vision board because I'd already brought that future to life for myself. That was the vision I'd imagined seven months earlier, now a reality. But in a month, maybe less now, my original vision board of a life in a house with a little redheaded girl would be a memory board.

I took the two posters from where they leaned against the wall on the dresser and carried them downstairs. I needed to know which of these visions was a closer match to the life Brigitte was looking for.

Of all the things I expected to find at the bottom of the stairs—that Brigitte had left in a huff, that Adam had stormed from the room and left her to drink alone, that they were quietly screaming at each other—what I faced was something that never would have made it onto the list.

33

ADAM

I wasn't sure if there was a word to describe how I felt at this moment. Relief was only a small part of it. It was like I could breathe again after having been holding my breath under an avalanche, compressed by three tons of snow, waiting to know if I'd be rescued or never found.

To say Brigitte surprised me would have been the understatement of the century. I was not normally an emotional man, but her admission moved me to tears. And when I stood to hug her, she accepted me with open arms and tears of her own.

A squeak on the stairs reminded me that we weren't alone. I looked up to see Lizzy staring at us, silent—until the poster boards fell from her hand and landed on the floor with a gentle *kathunk*.

I released Brigitte and guided her to turn and face Lizzy. We stood, shoulder to shoulder, wiping our faces in unison.

"Well, I guess I should go. Let you …," Brigitte nodded toward Lizzy without finishing her sentence.

She picked up her purse, gave me one more full-body hug, smiled at Lizzy, then let herself out.

"I, um, I …" Lizzy sat on the bottom stair and picked up

the posters. "I didn't mean to interrupt your ... your reunion. I'll go back upstairs."

"No, wait." I grabbed Lizzy's wrist before she was out of reach. She tumbled toward me and I caught her before she fell.

"Let go." Lizzy gave her hand a sharp twist and jerked out of my hold.

"Lizzy, wait."

"What? What do you want from me? You and Brigitte have reconciled. I assume that means she's not taking Olivia anywhere. I'm happy for you. Now, can I please go lie down?"

I waited until the bedroom door clicked closed, then followed. Before I'd pushed the door fully open, she said, "Please leave me alone." The tone of her voice was a virtual door slam in my face.

I hesitated but pushed into the icy wall.

"Adam, seriously, I don't want to talk right now."

"Not asking you to talk. But will you listen?"

"No."

"Yes."

She turned away and pulled both a pillow and the duvet over her head.

I would have laughed if she hadn't looked and sounded so miserable.

"Mona. Elizabeth. Sheila. Hillhouse."

A muffled yell came from the pile of bedding. "Bug off. Leave me alone."

Although she hadn't experienced it in the two months she'd been living with Olivia and me, I had loads of experience dealing with tantrums. And enough counseling conversations with Olivia's therapist to feel confident in my response.

I walked over to her side of the bed, pulled down the covers, wrestled the pillow from her hands, and pulled her writhing body up and into my arms. I whispered, "You're safe," and held her tight until she had no more fight left in her and she collapsed, sobbing against my chest.

Once her breathing was again normal, save a hiccup now and then, I let her go and encouraged her to face me on the bed. We sat cross-legged, and I pulled her knees over mine. I held her chin with one hand to keep her from leaning away, stroked her cheek with the other to strengthen our connection.

"It's over," I said, fighting every emotion known to man. Or at least every emotion known to this man.

"I know."

"You heard us talking?"

"No. I saw you kissing."

"What?" I recoiled at the thought of kissing Brigitte. "There was no kissing." I lifted her face to look at me. "There was a hug. A long-overdue hug."

"You're giving your marriage a second chance."

"Are you mad? No. God. Not even close. No, Lizzy, I am not giving it a second chance. She was hugging me to say thank you for having been as miserable as she was for the months after she left. She thought I was happy about her leaving. And that hurt her and made her angrier than anything, feeling like she meant nothing to me.

"And I was hugging her because she said she was dropping the guardianship challenge. She doesn't want to be a full-time mom. She never did. You were right. This was all about hurting me. But she's over it.

"You know what the funny thing is? If I hadn't married you, she would have dropped this two months ago. She started the challenge as soon as I sent her the divorce papers, to make a point that the only reason I had Olivia in my life was because she and I had been married. She said she wanted me to remember that."

Lizzy shook her head. "She could have just called and said so."

"She was hurt. She was angry. She was jealous that I got to have the perfect life and hers was falling apart. Again."

"And now what? She's not jealous of your perfect life anymore?"

"Well, no, since it's not a perfect life. Being a single dad, working as a volunteer gym teacher? I don't think that's anyone's definition of a perfect life."

"But …" Lizzy's eyebrows knit together and her mouth moved without sound for several seconds. "You're not a single dad anymore."

I was going to need a case of scotch to get through this day.

"I know. These last two months have given me the best summer of my life."

"So, let's have the best autumn and winter and—"

Lord have mercy. "Lizzy."

"We don't have to end it." She stared at my leg.

"But we do. I promised I'd be the strong one."

"But I didn't know—"

"Lizzy, you made me swear. We knew this would be hard, but I cannot, I will not let you give up your dream to travel."

"I was wrong. I don't want to leave," she whispered. Her face was flushed, and tears formed a solid line down her cheeks. She looked up and the pain in her eyes made me feel sick. "I love you, Adam. And I love Olivia."

She knew I loved her and it was what I wanted to tell her, but the phrase I knew I had to say flashed in my mind's eye. And even though I didn't believe a word, I made sure my voice was strong and confident when I lied, "Why? So you can turn out like your mother?"

The words tasted bitter on my lips.

She recoiled and her body contracted into itself.

I wanted to tell her that not one single ounce of my being believed she had one single narcissistic gene in her body. But I couldn't. I wasn't allowed. We'd made a deal, and as painful as it was to fulfill it, this was the agreement.

The anger I felt toward her mother was immeasurable and unproductive. I forced it aside. Since nothing in our agreement said I couldn't comfort her after I spoke those lies, I placed my hand on her back. She leaned into it. In my mind, I imagined the conversation I wanted to have, hoping she was reading my mind.

"You're right." She relaxed into my hug.

"Tired?" I asked.

"Exhausted."

"Me too." I pulled off my T-shirt, shorts, and boxer briefs. Once I was naked, I helped her out of her clothes and pulled the blanket over us.

I lay on my side, expecting to spoon her, but she faced me, then pressed her chest and stomach to mine, nesting her head in the crook of my neck. Arms wrapped around each other, we lay in silence until I thought she was asleep. Her breathing had settled. Her fingers had stopped moving across my skin. I was startled when she spoke. Even more so that her voice sounded totally normal, as if she were asking if I'd like cream in my coffee.

"Would you like me to move out now?"

Not now, not ever.

"No. Unless you feel like you need to," I said.

"I don't know. Will it be easier or harder to leave if I stay for another month?"

Sugar or Splenda? How could she sound so calm?

"Easier," I said, being one hundred percent selfish, not wanting to lose her any sooner than I had to. "Easier for Olivia since it will give us time to explain what's happening," I added, believing that.

"Yeah, you're probably right. Can we still have sex, or do you think it would be best not to?"

Would you like apple pie with your coffee?

"If you're sleeping in this bed, we're having sex."

God, I'm an asshole.

"Okay."

I'll be right back with your order.

She tilted her head and exhaled hot breath into my ear. She knew there was a direct line of communication between my ear and my cock—it rose. "I'm glad." Then she kissed my neck and leaned up on her elbow. "I'm so happy Olivia gets to keep her family."

She trailed kisses from my chin to my belly button. "And more than a little sad it means this has to end."

Her mouth moved below my beltline and lightly brushed against my hard-on. I moaned and arched my hips toward her lips. She pulled away. "But I'm happy that I got as much time with you as I did."

34

LIZZY

As I was about to take Adam in my mouth, he rolled away.

"Lizzy, stop. I can't do this." He pulled himself to sitting and lifted my shoulders with him, so I was straddling his legs, facing him. "Look at me. You're nothing like your mother. I don't want you to leave. Let's give this relationship a real chance. I honestly believe we have what it takes to be an actual married couple."

And just like that, all the blood that had been pulsing in my lower parts rushed to my brain, pumped hard in my ears. Pounding. Pounding. Pounding.

This was what I wanted, to make it permanent. To be Adam's real wife. But I didn't feel happy. Or relieved.

I focused on trying to label what I was feeling. It was just one thing: anger. *Come on psych degree, help me out here.* I'm angry because I'm scared. I'm scared because I've been hurt. I've been hurt because …

My mother's put-down answered.

You ruin everything.

I ruin everything.

There was comfort in the familiar thought that had done

a damn good job of keeping me safe. My heart rate slowed and my body relaxed. I addressed Adam without emotion.

"We had a deal. We *have* a deal. And for better or worse, whether I caused the problem or solved it or both, I held up my end. Olivia is safe, and now you have to tell me to leave."

"Lizzy, we didn't know—"

"Adam, I *do* know." I suddenly felt very tired. "So you have a choice. If you want me to stay for the next month, you have to promise you'll support me in leaving. If you can't do that, I'll leave now."

I pushed off the bed and hid myself in the bathroom since I was now shaking. It was exhausting being strong. I started the shower and stood with my eyes closed, focused on breathing, the voice in my head congratulating me for being so brave. Mom would be proud of me. Hell, I was proud of myself.

The glass door opened.

"Room for a big dick in here?"

I looked at his penis and shook my head. "I've seen bigger."

He smiled. "Yeah, well Belvedere's kind of freaked out. He just got yelled at. I think … he's saying that if you whispered a few nice words to him, he'd show you how big of a dick he really is."

"Worst blowjob sales pitch ever." I couldn't help smirking.

"Maybe an apology handshake?" He looked toward his cock, which was coming to life, then took my hand and wrapped it around his shaft. "He's saying he's sorry, in case you don't speak dick."

I gave him a squeeze, then dropped him. "All I can say is that I'm really glad the asshole I left in the bedroom didn't want to apologize too."

That made Adam laugh. It was contagious. I let him hug

me and accepted a kiss that recalibrated my circulatory system. Any blood that might still have been protesting in my ears beelined south.

"Gigi says she feels left out. She'd like an apology too."

"With pleasure," he said, turning off the water. He didn't bother with towels, lifting me from the shower and laying me on the bed.

"I'm wet," I whispered.

Adam dragged a fingertip from my neck, down my body. He grazed my clit and swirled around my opening.

"You certainly are." His eyes darkened and he licked his lips.

I mimicked the movement of his tongue with my own.

"I'd like to lick you dry."

I could barely breathe. I steadied my voice. "I think what you're planning will have the opposite effect."

He groaned and dropped his face to my folds. I grabbed his hair in my fists as the breadth of his shoulders pushed my thighs open.

Adam gave me a long, slick lick, top to bottom. I moaned, low and long. My back arched, seeking deeper contact, which Adam hungrily gave me. My hips lifted off the bed and I answered his attentions with an involuntary cry, grinding shamelessly against him, rocking against his mouth. The vibration of his growl against my core set me off, and I jolted, unable to breathe. And then lights and colors burst behind my eyelids, like fireworks going off in an R-rated Disney film.

Please don't let me ruin this.

The next day, the mail lady arrived with a registered letter for Adam, who was out with Brigitte, buying Olivia a new backpack and school supplies.

"He's not here. I'll sign for it," I said, reaching to take it.

"Sorry. Has to be signed by Mr. Rhodes himself." She scrawled on a delivery notice and placed it with the rest of our mail. "He can pick it up at this post office tomorrow between 8 a.m. and 4 p.m."

We spent the whole afternoon and night wondering what the letter could be. Adam called Brigitte. She swore she hadn't sent it.

"Have you entered a Publishers Clearing House contest? Maybe you've won one meel-lion dollars." I did my best Dr. Evil impersonation with my baby finger pressed to the side of my mouth.

"I'd throw you the best send-off party ever."

I deflated at the mention of my leaving and maybe even pouted a little. Adam stood from the table and motioned for me to stand too. I did. He pulled me into a hug and whispered, "You're going to have the time of your life."

Turned out the letter was from the school board. Adam's tenure as the volunteer gym teacher had come to an end, and they were giving him his official notice.

On the one hand, I was sad for him since he seemed disappointed. On the other, I looked forward to a full month of weekdays where he and I could hang out, just the two of us, while Olivia was in school.

Since I'd never been a tourist before, Adam suggested he teach me.

"That's ridiculous." I laughed. "What in the world do I need to learn about paying an entry fee and looking at things?"

"Here's your first lesson: that is not what being a good tourist is. It's settled. For the next four weeks, I will be your official Metro Vancouver tour guide. You are going to be a VIP tourist in your own city."

Adam created our itinerary, which had something to do virtually every day until the day before I left.

"This looks exhausting," I complained.

"This is traveling, darlin'. You're not going to be spending your time watching Disney movies in your hotel room. I hope."

"No, but—"

"No but nothing. Would you hike the Pacific Northwest Trail without first doing smaller hikes? Building your stamina? Breaking in your boots?"

"No …"

"Consider this your training period for nine months of trekking around Europe."

"I'll be exhausted before I even get on the plane," I argued.

"Prepared," Adam countered.

For three weeks Adam and I spent hours each day rubbing shoulders with tourists. He took me to all the places in the city I'd never bothered to visit and some that I had been to. But with Adam as my comrade in adventure even places that sounded boring—like the Maritime Museum—had me pee-my-pants laughing while he taught me the ins and outs of being a globetrotter.

"You want a picture of yourself in front of that sculpture." Adam pointed to a giant metal monstrosity. "Look around. Who are you going to ask to take it for you?"

"You dummy. The guy I'm sightseeing with."

Adam rubbed his forehead like he had a headache. "You want the handsome devil in the picture with you, so you never forget him."

I stuck my arm out to take a selfie. He gently pushed it down. "And you want the whole sculpture in the shot … work with me Hillhouse. Look around and pick someone to take our picture."

I pointed to an older couple. Adam made me ask them. The shot was terrible.

"Try again," he said.

Forty minutes, eleven photographers, and only one good shot later Adam asked, "So what did this lesson teach you?"

"That if I ever go traveling with you, I'm hiring a professional photographer to shadow us. Oh, and to not talk to handsome men, in case they end up being bossy like you."

Adam cocked his head. "I'll accept those answers."

After my lesson in how to get great tourist pictures, I asked people at every destination to take photos of us. Each evening I added something to the new holiday memory board collage I'd decided to make for Adam.

"You've slept in and are running late for the bus to take you to your scheduled entry time at the Guggenheim Gallery. You have five minutes to pack your day bag. Go!"

That was Adam's Week Three, end-of-week test to make sure I'd been paying attention.

"What do I get if I pass?" I asked, not making any indication I was about to jump out of bed and rush into action.

"Wrong question," he said with a wink. "What you *should* be asking is what you'll have to give *me* if you fail."

"A kiss, maybe?" I sat up, straddled his belly, then pressed my mouth to his. I loved kissing this man. Every kiss started slow and deliberate, like I was a new flavor he wanted to understand before he committed. My body responded, filled with tingling energy that increased as our tongues danced. His kisses left me breathless. Every. Single. Time.

He turned his head and whispered in my ear, "You missed your bus."

"I decided to take the underground train," I said, reaching behind me to find his fully engorged cock. I stroked him a few times, then positioned myself to take him in.

We made love, just like we had virtually every morning for the last two-and-half months. It was a beautiful way to start the day—skin-to-skin contact and a solid hit of dopamine, oxytocin, and serotonin—relaxed, happy, and connected.

As I caught my breath, lying beside Adam, his hand running along my collarbone, I tried to remember how my body and mind felt before this marriage of convenience so I could start to prepare for the after. The emotions that hardened in my chest caught me by surprise, and I gasped.

Adam's hand stilled. "You okay?"

"Just a little ..." I panted, "panic attack?"

"Come here." Adam pulled me into a bear hug. "Don't worry. The buses run every ten minutes. And whatever you've left behind can be replaced."

I knew he meant it as a gentle joke to help me relax, but my immediate thought was that I was leaving behind the only things I actually wanted to take with me on my adventure—my fake husband and stepdaughter.

And I was certain they were irreplaceable.

Olivia's sixth birthday coincided with the week she had her cast removed, which was only six days before my flight was scheduled to take off, so Adam organized a massive party with the whole family, including Brigitte.

Since still only Kama and Dylan knew our marriage was fake, people struggled to understand how and why I was leaving for nine months without my new-to-me family.

"Let me get this straight," Josh said. "You married Lizzy

knowing she'd be leaving three months after your wedding? That makes no sense, man."

Adam was quick and confident in his reply. "The heart wants what it wants. And Lizzy's heart wants to fulfill a lifetime dream of globe-trotting before she settles down for good. I respect that." He wrapped his arm around my waist and pulled me in for a public-appropriate kiss.

My mind was a mess. The very fact that I believed his implied message—that he expected me to come home to him, his unspoken lie that we would still be married when I stepped on the plane—made me question what the hell I was doing.

"Happy wife, happy life, right?" I said, looking up at him, wishing he could read my mind and tell me what I was actually thinking and feeling, since I was beyond confused.

My last week as Mrs. Rhodes passed quickly. We pulled Olivia out of school for several days so she could experience the tourist-in-your-own-town fun we were still having. But, on the Friday before my Saturday afternoon flight, we dropped her off for class, much to her displeasure.

Standing outside the building where we had a scheduled meeting, I plucked up the courage to say what had been on my mind every waking hour for the last week.

"I know that when I get on the plane, you'll be free to pick up"—I paused as my brain completed the sentence with *"other women"* but said—"your normal life. And I don't expect you to wait five years for me. Hell, I don't expect you to wait five weeks. Five days would be nice." I tried to laugh, but I could feel the downward turn of my eyebrows as the reality of what I was saying tore at my heart like blackberry thorns.

"You're far more likely to meet someone while you're

traveling. Hell, of course, you will. I have no doubt. I hold no illusions that you won't find someone to share your hotel room costs with by the time you're in France."

I shook my head. The very thought of sleeping with another man repulsed me. I was about to say, "What if we wait? Don't sign the divorce papers quite yet? Just in case …," but Adam interrupted the thought.

"Ready or not, right?" He took my hand, and we entered the law offices where Dylan worked.

35

____

ADAM

"Bro, you look like hell." Dylan put his hand on my shoulder. "You're sure this is what you want?"

I shook my head and sighed, tilting my chin toward Lizzy who was walking a few steps ahead of us toward his office.

Dylan raised his voice so she could hear him. "You don't *have* to end this, you know? You two seem pretty damned happy to me."

I wanted to answer, to say, "I am. We are. I agree. We don't have to," but Lizzy was in the driver's seat.

Lizzy turned around. "Yes, actually, we do." She looked at me with eyes that said the opposite. But I'd promised her I'd stay true to my promise, in case she lost the will to hold fast, which, last night, she admitted she had. She'd sat on the edge of the bed with her suitcase open and clothes placed in piles around it.

"I don't want to leave."

There hadn't been room for me to sit beside her, but I needed her in my arms. "Stand."

I picked her up, then dropped myself into the space she'd

left behind, pushed a pile of clothes over, and leaned against the headboard with her facing me on my lap.

I held her face in my hands. Stroked her cheeks. She closed her eyes and leaned the weight of her head into my palm. We kissed. Slow and intentional.

"Don't go." I breathed the words into her open lips, like a wizard casting a spell.

Lizzy froze, then leaned away. "You promised."

"I shouldn't have," I said.

Her eyes glazed over and she shook her head. "Don't. Adam, don't do this."

"I want a new contract. One that doesn't end. Stay. Please."

She pushed herself off my lap and spun so fast, her feet were on the floor before I reacted.

"Stop it!" she yelled. I was surprised the fire in her eyes didn't evaporate the tears.

"But you don't want to end it either. You just said you don't want to leave. So stay. It's what we both want."

"You know why I have to go," she snapped.

"Yeah, well, I think it's a stupid reason."

"Yeah, well, this isn't about you. It's about me. It's about Olivia."

"That's where you're wrong. This isn't about you, me, or Olivia. This is about your mom. And I don't know how many ways I have to tell you until you believe it, but you. Are. Not. Your. Mother."

She stared at me like she was trying to understand a foreign language. Her voice was quiet, but her tone was sharp.

"You have no idea, Adam. None. Maybe I'm not like her today, but that's because all this is new and shiny and fun. We haven't had to deal with one single challenge since we met. We have no idea how we'll do when we have to deal with emotionally hard—"

"Are you serious?" I snapped back. "We haven't had to deal with anything hard? Wasn't the prospect of losing Olivia emotionally hard enough for you?"

Anger filled my blood and pumped into my heart, which took the feeling and circulated it as exhaustion into my body. This come here, come here, go away dance with Lizzy was brutal.

Lizzy shook her head. Her posture and voice softened. "Adam, that's the thing. Olivia has never been mine, so she was never mine to lose. From day one, we both knew that whether you won or lost full guardianship, I was only a temporary fixture in this family. The stakes for me were the same, regardless of the outcome. So I was never *facing* the prospect of losing her; losing her was a done deal from the start. Was it hard? Yeah, of course, it was. But we didn't face that together. And that's what I mean. We haven't had to face any struggles *together*."

I knew she was wrong, but I couldn't think of any examples to prove it to her.

"Adam, I love you. And I love Olivia. You know that, right? And I knew that's what would happen if I put myself in this situation. That's what I do. I fall when someone shows me affection. But we both agreed that this relationship had an end date. You have your reasons, I have mine."

"My reasons were bullshit. I was wrong." I moved toward her with my arms open, inviting a hug.

She stepped away, crossing her arms over her chest. "But mine still stand. I can't stay. As much as I want to, in this moment, we'll both regret it when I change my mind and decide I don't want to be a mother anymore. And the person who will suffer most is Olivia. I love her too much to put her through that."

"Do you hear yourself? Seriously, do you hear what you're saying? That's crazy talk. She's going to suffer now, you know. You're not preventing anything. All you're doing is changing the timeline. Oh, and making sure something that might never happen does. Lizzy, let your fear go. Stay."

She inhaled a shaky breath then turned, pressed her back against my stomach, and wrapped my arms around her ribs. She pointed with her free hand to the vision boards standing on the dresser.

"Is that not proof enough?"

"A craft project?" I didn't even try to hide my derision.

"Do you see anything in common between our vision boards? One single thing?"

She waited for me to answer. I knew what she was trying to prove, but I still wasn't buying it. "There—" I pointed. "You have a picture of a yurt. I have a family camping. One thing in common. You want to go camping in a yurt? Let's do it. I'm all for it."

She pulled my arm away from her body and faced me.

"It's not enough, Adam, and you know it."

Now I was mad. "No, apparently I don't know anything. I love you. You love me. I thought what we had was real. Sure feels real to me. And you think, just because you have pictures of tourist destinations and I have outdoor adventure pictures, this"—I waved between us—"is all bullshit?"

"You're not hearing me."

"What am I not hearing, Lizzy? Tell me. Make me understand because I'm too stupid to see what's right in front of me."

"This, what we have, is not real. We did an amazing job making it seem real. And now, I have to go. That was the deal—"

"Screw the deal."

"No. You don't get to change the deal. You don't get to take that away from me." She pointed to her goddamn vision board. "I have wanted to travel to Europe since as long as I can remember. My mom used to show me pictures of all the places she would have gone if she hadn't had me. All the interesting, beautiful, historic places."

"That is your mother's dream."

"And then it became mine."

We stood in silence for a long minute, not touching each other.

"When you come home—"

"Adam, I want to sign the divorce papers. Do you think Dylan will do that for us? Tomorrow, on such short notice?"

"But we said—"

"I changed my mind. You broke your promise. You were supposed to be the strong one. I can't have this hanging as an open circle. You saw what it did to Brigitte. I don't want to end up like her."

"For god's sake, you won't end up like Brigitte. You're not like her. You're not like your mother. You are Mona Elizabeth Sheila bloody Hillhouse."

She stared at me, impassive in her expression, then walked to the bedside table and picked up her phone. She tapped a few times, then held it to her ear.

"Hey, can Adam and I sign divorce papers tomorrow morning?"

I wanted to scream. I wanted to grab her phone and throw it out the window. I punched the wall hard enough to get her attention, leaving a small but visible dent in the sheetrock. "Stop. Hang up."

She shook her head. "We changed our minds." She nodded. "Eleven is good. Thanks, Dylan. I owe you one."

And so started one of my top three worst night's sleep ever. Number one belonged to the day Dalton and Maggie died; number two was the night I spent in the hospital, keeping Nana company while Granddad was dying.

My brain knew Lizzy wasn't dead or going to die and that in nine months, maybe a year, she'd fly home. Probably. And I'd be able to talk to her again. But my brain was small and weak compared to all the tense muscles and heightened nerves in my body that were signaling that this was a death. And it wasn't wrong in the sense that when Lizzy got onto that plane, it would truly be the end of us.

Up until last night's conversation, we'd decided to leave the paperwork in place since it wasn't as if either of us planned to meet anyone or get married in the next few months. It was the path of least effort, and it suited me since it meant that at some point in the hopefully near future, we'd be forced together to have a conversation about how great a team we'd been and whether it still made sense to walk away from each other just because Lizzy's mother had infected her with crap ideas.

"Adam," both Lizzy and Dylan said.

I'd been staring out his window as Lizzy signed the papers. I turned to see that she had tears in her eyes.

"We don't have to—"

She put the pen in my hand, but it felt like she'd stabbed me in the heart with it. I didn't read the document. I didn't have to. I trusted Dylan. Hell, I trusted Lizzy. And if they'd pulled a fast one on me and had me sign over all my money, I didn't care. They could have it.

I signed, dropped the pen on his desk, and walked out before I acted on what I was feeling, which was to go toe-to-toe with Dylan and box out these emotions. Or more specifically, let him punch the shit out of me so I could feel the kind of pain I was much more comfortable with—a broken bone, bruised ribs, torn ligaments.

I left the law office as double divorcé and a promise to myself that I would never, *ever* get married again.

～

Our last evening together was quiet, aside from the singing we did with Olivia's favorite movie soundtrack. Lizzy and I went to bed at the same time we put Olivia in hers. We didn't have sex, didn't really even talk much. We just lay in each other's arms until we fell asleep, which for me was well after midnight.

In the morning we did make love, but it felt cautious, tentative. I stayed in my head since I was afraid of what I'd feel if I let myself.

The energy between us as we loaded Lizzy's suitcase into the van was also cautious, tentative. Up until two days ago, she'd seemed excited about the trip, but now she seemed sad. It didn't help that Olivia was making her views on this situation clear—it was the worst idea ever and wasn't fair. Neither Lizzy nor I argued with her.

Nana insisted we stop by for one last cup of tea.

"I don't understand why you feel such a strong pull to do this trip, Lizzy," she said. "What could you possibly do over there that you can't do here? With Adam. With Olivia. With the rest of your family."

Lizzy's eyebrows pinched together as she thought. "It's hard to explain," she finally whispered.

"I get it," I added. "Lizzy has been head down, working and going to school for her whole life. She's never had the chance to step out of her comfort zone, to do things on a whim, to set her own schedule."

"Well, it still doesn't make sense to me," Nana said, shaking her head.

"Me either," Olivia added.

"Thank you," Lizzy mouthed to me.

After saying goodbye to Nana, we drove to the airport.

I didn't want to be that guy in the movie who makes a scene, running to the departure gate, yelling his lover's name. And thank god Olivia was there to hold me back. I funneled my energy into soothing her, directing my thoughts to what *she* was losing instead of what I was losing.

I tried to remind myself that I'd not intended or wanted

this marriage to be more than temporary, a means to an end, which I'd achieved—despite the marriage lie. But that lie turned out to be truer than anything I'd experienced before.

I wished Lizzy were five years older and ready to settle down because I would ask her to marry me until she said yes—because marrying the same woman twice did not count as getting married again.

But at this moment, the only thing that mattered to her was expanding her life experience, not cutting it off at the knees with a husband and a kid. And I got it. I really did. My failed marriage with Brigitte was proof. But that didn't mean I had to like it.

I hated it.

I despised it.

I loathed it.

And I respected it. What choice did I have?

36

LIZZY

I checked my bags and the three of us walked toward the customs gate for international flights. There was a long lineup, but I had time, so I nodded toward a quiet space away from the crowd. Adam followed with Olivia in his arms. He placed the weeping six-year-old on her feet and stepped toward me. She clung to his waist like a spider monkey, making it impossible for me to get as much of my body in contact with his as I needed … which was all of it. Every skin cell screamed to connect with him.

The anti-anxiety pill I'd taken—"to calm my nerves for the long flight," I'd told the doctor when I went in for the prescription—was clearly doing what I'd hoped. As Adam stroked my hair and Olivia chanted, "Don't go," my mind wandered to my decision to not wear eyeliner, for fear I'd cry and it would run down my cheeks. No concern about that, it turned out.

"In case it isn't clear, someone is going to miss you more than you can imagine," Adam whispered in my ear.

"Give her a few days. She'll be fine. Kids are resilient."

"I wasn't talking about her." He pressed his lips to my cheek, then to the corner of my mouth, then to my lips.

My hands rose to his face. I pulled him closer, creating a tight seal between our mouths. I breathed him in and held my breath as we stood, barely moving, holding on to the connection, the moment. Olivia's pleas blended into the hum of white noise around us.

Someone jostled me, excusing herself. The spell was broken. I leaned away and inhaled a quick, sharp breath.

I still wasn't crying. Was the pill really that powerful, or was it the inevitability of this ending that made me feel nothing except what was at this moment? No longing for the past to continue. No regret about a future that could have been. Just a deep calm, knowing that everything was as it should be.

I crouched to Olivia's height and opened my arms for a hug. She fell against me and squeezed me hard.

"I'll send you postcards. And when I get home, we'll have a girls' night and you can show me all the tricks you've taught Apricot and Marmalade and tell me all the funny stories about making Dadam laugh so hard he pees his pants and we'll do a puzzle, maybe draw some pictures. Sound good?"

She nodded, but the only sound she made was a quiet sob.

I stayed in my crouch, hugging Olivia until my thighs burned. When I finally let her go and tried to stand, my legs rebelled and my butt dropped to the floor. Instead of bouncing up like I normally would have done, I stayed seated. The beauty of an airport, where people could cry, kiss, sleep, and be their most vulnerable selves in public without shame. I pulled Olivia down onto my lap.

"I will miss you so much, pumpkin." I kissed her red curls. "Take care of Dadam while I'm gone, okay?"

Another silent nod.

Adam dropped to the floor and joined us. "Are we having a sit-in? A protest against Lizzy leaving?"

"Yes! You can't go, Mona. Dadam, help me hold her down."

Adam grabbed Olivia and me as a single unit and lifted us into his lap. I imagined we looked ridiculous. And I didn't care.

Live in the moment. Appreciate the moment because that's all that matters. Nothing to mourn. Nothing to regret. It was oddly comforting and entirely unexpected to feel so relaxed about this whole situation.

With a kiss on Olivia's head and one on Adam's lips, I twisted myself out of the human Jenga pile and rose to my feet.

"I guess I should get in line. Wish me luck."

Adam and Olivia stood with me until I had to show my boarding pass to a security guard. And then they stood to the side of the line and waited until I was well and truly on the other side of customs. We waved and blew kisses to each other and then … I walked away. Toward my trip of a lifetime, made entirely possible by having forfeited my freedom, living as a wife and mom for three months. From one extreme to the other, and as easy as stepping into an international flight waiting room.

37

LIZZY

I distracted myself with a word game on my phone while I waited to board. Since I was flying business class—one of the many perks of having the extra money—my section was the first called.

I arrived at my seat while my seatmate was pushing her carry-on luggage into the overhead bin. Before she sat, I tapped her shoulder.

"I'm the window."

"Hello, window." She gave me a big smile. "I'm the aisle. Also known as Claire."

"Lizzy."

We got settled, and she was the one to start the conversation.

"I saw you saying goodbye to your husband and daughter. Is it hard to leave them, or do you travel often?" She laughed. "I suppose it could be both."

"Or none of the above?" I debated how much to say, whether I wanted to talk. Claire filled the short silence.

"Not your husband? Not your daughter? Not hard to leave them? You don't travel often? I need more to work with, or it's going to be a long flight. I hate takeoff. I promise, I won't talk as much once we're in the air. So if you can entertain me with tales of love until we're safely off the ground, I'll be your friend forever." She laughed again, and it made me laugh since she really did sound like she was trying to make the best of a stressful situation.

"Short answer is yes. To all. I guess."

She rolled her hand, indicating she wanted more.

"Okay, well, Adam was my husband until yesterday—"

"Oh! I'm sorry? Not what I expected." She laughed again, then apologized. "I laugh when I'm anxious. It's a terrible trait. You should see me at hospitals. I'm a nightmare. Worst visitor ever. I have to say, you and your ex-husband look like you're still in love."

"Mmm … it was a marriage of convenience with an end date. Today was the end date. So, love or not, this is how it was supposed to go."

"He wouldn't change the arrangement? That's heartbreaking. I'm so sorry."

"Actually, he wanted to change the deal. I'm the one who wanted to end it." I waved the air as if to clear it of messy energy. "It's complicated."

"Complicated is good on an eight-hour flight. Let me buy you a drink." Claire laughed and waved down a flight attendant.

I was four tiny vodkas into my story when the anti-anxiety pill stopped working and my emotions bubbled up and out of my eyes, nose, and mouth in a messy display of the truth.

Claire, who had been leaning forward on our shared armrest, pushed herself away from me with a smirk.

"You don't regret your decision at all, do you?"

"I think I just made the biggest mistake of my life."

38

ADAM

Lizzy had only been gone three days, but I knew I'd never want to replace what we had. Dylan had been right. I was an idiot to have followed through with the divorce. I should've let her leave the way I'd let Brigitte leave, still tied to me. But nothing about this divorce felt the same as my first. Nothing at all. Lizzy had risked so much to help me. I'd have been an even bigger asshole if I'd kept her legally tied to me when we were both free to move on. In theory, at least.

Olivia still wasn't understanding the finality of Lizzy's departure, and I didn't dissuade her of her false belief that after she finished her trip, she'd be moving home with us again. Why would I? I knew that time would make the reality easier to accept, and that to a six-year-old, time and thinking about the future were still too abstract to fully grasp.

I kissed her on the head at the front door to the school and wished her a good day. I got into my van—which still carried the ghost of Lizzy's presence because I'd bought a bottle of her trademark Fuji Green Tea perfume at the airport to use as car freshener—and just sat. I had nowhere to be, nothing to do. Nobody needed me. For the next seven hours I could vanish off the face of the Earth and I'd not be missed.

So I drove, since driving was good thinking time. With no particular destination, I decided I'd turn around when I needed to stop for gas. The gauge showed I had just under a quarter tank—an hour out, an hour back.

In life before Olivia I drove a Miata. If I wasn't on a mountain I was free to do whatever I wanted, when I wanted. I couldn't count the number of spontaneous road trips I'd taken just for the hell of it. Because I could. Sometimes on my own and other times with one of the guys or my boarding family. I hadn't traveled at all since becoming a dad. I missed it and that made missing Lizzy even worse.

I reached the exit for the American border, pulled off to refuel, then headed back home feeling no better. A drive had been a bad idea.

The thought of entering the empty house haunted me so I spent another long period sitting in my driveway. The painted tree had long since lost its color but I hadn't missed it until now. Staring at the house, I considered painting it multicolored to make it more welcoming. In the front window, the kittens exchanged turns on the top shelf of the cat tree. I wondered if they were lonely in the quiet.

Forcing my legs to move, I got out of the van.

I remembered how I'd sigh with relief for time alone, when Olivia was with Nana or one of my brothers. But no matter how hard I tried to conjure that feeling, it wouldn't come. Quiet time alone was the last thing I wanted.

Loud music didn't help drown out the voices that had invaded the empty spaces in my head. Showering and jerking off with an image of Lizzy bent over under the water didn't relieve the tension in my body. I dragged all my weights up from the basement to the living room. I used them. I went for a run. I cleaned the oven. I ironed dresses.

Nothing I did reduced the intense loneliness. Olivia's three o'clock pickup time couldn't come fast enough.

On the way home from school, we stopped for ice cream. Not because Olivia wanted it but because I needed it. Pulling into the strip mall, I parked beside a MiniMaid service car.

"Dadam, can we please, *please* trade this ugly van for a car like that?"

"Only if one of us gets a job cleaning houses. Do you want to quit school to clean other people's toilets?"

Her scowl made me laugh.

"But it's *so* pretty."

Pretty was one way to describe it, though gaudy would have been my first choice.

"You said we couldn't paint the van pink, so how come that person could paint their car purple with pink letters?" Her hands were pressed to her hips. I mimicked her pose, and she scowled harder.

"Technically, that car isn't painted. It's a wrap, like wrapping paper."

Then I scooped her into my arms and carried her fireman-style over my shoulder into the ice-cream parlor with her complaining the whole way across the parking lot that she was too big to be carried that way.

Without thinking, I said, "Not even close. Even Lizzy isn't too big to carry like this."

Olivia slumped against me. "I miss her."

"So do I, pumpkin."

"I know what we should do," she said, pointing a finger in the sky. "We should ask the person driving that car where they got the wrapping paper and then we should make our van pink so when Mona comes home, it's a surprise for her. She'll love it!"

"She would love it," I agreed. I made a mental note to call the therapist for advice on how to handle thinking and talking about Lizzy—asking for my kid, I'd say.

We had our ice cream—I tortured myself by ordering Lizzy's favorite—then we left. The MiniMaid car was still parked beside us. Olivia ogled it some more.

I wondered how much it would cost to wrap a Honda Odyssey. Instead of MiniMaid lettering, I pictured *Rhodes Trip* written on the side. Taking Olivia on a road trip would certainly be a good distraction from all the free time I was facing. A drive to Disneyland, two weeks away from the monotony of daily life might be just what the doctor ordered.

But given the joint guardianship agreement I now had with Brigitte, I'd have to run it by her first. And what if she decided she wanted to come along? How could I say no? I decided it wasn't worth the potential hassle.

Olivia and I had a quiet night working on math worksheets and a new puzzle of rainbow-colored unicorns she got for her birthday. Suggested for ages eight and up, it was a little trickier than the ones we were used to but a fun distraction, even for me.

The next day we had a boring morning getting ready for school. Everything felt flat without the background soundtrack of Lizzy's humming and singing. The mornings were darker, and not because of the slant of the earth but because the big, beautiful smile that I usually shared my coffee with was on the wrong side of the planet.

Half of me hoped she was having a great time, but my inner asshole hoped she was miserable and trying to figure out how to cancel all her prepaid travel tickets to get on the next plane home.

"All right, kiddo, time to roll," I called up the stairs. "Teeth clean?"

"Yup." She stood at the top and gave me a toothy smile.

"Hands clean?"

She held them in front of her for me to see as she descended. "Of course."

"Underpants clean?"

Olivia groaned. She was close enough to pick up, so I scooped her into my arms.

"Dadam! Put me down."

I tickled her just to hear her laugh. I needed to record that sound and have it playing on a soundtrack loop as I went about my day doing nothing.

The mail dropped through the slot in the front door, and the kittens appeared from nowhere to attack it. It was an amazing talent they'd developed, and we'd learned that if one or both was ever hiding, all we had to do to find them was push some paper through the mail slot, and they'd come running.

I placed Olivia on the bottom stair and turned to fight the cats for the mail. Normally all they had to pounce on were boring white envelopes filled with bills, but today there was something colorful. A postcard.

My heart did a double beat when I realized what it was.

"Olivia, look. Something from Mona." I hesitated handing it to her since I was looking at the picture. It was a tourist postcard, but with a twist. Lizzy had glued a picture of Olivia in her rainbow onesie, holding her kittens, on it. Olivia grabbed for it, but my fingers didn't release.

"Dadam! Let go!" She tugged the card from my grip.

"I can read it to you if you want." It was a lame attempt to get it back.

She looked down her nose at me and flipped it over, reading aloud.

Dear Olivia,

I visited the London Eye today, but didn't go for a ride since I don't like heights. It looked exactly like the picture on my vision board, so kind of boring, actually. I thought it would look much better if it had a cool kid and a couple of kittens as one of the capsules.

"Dadam, what's a capsule?"

"Turn the card over and you'll see. It's one of the cars you ride in." I reached to take the postcard from her again, and she swatted my hand away.

Her smile turned to a giggle when she noticed that she and Apricot and Marmalade were riding the giant Ferris wheel.

"What else does the postcard say?"

Tomorrow I'm off to see Big Ben, which I'm pretty sure will also look better with a Kid Kong and Kitten Kongs hanging off the top. Give everybody kisses for me. Xox, Mona

Olivia picked up both kittens and kissed their heads. "This is from Mona." Then she looked up at me. "Bend over so I can give you a kiss."

I gave her my cheek, and she delivered the gift from Lizzy.

"Let's put that on the fridge." I reached out again to try to get the card from her, but she held tight.

"No, I'm taking it to school to show my friends."

"But …" I stopped myself from arguing despite my intense need to possess her mail.

I dropped Olivia at school. She told me I was lucky that I didn't have to go anymore. I told her she was lucky she didn't have to hang out at home with a grumpy dad. She told me to play with Apricot and Marmalade and I'd feel better.

The cats got a few pats from me, but I spent the day online researching ridiculous things, like whether I could get a wrap made for the van. Apparently it was possible, and a simple design could be done in under a week. Then I lost my mind and looked up how long it would take to ship a bright pink minivan to the UK. I was stunned to learn it could be done in as few as six days, assuming there was a ship in Vancouver harbor heading that way. So that was how I spent several hours—calling shipping companies and brokers to find out when I could get space in a cargo container.

By school pickup time, I had a solid plan. I hadn't booked anything, but if the idea sounded even three degrees less insane in the morning, I'd call Brigitte and tell her about it. No point getting too excited if she wasn't on board.

39

LIZZY

Three weeks into what I'd planned to be a nine-month, nine-country adventure, and I was already missing home more than I was looking forward to my next destination.

At my insistence, Adam and I were not allowed to call or text each other. It was good luck that neither of us had thought of old school mail so the postcards to Olivia were my tether to home—a tether I wished Adam would grab onto and use to haul me back. Or better, follow to find me.

Because I knew how literal Olivia would take it if I ever wrote 'wish you were here' on any of the daily postcards I sent, I sought out images that had the words printed on the card, giving Adam an explanation lifeline. But in my heart, I hoped he'd notice the theme and act on it.

With one week left in England I was visiting the Lake District at the northern tip of the country. I traveled on my own by train to get there but decided to join an organized tour for five days to make the best use of time and to make sure I saw all the best sights. That, and I was lonely, tired of experiencing everything on my own.

The tour was promoted specifically for singles—not that I

was hoping to hook up with someone; I just didn't want to be the only person who wasn't on my honeymoon or celebrating a milestone with a spouse. It seemed the universe was having a great laugh, dropping happy couples in my path. A singles tour sounded like a good "screw you, I'm in control of my life" to the big, mean universe.

The tour company was in a cute little town called Bowness-on-Windermere, which was to be our home base. We'd make day trips from here and for all but one night, we'd sleep in our guesthouse accommodations. We were to arrive between 2:00 and 4:00 p.m. to get signed in and given our rooms. Then we'd all meet in a local pub that offered a free pint to anyone who didn't use their phone for the duration of their time drinking.

Shortly before six o'clock, the front desk staff pointed me in the direction of Off the Blower, the pub I was directed to, to meet my group. It was a five-minute walk down a cobblestone side street. The scent of fresh-cut grass and rich soil was so different from London, Manchester, and Liverpool, which all smelled like pee and compost. After these five days, I'd be back in London for two days and then into the Chunnel to start my month of tootling around France.

I arrived at the pub and looked around from the door. To my left, dark wood tables had been set up to make one large horseshoe. Half a dozen senior citizens sat at one end. To the other side was a different table setup with heavy, square tables pushed together to form an even larger square with four chairs along each side. Like the other table, six people were already seated. They looked closer to my age, so I put on my friendliest face and made my way over.

They all stopped talking and watched me approach; a few of them smiled.

"Hi! I'm Lizzy," I said to the woman, who looked most interested in being sociable.

"'Allo, Lizzy. What can I do for you?"

"I'm with the tour."

She shook her head and pointed to the other end of the pub. "Wrong table. That's you over there, love."

My eyes followed her hand to the table of senior citizens while she spoke. I was confused.

"That can't be right. It's a tour for singles."

That's when the guy sitting two seats over laughed. "Maybe you'll find yourself a nice widower to hook up with. Stay away from the divorcés. They're usually too broke to be a sugar daddy."

"Don't be an asshat, Dirk," the woman said. "Never mind him. You staying at the Field's End Guest House?"

I nodded.

"Then that's who you'll be partying with." The furrowing of her brows suggested she wanted to be sorry but the rise of the corners of her lips made it obvious that she thought it was funny.

"Thanks."

As I walked toward my group, Dirk called across the pub for everyone to hear, "Don't kill the poor guy!" As I reached my table, everyone had stopped talking and was looking at me.

"Hi. I'm Lizzy. And it looks like I'm on the tour with you all."

It wasn't what I'd expected, but in the end, it was actually quite nice to explore the historic sites with a group of seniors. The mistake had been all mine. The website was clear that these particular dates were for singles sixty and older. I'd overlooked that detail and wished I could call Adam to tell him how I'd failed the "pay attention to the small print" part of his pre-trip tourist training. I imagined how hard he'd have laughed at my mistake and it made me feel better.

The tour operator offered to refund my money but said I could come with them if I promised not to act like a twenty-something. I might have been offended if I hadn't met Dirk and his gang first. Twenty-somethings in this town didn't make a very good first impression.

Three ladies had come on the tour together. All were widows in their eighties, friends from California who'd never traveled internationally since, as Hazel put it, "Our husbands, bless their souls, hated flying." Hazel's husband was the last of the three to die, and that's when the widowed friends decided to go on their big traveling adventure together. Janet and Greta were the other two.

The three ladies took me under their wings and made me a welcome fourth in their small gang. Not only did I always know I had a seatmate on the bus, but these three took it on themselves to offer me never-ending surrogate grandmother advice.

They'd asked why a pretty young thing like me was traveling alone. At first I made up a story about this being my postgrad gap year. But on the fourth night, the four of us having dinner in a quiet restaurant in Pooley Bridge after an afternoon sitting in the sun, floating along Lake Ullswater on a hundred-year-old boat—and with two Gin Gin Mules loosening my lips—I spilled the whole story about Adam and Olivia and Brigitte and me.

They didn't interrupt to ask questions even once. Not until I said, "And that's why I'm here with you now," they gave each other knowing looks and let fly with their opinions. They spoke like I wasn't even there.

"You know what this reminds me of?" Hazel tapped the table.

"My granddaughter," Janet said, shaking her head with an air of disappointment.

"Exactly! But I don't remember what we recommended. Did we help fix that mess? Or ... did we make it worse? I can't keep track anymore," Greta admitted, looking embarrassed.

Hazel and Janet sighed and exchanged glances.

"Depends what you consider success, doesn't it? They're happily married with two children, and I'm the on-call babysitter. Not sure we thought that through."

"I'm sure little missy over there has her own grandmother."

I cleared my throat, about to tell them that I did not, in fact, have a grandmother, but Hazel waved at me to be quiet.

"Regardless, the babies won't be ours to deal with. I think we need to convince her it's time to go home," Janet said.

"I disagree." Greta bumped a shaky fist to the table.

"What? Don't be ridiculous. Look at her." They all gawped at me as if I were a zoo animal, tsk'ing and shaking their heads. "She's miserable. She should go home and tell the young man how she feels."

"Nope. She should continue with her travels, just like she planned, until she has him out of her system. She's going to Paris in three days, for goodness' sake. A few nights in the city of love, and she'll be over that man in a heartbeat. You heard her. She's only twenty-five. Far too young to settle down."

"And how old were you when you married George?"

"That's different and you know it." Greta placed her elbows on the table and leaned forward. "I was mature for my age."

Hazel and Janet looked at each other with unbelieving eyes and then guffawed.

I listened to them bicker about what the right age to settle down was, drawing on their own experiences, which started out quite differently and then became very similar. Each had only been married once, and that marriage had lasted until death did them part. It occurred to me that they were playing some strange relationship advice version of good cop, bad cop, dumb cop.

When our food arrived, they stopped jabbering, and I became aware of the song playing in the background. It was from the animation Olivia loved, of the little girl and her snowman friend, the one that made me cry every time I watched it. I tried to block it out but failed. When it got to the chorus, I excused myself to the bathroom, feigning something in my eye.

Every line of the song was accompanied in my mind's eye by an image from the short movie. The phrase, "I will follow you, will you follow me?" played on repeat, even while the song moved on to other parts. I imagined myself as the little girl who grew up and left her beloved snowman in a deep freeze, forgetting about him for years. But then I thought, *no, I'm the snowman, locked in the freezer, waiting for someone to remember that I'm there.*

I pulled out my phone, desperate to chat with Adam. I had to do some extreme sport mental jujitsu to make it okay to type Adam's phone number into a text. I logicked that since I'd never explicitly said I wouldn't message Olivia it was a fair loophole. I found the video on YouTube and copied the link into a chat with the message:

> Tell Olivia I'm in a pub listening to this song.
> Wish you were here. xo

I stared at the message for several seconds, knowing that to send it wasn't playing fair. The song ended. I hit Send anyway since the whole point of this stupid 'no contact' rule was so that I'd stay focused on where I was and who I was with. Since it wasn't working, what difference would it make if I sent one dumb text?

I'd been thinking about Adam virtually every minute of

this trip, wishing I were spelunking with him, climbing to the top of a church bell tower with him holding my hand and telling me I was safe, drinking Guinness with him, experiencing all the things with him and Olivia. There was very little that we couldn't have done with her. Even the pubs allowed kids until well past her bedtime.

The last three weeks had given me a whole new perspective on my mom's mantra that "kids ruin all the fun." I splashed water on my face, applied fresh eyeliner, and returned to my new friends with a question.

"When you look back to when your kids were small, what's the one thing you didn't do that you still regret today?"

Greta answered before I'd even finished the question.

"Have more of them," she said.

"As if five wasn't enough?" Janet shook her head.

"Well, it's true that if *you'd* had five, that would have been three too many," Greta replied. "But *my* children were perfect angels."

All three laughed at what was clearly an inside joke.

"Honestly?" Janet said. "The only regret I have is that I waited until I was thirty-five to have mine."

"Why's that?" I asked, leaning in close to really absorb her words.

"While these two were able to go on romantic holidays before their husbands needed Viagra—"

"Speak for yourself! Clint was virile until the day he passed, bless his soul."

"As I was saying, they were free to go to adult-only resorts ten years before me. I suppose we could have left the kids on their own when they were teens—"

Raucous laughter from Greta and Hazel interrupted Janet.

She scowled. "But we probably would have come home to a house burned down. They were a handful, my two. I wouldn't have traded them for the world, though. And you know what they say, about karma being a bitch?"

Now she was laughing.

Hazel leaned my way. "Her grandkids are absolute hellions."

"What about you, Hazel? Did children make you miss out on anything you regret now?" I asked.

She got serious and took my hand in hers. "Dear, you are not responsible for your mother's unhappiness with her life. It was horribly wrong for her to make you feel that way. My regrets are mine alone. They won't be the same as yours. And no matter what decisions you make about love and marriage and kids, there will be things you'll regret. There always are."

"A piano rehearsal you missed because on that day, it felt more important to work late," Greta said.

"Or a cruel word said in anger that wasn't even true." Janet hung her head.

Hazel continued, "Between the three of us, we have over two hundred years of life experience—"

"Bite your tongue!" Greta interrupted.

"We may not agree on everything, but I think we can all agree that if you listen to your heart above all else, your regrets will be relatively inconsequential."

The three ladies lifted their pints and clinked glasses. Then Janet added, "Though sometimes it's good to listen to your lady parts too."

40

———

ADAM

My phone pinged as I was making Olivia lunch.

"Can I check it?" she asked, reaching for the device on the counter.

She was in a phase where she wanted to read everything with words on it, from the ingredients on the can of chicken noodle soup she was having with her grilled cheese to the instruction manual for the air fryer we'd given Nana, to every message my phone told me I'd received. My family WhatsApp group had become an exercise in reading between the lines since it was now an all-ages chat.

"Sure," I said, flipping the sandwiches for a few more seconds to make them the perfect shade of golden.

"It's from Mona," she squealed.

I dropped the spatula and dove to grab the phone from her. Not that I expected Lizzy to write anything X-rated. I just wanted to be the first to read her message. I never got to read anything first. The cats no longer had to announce the arrival of the mail since Olivia and I were more excited than they were about mail and fought to be the one to see what the delivery lady had brought us.

Even though I had the advantage of strength and height,

my dear daughter had become sneaky. Yesterday, while I sat on the bottom stair at the front door thinking she was in the bathroom off the kitchen, she'd snuck out the back door and had been waiting to intercept the post card right from the mail lady's hand. Olivia was giggling, the Canada Post employee smiling behind her, when I opened the door after the bell rang. Olivia had read the card to the post lady before I saw it.

"Looks like somebody is missing home," the mail carrier said. "I have to admit, I'm enjoying all the fun collages."

Before I could wrestle my phone from the squirming bundle of happy energy, she'd opened the message and declared, "It's for me, anyway."

"Read it," I demanded.

"It says, *Tell Olivia I'm in a pub listening to this song. Wish you were here. xo.* And there's a link. Can I click it?"

"No."

She swung the phone behind her. "But if it's from Mona, it won't be dangerous. Please, Dadam?"

"Brat."

Olivia giggled and shrugged one shoulder.

"Fine. Open it."

As soon as I heard the first note, I knew what it was, and any concern I had about our plan to surprise Lizzy by showing up in London with our shiny, pink-and-purple *Rhodes Trip*-wrapped van went up in smoke—along with the grilled cheese sandwiches, which the smoke detector told me were now burning on the stove.

The doorbell rang, then the front door opened.

"Hello! Is lunch ready? I'm starving."

"Auntie Brigitte!" Olivia kept my phone in her hand and ran to the front door.

"Just had a minor setback," I called. "Soup's ready. Sandwiches will be a couple minutes."

At first, Brigitte had been reluctant to let me take Olivia

out of school indefinitely so she and I could traipse around Europe in a pink family van. Turned out, she wasn't upset about Olivia missing classes; it was being left behind that upset her. But once we figured that out, finding a suitable solution was easy.

Olivia and I were all set to fly to London in two days. The van was already in London, temporary import paperwork all in order. The platinum service I paid for would even have a chauffeur waiting with the vehicle to meet us at the airport when we arrived.

How we'd spend the first two weeks of our trip was a bit of a gamble, but on November 7, the deal was that Olivia and I would meet Brigitte at Heathrow where they would board a plane for Germany to start a two-week, guided tour of several castles that had inspired the homes of some of their favorite fairy-tale princesses. The two of them would take trains across three countries, sleeping in princess-inspired hotel rooms, traveling with a dozen other families who had kids between the ages of five and eight.

Olivia was beside herself with anticipation. With Brigitte's help, she had created a new vision board reflecting all the places she'd be visiting on her princess paradise adventure.

The only outstanding question was whether I'd get my prince's version of a happily ever after, or if I'd find myself on a solo Rhodes trip in a pink van. The last message from Lizzy made me more confident that little birdies would indeed circle our heads, singing love songs. I sure hoped so.

The overnight flight from Vancouver to London landed right on schedule. Olivia had slept most of the time; I had not. But we didn't have far to go—and I wouldn't be driving. The van and a driver were set to meet us at the arrivals pickup area. Neither Olivia nor I had actually seen the van, since timing was so tight to get it wrapped and then to the docks to ship. I had to take a leap of faith that my vision of it would be as good as the reality.

We left the building, into the weather at Heathrow Airport, but didn't notice the rain. Olivia saw it first, a few vehicles up the walkway, in the limousine pickup area. It looked like a gaudy Hawaiian shirt among a sea of black tie tuxedos. I laughed out loud, not sure if I was proud or horrified to claim ownership. Since Olivia was beside herself with excitement, I opted for pride.

The driver approached with an outstretched hand. "Mr. Adam Rhodes?"

I took his hand. "Yes." I could conjure no other words. I could not take my eyes off the giant Barbie-pink van with purple trim. What had I been thinking, plastering my name across both sides?

I questioned my sanity for a fraction of a second until Olivia said, "This is savage."

"Savage?" I couldn't think of anything less savage, but what did I know? "You think Lizzy will like it?"

She shook her head, rolled her eyes, and made a face that wordlessly communicated that I was clueless.

"Hey. Don't give me that savage look," I said, dropping our carry-on bags into the van.

Her car seat and a crap load of camping gear and clothes had been shipped in the vehicle, so we were ready to roll.

She clicked her seat belt, and I slid her door closed. It wasn't until my hand was on the latch to open the passenger door that I saw the extra little detail I'd asked the shop to add at the last minute. It was one word, painted on top of the wrap in Lizzy's handwriting—her name in gold. I ran my fingers over it and muttered, "I hope you think it's savage too."

Lizzy had no idea we were here or that I'd even

considered this surprise. I'd promised not to tell her if I missed her, not to message her with news of what Olivia and I were up to, and under no circumstances would I call her. I'd kept all my promises for four painful weeks. And now I was going to break one.

I pulled out my phone and typed a message.

Me: *Where are you?*

I assumed she'd be awake since it was eight thirty in the morning. I was ninety-nine percent sure she'd still be in London. I just prayed she'd be alone.

The driver looked at me. "Hotel?"

"I'm confirming that now," I said, hoping it was true. The backup, if she didn't reply, was the Mayfair, the hotel she'd booked for these days when we were coming up with her travel itinerary

Olivia kicked my seat. "Come on! Let's go. I want to see Mona."

I looked over my shoulder and tapped her leg. "Patience."

My phone pinged.

Lizzy: *At my hotel. Why, what's wrong? Is Olivia okay? Are you?*

Me: *The Mayfair?*

Lizzy: *Why?*

Me: *I'd like to have something delivered to you.*

Lizzy: *Adam …*

Me: *Please?*

Lizzy: *Grr. Yes.*

Me: *Stay put. Okay?*

Lizzy: *For how long?*

I asked the driver, "How long to get to the Mayfair?"

"Forty minutes, give or take."

Me: *One hour. Max. Can you wait?*

Lizzy: *For you? I'll wait.*

Music to my ears. The forty-five-minute drive felt like

hours since I must have checked my phone four dozen times.

I had the van parked in the hotel's underground lot, then thanked and tipped the driver. Olivia and I took the elevator to the lobby and asked the front desk to call Lizzy's room and let her know there was a delivery for her on parking level P3. I stood and listened to the one-sided conversation.

"No, ma'am. I haven't seen what it is. I can only tell you that a gentleman has asked for you to collect your delivery in the parking lot." There was a pause. "I agree. It is quite unusual. Would you like a porter to accompany you, ma'am?" Another pause. "Have a nice day." She hung up and said, "She's on her way."

Olivia bounced on her toes and pulled me toward the bank of elevators. "Hurry up! We have to get there first and hide."

We had loads of time, it turned out. A solid ten minutes before the elevator delivered the tourist we were waiting for. We'd chosen P3 since there was a spot close enough to the elevator to see whoever was coming out. Four parties arrived before Lizzy. Olivia was so amped, I thought she was going to have an aneurysm.

Our plan had been to let Lizzy find us, not to push open the van door and scream—or in my case, holler—her name as soon as we saw her. But that's what happened. Olivia jumped out and ran toward her yelling, "Mona!" I was only a little less uncivilized. I didn't run, but I moved quickly with my arms wide open.

The expression about a deer in headlights? That. She stood motionless, arms at her sides, eyes doing the best impression of a tarsier I'd ever seen.

Olivia crashed into her legs and grabbed on tight. Lizzy started to fall backwards, but I was one step behind and caught her, pulling her hard and fast into my arms, crushing my child between us—just a little.

She didn't say a word. Didn't smile. I couldn't read her expression.

Olivia squeezed herself free and grabbed at Lizzy's limp arm.

"Look, over there." She pointed. "We have our van. For a Rhodes Trip. Get it? And you're coming with us."

Lizzy's eyes followed Olivia's hand. Her mouth fell open. As impossible as it seemed, her eyes opened even wider. And that's when she reacted.

41

LIZZY

I was afraid to move. I didn't want to wake myself from this dream. Adam held me tight and, despite my intention to only observe and remember how it felt to be wrapped in his arms, my body started to melt. My knees buckled. My shoulders dropped. I closed my eyes and waited for the dream to end and for me to be lying alone in my stupidly expensive hotel room when I opened them again.

But it didn't end.

Dream Adam's arms scooped me up and carried me toward the sound of an overly excited little girl calling, "Put her on the bed."

I looked toward the voice and saw a bright pink van—definitely a dream—with Olivia bouncing on what looked like a mattress where the right rear passenger seat would normally be. Dream Olivia scooted deeper into the dream van as Dream Adam leaned forward to put me down.

My brain buzzed like a beehive. My heart beat a staccato rhythm. It didn't seem to know if it should stop or explode. All it knew was that as soon as my body lost contact with the man carrying me, I'd wake up. So I wrapped my arms tight around his neck and pulled myself to meet his lips. I needed to kiss him before this dream ended.

My mouth met his. He felt so real I moaned, pulling him even tighter against me. We tumbled, me still held tight in his arms, and I gently landed on the mattress. He tried to pull away, but I wouldn't let go. I'd decided I was never letting go. Dream Adam fell on top of me, and in the seconds that I couldn't breathe from his body weight pressing down, I knew this was how I wanted to die. No regrets.

The pressure lifted, but his mouth was still attached to mine.

"Get a room!" Dream Olivia laughed.

And then Dream Adam was gone. I was afraid to open my eyes. I could feel the mattress under me. My hotel mattress. I pulled in my bottom lip and could still feel the abrasion from his beard, smell his spicy energy in the surrounding air.

"Why is Mona sad to see us?"

"She's not sad, pumpkin."

"Then why is she crying?"

This was torture. I steeled myself to be taken out of the fantasy. I opened my eyes and saw a mess of red hair hanging loose over a face that was filled with concern. Moving only my eyes, I looked past the curls to see more hair—a beard half covering the lips I'd just been kissing, now smiling.

I looked from the concerned face to the smiling face. Back and forth three times.

"What's wrong with her?" Olivia whispered.

"Nothing's wrong with her. I think this is a case of if something is too good to be true, don't believe it. And I think that seeing you is too good to be true."

That's when I pinched myself. Then I pinched Olivia's cheek.

"Ouch!"

Adam laughed and stuck his arm out to within my reach. I pinched it too.

"In the flesh." He grabbed my hand, pulled it to his mouth, and kissed my palm.

I rubbed his cheek, and the electricity from the touch kick-started my heart, which I realized at that moment had stopped beating the minute I got onto the plane back in Vancouver.

42

LIZZY

The next two weeks were like a fairy tale. I canceled all my bookings in France and beyond, since Olivia wanted to visit the places I'd sent postcards from. I was more than happy to experience the sights with my family. Adam said he didn't care where we were or what we were doing as long as it was together.

And as much as I loved visiting the sights with both of them, I'd have been lying if I said I wasn't also looking forward to the two weeks of time alone with Adam. We'd been staying in hotels with Olivia, but once she was off on her adventure with Brigitte, he and I were going to make use of the kitted-out Barbie camper van, which was what we were now driving to meet Brigitte at Heathrow Airport's Terminal 2.

Brigitte had taken an overnighter from Vancouver and had a four-hour layover before the flight she was taking with Olivia to the first castle and country on their princess tour: Bavaria, to see Princess Aurora's home from *Sleeping Beauty*. From there, they'd travel by train, often at night, to wake-up in a new country and at a new fairy-tale castle. Over the two weeks, they would have lunches with the Little Mermaid and Prince Eric at his castle in Switzerland, Beauty and the Beast at the Beast's castle in France, with Rapunzel in Normandy, then with Snow White in Spain.

Then it was onto a plane over to Scotland for the last two castles, Merida's from *Brave* and the castle-of-all-castles, Cinderella's. The tour would end with a grand ball and each of the young princesses being whisked away in a pumpkin-shaped carriage—though not quite at midnight as the clock struck an age-appropriate carriage-into-pumpkin hour.

After Scotland, we had planned to meet Olivia at Brigitte's flat in London. Brigitte was going to stay for a few months to wrap up her life before making the move back to Vancouver on a more permanent basis.

Adam had arranged with Apricot and Marmalade's first human mother to care for them while they were away. Olivia said she would miss them but knew they would be happy since they were going to spend time with their mom and one of their brothers.

Adam had thought of everything to make sure everyone would have the best holiday of their lives.

I kissed and hugged Olivia as best I could, given how she never stopped bouncing and tugging on Brigitte's arm to hurry up so they wouldn't miss their flight. Adam waited for his little tornado to touch ground before grabbing her in a hug so tight, it made her squeak.

"I'm going to miss you, pumpkin."

"I'll miss you too, Dadam."

Brigitte and I laughed at how unconvincing Olivia was.

"Now put me down. I have to go." She wiggled free and ran to Brigitte.

"Have a fabulous time." Brigitte gave us a warm smile. "And I'd say there's no need to worry about this one." She ruffled Olivia's hair.

Olivia shook her head and sighed. "Come. On."

Adam and I stood, arms around each other, and waved until they were out of sight.

"You okay?" I asked.

"Yeah. I'm going to miss the hell out of her, but I know she'll have a good time with Brigitte."

"You think?" I poked him. "I guess I've got my work cut out having to distract you."

He looked at his wrist as if wearing a watch. "We have time. I'm thinking we should test the mattress, you know, to make sure it's working before we leave England. It might be hard to find parts in France."

My blood swirled downward through my body right to Gigi, making her ache. "So tempting. We can't, though. Can we?"

"We can do anything we want. We're on holiday."

Adam walked and I skipped to the van, but I changed my mind as soon as we got there.

"I can't. Too many people around."

"You know, there will be people around when we're camping," he reminded me.

"But, not like right beside us. They'll be at least a few car lengths away."

Adam opened my door and kissed me in a way that didn't help reduce my longing. I moaned.

"Hold that thought for five minutes."

Adam navigated toward the exit of the short-stay lot and paid the fee. Instead of driving out of Heathrow, he took an exit toward the long-stay parking lot. We drove a few minutes, then he took us to the farthest corner of the lot, at least a dozen car lengths from any other vehicle.

"Cheaper than getting an airport hotel for an hour," he said, turning off the van's ignition and then igniting mine.

The mattress worked just fine. Better than fine. It was a dream-come-true mattress.

There was no need to stop anywhere before heading out

on the ninety-minute drive to the Channel Tunnel to board a train—with our pink Rhodes Trip van!—for the half-hour trip from England to France, where we arrived shortly after lunchtime.

Given the temperature in early November, we'd decided to drive from chilly Calais at the northern tip of France to the French Riviera and the Côte d'Azur in the south. We'd stay for five or six nights and then do the two-day drive to Sicily, Italy, for another five nights. The plan was to sleep in our van, hike or lounge on the beach during the day, and eat dinners in fancy restaurants. That was as much as we knew. Basically, we had a direction but no expectations beyond enjoying every moment together.

43

ADAM

Before I met Lizzy, I'd logged tens of thousands of miles flying all over the world to snowboard. I'd stayed in the best hotels and eaten in the most to-be-seen-at restaurants. At the time, I thought I'd been living my best life. But spending two weeks sleeping on a foam mattress in the back of the van, eating fresh mussels from fishermen on the beach, and singing Disney cartoon duets while we explored quiet walking trails made me realize I didn't miss one single perk of being a sponsored athlete.

Brigitte called a few times so Olivia could share excited stories about their castle adventures. She told us, in no uncertain terms, that when she grew up, she was going to get a job as a princess and go to balls every night. So much for my idea that she'd become a heavy-duty mechanic. Lizzy reminded me that she could be both a princess and fix giant equipment.

"You know one thing I absolutely adore about you, Mona Elizabeth Sheila Hillhouse?" I asked as we lay on blankets under a clear Sicilian sky.

"Tell me," she said, but immediately prevented me from speaking by pressing her lips to mine. She kept me tongue-tied until I saw stars, whether my eyes were open or closed. When she finally pulled away, she collapsed laughing. "You were saying?"

"With you, anything feels possible. You know that?"

"All I know is that when I'm with you, things don't just *feel* possible, they *are* possible. In the last four months, you've helped me fulfill every single dream and wish I've ever had, some a teeny bit ahead of schedule." She held up her thumb and forefinger, pinching a small amount of space between them.

"We can use the next four years as practice, so that when you reach your magic age, you'll be good and ready to—"

"Twenty-six," she interrupted.

"Pardon?"

"My magic age. It's *actually* twenty-six."

I gave her a questioning look.

Lizzy placed her mouth by my ear and whispered, "I'm quite mature for my years."

"Is that so?"

"Mm-hmm. At least thirty-two by normal standards."

Was she saying what I think she was? It was time to take a gamble and find out. What could possibly go wrong?

"Hold that thought," I said, extracting myself from her hug. I opened the van door and climbed in, dug to the bottom of the tote box that was home to my clothes, and found a small velvet box. I held it in my hand and checked in on how I was feeling.

My breathing? Slow and steady. Heart rate? Normal. I ran the fingers of my empty hand over my palm. Dry.

I hadn't expected to be so calm. But why wouldn't I be? I closed my eyes and was taken to the top of a cliff with a drop-off that would kill 99 percent of people who dared jump. Trained to envision success, I never felt fear in those situations. And that's what my mind and body were doing now.

I envisioned myself kneeling in front of Lizzy. Heard myself ask the question. Saw her smile. Felt her arms wrap around my neck, her voice whisper, "Yes," in my ear. I felt myself smile, my real smile, not one in my mind's eye.

"Time to jump," I said.

I hadn't heard Lizzy approach. "Where are you jumping to? Or what are you jumping from?" Her expression was a mix of amusement and concern; her lips curved up, but the corners of her eyes crinkled, unsure.

I slid out of the van and took her hand, walked us over to our blanket with the clear view of the star-filled sky. I pointed up. "To infinity and beyond," I said, without the cartoon accents. "As long as you're with me."

I knelt.

Lizzy gasped.

"I need one of those." I pointed to the hands she had pressed against her mouth.

She dropped her left arm, and I opened the ring box before taking her hand. "Mona Elizabeth Sheila Hillhouse, will you do me the honor of becoming Mona Elizabeth Sheila Hillhouse Rhodes?"

Her smile rose to her eyes, but after a few seconds without moving a muscle, she shook her head and pulled her hand from mine; held it over her heart.

"No."

"No?" My voice sounded distant behind the roar of the avalanche in my ears.

She motioned for me to stand. We faced each other holding eye contact for a lifetime before she took my hands and kissed my knuckles. "If you're okay with it, I'd much prefer to embrace the 1950s values Nana taught you." She stood on tiptoes and exhaled hot breath against my ear. "Well, one of them at least."

I was in free fall.

Then she dropped to her knee and looked up. "Adam

Jones Rhodes, will you do me the honor of allowing me to become Mona Elizabeth Sheila Rhodes? To let me be yours, for now and forever? I don't want or need to keep a backup family name."

I fell to the ground and pulled Lizzy into a tight hug. "Mine."

"Mine," she repeated.

Thanks for reading Rhodes to Love: Daring with the Single Dad.

If you're not quite ready to say goodbye to Adam and Lizzy, I have a treat for you—a bonus epilogue that takes place ten years later and is only available to people like you, who've read to the end of this story!

Geni.us/rhodes-bonus

Have you read all the brother's journeys to their happily ever afters?

- Nick & Sophie, small town, his and hers firefighters, in FIRST IN: Cheeky with the Fire Chief.
- Dylan & Kama, rivals with chemistry, in SECOND BREATH: Dazzled by my Blind Date.
- Josh & Paige, the love that never waned, in THIRD PARTY: Merry with the Millionaire.
- Adam & Lizzy, fake marriage, true love, in RHODES TO LOVE: Daring with the Single Dad.
- Morgan & Tamara, forced proximity, friends to lovers, in FRISKY WITH MY BESTIE.

GET A BONUS EPILOGUE!

Thanks so much for reading *Rhodes to Love: Daring with the Single Dad*.

If you're not quite ready to say goodbye to Adam, Lizzy, and Olivia, I have a treat for you—two bonus chapters in the form of an epilogue that takes place ten years later. It's only available to people like you, who've read to the end of this story!

Geni.us/rhodes-bonus

love&stuff,
Danika
DanikaBloom.com

ABOUT THE AUTHOR

Danika Bloom is a *USA Today* bestselling author who always wanted to be the mom in The Partridge Family or The Brady Bunch ... since she only had one child, she lives out her mom-of-many fantasies in her rom-com series about bands of brothers ...

Actually, that's kind of creepy when you think about it ... Shirley Partridge (aka Shirley Jones) writing spicy stories about her hunky son Keith (aka David Cassidy, her real-life stepson) and his brothers ... ?

Hmm, she might want to rethink this bio.

Danika Bloom lives in a small village in BC, Canada. One of her bucket list dreams is to rent a suite at Disneyland and have Goofy officiate her 25-year anniversary. She falls in love with all the heroes she writes and has a very patient husband.

Find all her books at DanikaBloom.com